GETTING EVEN.

EVENTUALLY.

S. Featherstone

Cenizas
Books

This book is a work of fiction. Names, characters, places and incidents are either the product of the author's imagination or are used fictitiously, and any resemblance to actual persons, living or dead, business establishments, events or locales is entirely coincidental.

Cover design by: Don Barnes – Cellar Ideas Inc.
www.cellarideas.com
Cover photo by: Addison Pemberton

First Printing: September 2003
10 9 8 7 6 5 4 3 2 1

Library of Congress Cataloging-in-Publication Data
2003094374

Featherstone, S.

Getting Even. Eventually. / S. Featherstone

ISBN 0-9742616-0-2

1. Bush flying – Mexico – Action/Adventure 2. Featherstone, S.

BISAC – FIC002000 – FICTION/Action & Adventure

PRINTED IN USA

Acknowledgments.

There are too many people I would like to thank for inspiring me.

First and foremost I want to thank My Wonderful Wife Evie Einstein who has been a source of motivation and inspiration. Her love and support has kept me going through the good times and the bad.

My Great Mum Penny and my Dear Friend Sandra Burch who's editing skills and patience I am eternally grateful for.

My Real Bush Pilot Friend Oscar Zepeda (Mr. Land-Anywhere). Without his stories, ideas and utter love of flying would have made this story impossible to write. Please be aware that all the approaches described are factual and are performed on a regular basis by Oscar.

And to a man who I could only aspire to become, My Father In-Law Dr. Hans E. Einstein.

A special thanks goes to Barbara and Steve Schapel for believing in this little venture!

AND LAST, BUT NOT LEAST

Thank **you** for taking the time to read these words.
I hope you enjoy reading it as much as I enjoyed writing it!

Cover Design courtesy of:
Don Barnes – Cellar Ideas Inc. 408-265-5488
Cover Photo courtesy of: Addison Pemberton – Thanks!!

In memory of

Gilberto Zepeda Luna

And all our fellow pilots
who have gone before us.

"When once you have tasted flight, you will
always walk with your eyes turned skyward, for
there you have been and there you will always
be."

Leonardo da Vinci
1452-1519.

GETTING EVEN.

EVENTUALLY.

S. Featherstone

Chapter 1.

Am I Insane?

In a magical instant what was once a cumbersome ground vehicle became a graceful air vehicle. It really didn't matter how many thousands of times Jake took off in an airplane under his own control it still excited him as much as the first time. He recognized that this could be said of very few things in life. Problems seemed to become insignificant and distant, almost in proportion to the altitude between himself and the surface of the earth. Cynics might equate his love of flight to escapism. You can call it what you like as long as it works.

Escape, the word kinda lingered in his mind. It was a powerful word with a strange unfamiliar connotation, traditionally criminal, possibly cowardly and in a way comforting. Jake McInnes certainly didn't consider himself cowardly and as far as he was aware no one who knew him would describe him as such.

Based on the circumstances surrounding his departure Jake settled for criminally comforting as the best way to describe his escape in the stolen, or as he preferred to describe it, borrowed Cessna 185. If things worked out the way he hoped, and he realized that things rarely worked out the way he hoped, no one would miss the old aluminum bird for a long time. Maybe never.

The soothing drone of the freshly overhauled engine before him and the easy feeling he always had when he was flying allowed his mind to wander farther and deeper than before. Jake continued to hash over the word. Escaping was exactly what he was doing. It wasn't a real criminal escape, like in the movies, well not entirely. It was an escapade to a richer more fulfilling life, or so he hoped. He was getting away from a mediocre existence. At least that is what he had told himself as the plan began to take shape almost a year ago. For better or worse, but at the very least not more of the same. It had taken months of planning and meditating. Weighing the options and possibilities. After all, it had taken Jake many years to get into the trouble he had created for himself. Sure, you face the problems you create for yourself, but there comes a time to say, "I'm ready to put this, and everything else behind me and move ahead – good or bad".

Maybe his privileged and comfortable middle class Southern California surfer dude upbringing, totally devoid of responsibility was partially to blame. Possibly if he had've been born a street smart Katmandu kid he wouldn't have made so many dumb decisions and brought his life to the muddle it had been for most of his adult life.

Who knows, who gives a shit? This was his opportunity to start fresh. After all, he would still be doing what he loved most. Flying. And making a hell of a lot more money for his efforts. Furthermore, this was really flying, not going around in circles at ridiculously low speeds fish finding, but bush flying in the Mexican Sierra. Hell, it sounded like some movie Humphrey Bogart or Jimmy Stewart should be in.

At 2 o'clock in the morning the brilliant stars generously shared the crisp clear air with Jake, Amber and the 1969 Cessna 185. Its new engine growling effortlessly as they climbed at 1200 feet per minute at 100 knots indicated airspeed. In ten minutes or so they would reach their cruising altitude of 9,500 feet for this particular direction of flight.

"SoCal departure X-ray Alpha Tango Alpha Papa," Jake said professionally.

"SoCal departure go ahead Tango Alpha Papa." The response came back quickly since there weren't many other planes to control.

"SoCal Tango Alpha Papa is departing Carlsbad Charlie Romeo Quebec at 1,200 feet, I'd like to open my flight plan."

"Roger Tango Alpha Papa stand by. I'll have a squawk for you in a moment.

Tango Alpha Papa squawk 5234, ident. Confirm your destination: Ciudad Obregon, Mexico."

"That is correct for Alpha Papa."

"Tango Alpha Papa climb and maintain 9,500 own navigation."

"Alpha Papa."

The Lycoming six-cylinder 540 cubic inch turbocharged engine stumbled slightly, he instinctively checked the engine monitor, all temperatures looked fine. Probably a speck of dirt or drop of water in the system. Better put the engine monitor on scan, it would quickly show any bad trend. Amber, Jake's Australian shepherd snoozed unfazed, with the confidence of a dog with more flight time than many humans.

Few things in his life had been more exhilarating or had called to him as loudly as flying. He knew how fortunate he was to be privy to sights only pilots have the opportunity to see. Like now, at this moment in time, a full moon gently illuminated the ocean, creating unique lazy reflections off the ripples. Jake concentrated and tried to etch the beautiful Southern California coast into his mind, since it might be a very long time before he saw it again.

What may have been bright head beams from a few cars and trucks on the freeway flickered only dimly from his vantage point. It was unbelievable how this area had grown since he was a kid. There used to be so much empty space and now everything was overgrown with ridiculously expensive yet tiny housing.

"Tango Alpha Papa, fly heading zero three zero to avoid traffic. Same altitude descending at your 2 to 3 o'clock."

"Tango Alpha Papa willco, no joy on that traffic," he smiled, it would be a long, long time before he heard any traffic warnings where he was going.

Sure he was apprehensive. It was a manifestation of the uncertainty of what he was doing, the risks and not knowing what the future had in store. Sort of like when you soloed for the first time. It was a memory most pilots remember vividly. He remembered, as clearly as if it had happened yesterday. Ted had told him to pull to the side of the taxiway and let him out. Jake had turned and looked at him with huge eyes and simply said. "Are you sure?" He hoped Ted would laugh and say it was a joke, but instead the reply came: "You're ready. Do three touch and goes and we'll call it a day." Everything was fine for the first take off and then the overwhelming thought came to his mind, "Now I have to land this bitch." In hindsight it wasn't a huge ordeal, but at the moment it was huge. Now he realized just about anybody could make a half decent landing in a Cessna 150.

It would be a serious understatement to say that Jake McInnes had accomplished less in his life, thus far, than he had hoped for. It was evident to Jake that his father at his age, 45, had been much more successful than himself. But then, who in his right mind would want to live his father's life? A claims adjuster for a transnational insurance company, pushing paper day after day in some windowless cubicle, in some high-rise. The only way to remember what the sun looked like was from the photograph on your desk or the mental image carried with you from last weekend's barbeque.

Sure it was a safe, moderately well paying job with full family benefits; but that was it. Jake never belittled his dad's life or what he did, he was simply saddened because it seemed a waste. No thrills, no excitement. Sure there were some exciting days, good and bad. You marry, you have kids, there are surprise birthday parties, maybe someday you're involved in a car crash. But that was not the excitement he had in mind. It was the thrill of going out there and purposefully putting your balls on the line, for the whole bag of marbles, win or lose. But you did it.   In search of adventure, a unique experience, something no one can take from you. In a way, like the first time you got laid, the excitement and the jitters. You did it, it's yours forever.

To make matters worse his father had lived a short life. Only fifty-two, seven more years than Jake was now, he had died of lung cancer. You only live once and you never know when your time will come and that was just a few of the reasons why Jake was hell bent on living his life as fully as possible.

The King 155 comm. crackled to life awaking him from his thoughts. "X-ray Alpha Tango Alpha Papa contact LA center on 123.25"

"Tango Alpha Papa 123.25" Jake dialed in the new frequency, and flipped it over to the active and listened for a few seconds, making sure he didn't interrupt someone else's call. "X-ray Alpha Tango Alpha Papa 9,000 on my way to 9,500"

"Tango Alpha Papa confirm your destination as Ciudad Obregon this morning, and confirm you have international advisories."

"Tango Alpha Papa confirms Ciudad Obregon and has international advisories, thanks."
Jake looked at his King 89B GPS to see his time enroute to Ciudad Obregon. He didn't want to arrive before 7am. If he did it would mean paying overtime to the controllers, even though they were certainly there already attending other traffic. Jake was aware that Mexico had a great deal more restrictions on flying than the US. Before take off, that is, because once you depart, with their limited radar coverage, you would virtually disappear until you reached your destination.

Settling in again he rechecked all his gauges, six egt's, six cht's, oil temp, pressure, amp meter, voltmeter, suction, fuel flow, and fuel level. Course was right on, 102 degrees, which included 5 for wind correction. Six minutes to KUMBA intersection which would put him on the edge of the restricted area over the Great Salton Sea.

Warmth from the engine, smooth clear night, the rhythmic purr from the big Lycoming quickly put Jake back into the trance he had just come out of. His mind drifted pleasantly to thoughts of Mazatlán. Only an hour and a half from Durango. It may be minus forty degrees in Fargo, North Dakota. Mazatlán would be a pleasant 87 degrees, with just the right tropical humidity. Gorgeous turistas would be looking for a good time during their getaway. He could already hear the lapping of the warm ocean, the rustling of the palapa overhead, the rich unique smell of the coconut oil baking on the back of the lovely girl he just had the pleasure of spreading it on. Her voluptuous round butt barely covered by a so-called bikini. It's all he could do not to reach out and get himself in trouble. Within arms distance is a bucketful of ice, cold bottles of Pacifico beer protrude just above the rim, sand clings to the bottom of the bucket as it sweats in the heat. 'Now I've gone too far, the last beer I had was eight months ago. Sober since then. It was and still is the most difficult thing I have ever done. The cravings are constant, it's getting better but I still think about it every single day without fail.'

Jake reached over to his shoulder pocket and pulled out another Camel Light tearing off the filter, lighting it with the Zippo and inhaling deeply in one very well choreographed motion. It wasn't a shot of good Don Julio Añejo Tequila, but it would do.

A slight shudder, followed by a little roll with a change in pitch brought him back to the present. 'Good. This will help me keep my mind off the booze.'

The Cessna 185 was just passing over the highest portion of the 6,000 foot range, which divides Southern California's coastal section from its desert interior. Just a little wind can create significant updrafts and even worse downdrafts, but Jake knew very well that on a night like tonight it wouldn't be bad. Just as he expected, as soon as it started it was gone, replaced by glassy smooth skies.

This radical change had been 10 months in the making. 'Am I insane? I've asked myself this question a thousand times, and I'll probably keep asking until I change the question to: Was I out of my mind? Or maybe. What the hell were you thinking? Are all the horror stories I have heard over the years about Mexico true? My friend Omar swears they are not. Neither my plane nor my radios will be stolen if I leave them unattended for two minutes. I won't be kidnapped at gunpoint and forced to run drugs 'al norte'. So how do these stories and rumors get started? It's probably fear of the unknown and a great excuse not to be adventurous.'

One of the great advantages about flying a 185 is that most drug runners don't fly taildraggers for some odd reason. They prefer the Cessna 206, 207, and 182's, which also happen to be the most frequently stolen airplanes in the world. These aircraft have good short unimproved runway characteristics and a nose wheel which most 'mules' prefer. Another consideration, it takes some practice to fly a tail dragger and many young drug runners just don't have the time to invest in learning the nuances and complexity of a tail dragger, even if they do make a better bush plane. In fact a lot of runners die before getting any type of experience any way.

Cessna 185's are still the workhorse of the Alaskan bush pilots. In terms of take off and landings it can outperform most of its counterparts, and if you add tundra tires, or skis, or floats, you can land just about anywhere. Maybe when they see the performance of Tango Alpha Papa they will be convinced and everyone will want one. Too bad they don't make them anymore.

Billions of brilliant stars, a full moon, and the fact that it was a clear night allowed Jake to distinguish some faint features and silhouettes far below as California's Imperial Valley and the Great Salton Sea lay off to the left almost two miles beneath the wings of the 185.

Even though he constantly questioned his decision, it would be safe to say he had made up his mind months ago. There was one certainty to all this. He wasn't escaping life. He was recreating his life. And recreating it in a manner that he truly believed would be fulfilling. It had always saddened him to see how many people live their lives wishing and hoping for something. Something different, something exciting. The lottery maybe. Few take the bull by the horns and actually force a change. For many it's a fleeting thought and then it's back to driving to work on an ever more crowded freeway. Sure, most people have complicated lives, loaded with mounting responsibilities like mortgages, kids in school, hobbies, friends and added all together, even if you'd like to make a drastic change, the task seems insurmountable. Jake didn't have such a complicated life. So eventually, he concluded that he didn't want to be sitting alone in some crappy old folks' home in Riverside, or even worse, as he took in that last breath of precious air and have the ultimate question pop into his dying mind, 'What would my life have been like if I had taken a chance and actually pursued my dream and gone bush piloting in Mexico? If nothing else I am determined never to ask myself that question.'

Jake's friend Omar Carrillo y Salas had painted a very exciting and tantalizing picture. He had been a bush pilot in his native state of Durango, Mexico since he was around fifteen. He specified 'around' because the determining factor was when he could reach the rudder pedals and see out the window with the assistance of only one pillow. (Who makes these rules anyway)? Of course his pilot's license showed him to be 18. Nobody really questioned this short 18 year old since there are a lot of short people in Mexico.

Twenty-four years of bush piloting. Omar was calm, collected and had a happy disposition towards life. He and Jake had met a couple of years ago when he was ferrying an airplane back to Mexico for one of his customers. The Centurion 210 he was flying started running very rough and landed at the nearest airport, which happened to be Palomar Airport KCRQ in Carlsbad, California.

Between Omar's limited English and Jake's baja-surfer/high school Spanish they managed to understand one another. The magnetos where shot and he might as well replace the plugs and harness at the same time, so Jake had invited Omar to stay with him in his old aluminum Airstream. It was by no stretch of the imagination a palace, but it was home, it was comfortable and it almost had an ocean front view. It kept him dry during the few days that it rained and it kept him warm during those few winter months. Best of all it was paid for and in Southern California 'Paid For' isn't in very many people's vocabulary.

During Omar's three day stay with Jake and Amber he told a dozen stories of his best flying exploits around the beautiful and breathtaking Mexican Sierra, the interesting characters, the cargo and the gold. Primarily, Omar flew gold bullion from Mineria San Patricio deep in the heart of the Sierra to Durango where he met up with an armored truck for its delivery to the bank. It was very treacherous flying, if you had an engine problem there were very few hospitable places to land. Mountain tops pushed ten thousand feet, while the canyons between each fell away in sheer cliffs three to four thousand feet deep. It would be virtually impossible to make a survivable forced landing in the area.

There are literally thousands of tiny little towns scattered around the countryside, they are so inaccessible even the poorest of people have no choice but to fly in or out. It's either fly or expose yourself to five or six days of harsh dirt roads and who knows what else. Many of these people have never seen a city the size of Durango, which only has 350,000 inhabitants, let alone get on an airplane. In fact a great many indigenous people in the Mexican

Sierra don't speak Spanish, they speak Indian dialects. Huichol, Cora, Mexicanero and Tepehuano among others.

Over the years Omar asked for Jake's help in finding or checking aircraft for sale. This association eventually gave them the idea of doing some business together. Possibly an air taxi and cargo service, after all Omar had been in the business of managing and flying for that type of operation his entire life. The biggest problem would be amassing the amount of money necessary to buy an airplane outright and have enough change to make sure they could survive the startup. Credit was impossible in Mexico, with rates as high as 40% per annum you would have to be totally insane to even try.

It seemed like an impossible dream. Omar had a very nice boss and more toys than most. His primary objective had always been to provide for the well-being, comfort and education he believed his eight year old daughter deserved. One day she would become a professional. A member of society to be admired, a success, and he was going to make sure he did everything to obtain this objective.

During one of Omar's many visits, in particular one a year ago, Jake dropped a hint about possibly being interested in an extended visit to Durango. See how he liked it.

"Do you think I could get a flying job in Mexico?"

"Sure. The pay probably won't be to your liking though," Omar said matter of fact.

"Life is cheaper in Mexico, maybe I can make do."

"Yeah, we would have some fun." Omar thought of the implications of teaching Jake to bush pilot in the severe environment and without a full knowledge of Spanish. After all the last pilot he had trained for the challenges of bush flying was his younger brother Enrique and he had died a year and a half ago in an airplane accident. "You would have to get a Mexican pilots license. But that wouldn't be a problem."

"How about if I brought my own plane with me? That would probably help. We could both fly it." Jake knew this would pique his friend's interest.

Omar was now warming up to the idea. "You would have to register it in Mexico. You can't work with a US plane in Mexico. As long as you are willing to register it in Mexico and pay the import duty, that would be great!"

Jake was also getting excited with the prospects. "Maybe we could start our own cargo and air taxi service? Would you be interested?"

Omar's eyes lit up, "Of course I'd be interested!"

With these words the idea was hatched. Now all they needed was a good bush plane with no money down, zero interest and zero payments. Jake realized this was a bit of a tall order.

LA Center came loud over the radio jolting him from his thoughts. "X-ray Alpha Tango Alpha Papa you are about to depart United States airspace. Radar services are terminated. Squawk VFR. Suggest you contact Tijuana approach or Mexicali tower. Good night."

"Thanks LA Center have a great morning. Switching to TJ approach." And that was it. 'Now I am truly venturing into the unknown. I can't honestly say that this is where my adventure begins because it really started when I found the noble steed I'm flying at this very moment.'

Jake reached into the shoulder pocket of his black military surplus flight jacket and extracted the crunched pack of camel lights. As always he tore off the filter and lit the remaining cigarette with his classic plain Zippo. At least that's how the Zippo box that once contained it had described its contents. Jake could never remember who had told him it was the filter and not the tobacco that kills you. It made sense at the time and the custom had stuck. If nothing else it was kind of interesting to see the inquisitive looks from people as he performed his ritual.

"Mexicali tower, Xtra Alpha Tango Alpha Papa entering Mexican airspace at Calexico-Mexicali," Jake said in Spanish. Might as well get started now.

"Tango Alpha Papa state departure point and destination."

"Departure point is Carlsbad, California and destination is Ciudad Obregon."

Smoking was one thing Jake was not about to quit. He had just kicked the hardest thing ever – booze. He wasn't about to lose all his vices in one year. Hell! If he did, he might just as well become involved with some weird religious sect or join a monastery on a mountain top somewhere. God forbid!

Once he had made up his mind that he wanted a future in bush piloting around the Mexican Sierra, next question was, how do I get my hands on a good bush plane with no money? This would be the biggest dilemma. It had filled his mind for months on end. He came up with a thousand hare-brained schemes. But sometimes the best solution is right under your nose and will work the best. Jake recalled the day he walked to the airport restroom, and an old Cessna 172 came into focus. The decrepit old airplane with its three flat tires had sat collecting dust for as long as he could remember. In fact, it had been there so long, he didn't even notice it anymore. A paint scheme, which in it's time would've probably been the rage was now bleached white by the sun.

Suddenly it hit him, he realized that every airport he had ever been to had one or two such airplanes, and for an airplane lover that was truly a sad thing to see. Most pilots believe an airplane, in some strange way, has a soul. If you aren't going to use it, or worse, neglect it, then you don't deserve it. Jake was torn by these thoughts but he had a need, a desperate need to try and make something of his life. Not just something mundane, something exciting, special. If somebody just didn't care enough to take care of such a wonderful possession then they certainly didn't deserve it. Period.

Now the problem would be to find the right airplane, and a 172 just wouldn't cut it. A good bush plane would be a Cessna 185 or 180, a Pilatus Porter or maybe a Helio. Jake's preference would be a Cessna 185. With his mind made up it was time to go searching. He decided that the best location to find a neglected airplane in good condition would be the desert. Between the heat and the bone-dry conditions it would be the best place to mothball a plane.

Jake's boss allowed him to use the little Citabria with its huge underbelly fuel tank for his weekend getaways. After all a good employee was hard to find, and especially one with Jake's eyesight. He could spot a swordfish miles away. He had been the best fish spotter his boss had ever hired. It was a very tough job. Not only did you have to fly 14-hour days with only one refueling stop. But you had to piss in a coffee can while flying just above stall speed. To make matters worse, a few years back some competing boats that didn't have their own airborne fish spotters would shoot at you! That really sucked! On one such occasion Jake didn't notice that his fuel tank had been perforated and had run out of fuel. He ditched the plane right next to the fishing boat.

On the fourth weekend of his search for an abandoned plane he landed at Overton, Nevada, just outside of Las Vegas and came across a Cessna A185E. It was a really sorry sight, it looked even worse than the 172 at home but at that moment Jake decided this plane would be perfect, it was even equipped with an underbelly pod for extra cargo.

Jake waltzed into the manager's office. Every single floorboard creaked as if it were about to give way. The manager was a caricature of himself, Walt Disney couldn't have done better. In his late 80's Hamish, a British expat, exRAF pilot had been the Overton Manager since the mid 50's. His long well kept handlebar moustache and huge red pock marked nose were the first things one would focus on and it was very hard to tear your eyes away.

Hamish snapped to attention, and in a beautiful English accent said: "Will you be needing some fuel today Saaaa?"

Jake bit the inside of his cheek. Amber sat down next to him and with her typical inquisitive look inspected her surroundings. He didn't really need any but he could see the expectation in the old gentleman's eyes. "Sure, I could do with a few gallons."

"I'll get right on it."

"No need to hurry. I also wanted to ask you about the white and red 185 at the end of the last row of hangars. Do you know who owns it?" Jake tried his best to not sound too interested.

Hamish quickly looked through a set of yellowing index cards. "Let's see. I believe its tail number is N54NE?"

"That's right," Jake helped.

"Ah yes right here. That plane hasn't flown in over ten years. Nice old chap passed away and left it to his son. Awful shame isn't it?" The manager got a longing look in his eye.

"Do you have a phone number or a name?"

"Let's see. The number I have has been crossed out but I can provide you with an address. You know the son owns it now but he's not a pilot. As a matter of fact, lots of people have asked about the plane. Seems he can't bring himself to sell it since his father used to take him on camping trips when he was a lad. Awful shame to see it just rot away."

"So the son hasn't been out to see his plane in a long time then?" Jake asked.

"I'm quite sure he has never been out. According to my records he sent a check to cover five years worth of tie down fees. Still has two to go."

"Well there's no harm in asking if he'd consider selling, right?"

"Certainly Saaaa. Now, how about that fuel?"

It seemed that Jake had found his plane. His first reaction was to come back to the airport, do some quick fixes and get the hell out before anyone noticed. But on second thought that would only raise suspicion. Not only that, it could also be a very dangerous proposition. A hundred things could go wrong with an airplane that hadn't flown in who knows how many years. No. He'd calmly show up with tools and the parts he knew with certainty would be needed. Then he would rent a hangar and do a thorough annual inspection. It probably hadn't been fully inspected in ten years, maybe more!

A full month of fish spotting, day in day out, sitting on his keister. Flying a few hundred feet above the waves, no land in sight. Spot a nice big swordfish, slow the plane way down and circle it until the boat could catch up to harpoon it. And then it was off to search for another. It was a bumper month, the catch was good and Jake got a nice commission for every fish caught. Since it was the end of the season it would be a perfect time to go fix up the old 185 and give it a more dignified life.

Jake spent the first week scrounging all the items he knew he would need for the 185's annual. Tires, bearings, plugs, grease, oil, oil filter, and an array of other items. His tools would wait 'til last. The little old Toyota pickup was at its maximum capacity. He hoped it would make it the full 320 miles to Overton.

The desert was hot as can be, 120 degrees to be exact. Strange place the desert, millions of square miles virtually uninhabited covered with dirt, or at best a shrub or two. Jake's left arm and the side of his face were burned red and parched from the dryness. Amber sulked, with her full coat of fur she was not a happy camper.

Jake parked in the shade beside the manager's office and walked around to the front of the old weathered building, Amber in tow. As he passed the office window he saw Hamish reclined in his old institutional green metal office chair, circa 1930, his feet resting upon the shabby old institutional gray metal desk. A floor fan whizzed frantically back and forth attempting to attenuate or at least disperse the violent heat. As Jake pushed the screen door open, it came in contact with the little bell. Hamish peered suspiciously through one disinterested eye and closed it again in hopes it was either a dream or whoever it was would go away.

Jake realized that the old man would probably prefer to continue sleeping but he hadn't come all this way just to sit around. "Hi, I was here about a month ago looking at the old run down 185."

"Hmmm," Hamish replied still asleep.

"Well, as it turns out the son was willing to sell it to me."

"Really?" This started to wake the old man from his rest.

"Do you have an empty hangar you could rent me for a month?"

"Sure, take #19. It's at the end of the row where the 185 is now. We'll talk about the price later."

Despite their age the cracked old tires were still able to hold 35 lbs. of pressure without blowing. As Jake filled them he did turn his head away just in case.

He rolled the graceful old lady into her hangar and got down to business. First, every inspection panel was removed and placed into a baggy with its corresponding screws. There are few more frustrating things than to have a bunch of parts and not remembering where the hell they go. Next task, the interior, but that would have to wait for tomorrow morning.

Amber looked at him inquisitively as he placed the cot in the rear of the hangar. Jake could swear he saw a definite expression of "are you shitting me? We're not sleeping in a hangar?" Money was tight, not that it had been plentiful at anytime. Anyway, sleeping in a hangar would be a big incentive to get things done and get on down to Mexico and start working. Sleep came quickly as the satisfaction of a days work towards his objective came to a close.

Morning appeared and so did the immediate need to find a cup of coffee, a couple of sandwiches for breakfast, lunch and dinner. Finally on the list was to find a state park where he could start his day with the 3 Sh's. Amber seemed a bit put out by the situation, at eight years of age, she was slowing down a little and more than ever seemed to appreciate some comfort.

When the cowl came off, he noticed that instead of a Continental IO-520 he found a Lycoming TIO-540. The logbook confirmed the STC. SA2118NM. The first order of business was the removal of four birds' nests. It appeared that many families of birds had lived under the protection of the old Cessna. The nests were so entwined in the engine that it took hours to remove them. Then of course came the clean up which pretty much took the rest of the day. It was a task he was very happy to have behind him. He was literally up to his elbows in bird shit.

Even though they checked out, it wasn't something he was willing to short change, Jake had just started replacing the Bendix magnetos, harness, and sparkplugs. As he gazed outside momentarily, he realized what a nice quiet airport this was. Maybe ten airplanes had arrived and departed during the whole day.   No jets like Palomar, with their obnoxious auxiliary power units buzzing loudly all day.   There wouldn't be any traffic at night since there was no lighting system. As the sun dropped behind the barren hills to the West, it cast long playful purple shadows around the tiny valley. Amber suddenly gave off one of her low level warning growls and Hamish peered around the corner of the old rusty hangar door.

"Good evening. I just wanted to see how you were making out with the old bird. Don't mean to interrupt or anything," Hamish said tenuously.

"No, no, I was just about to call it a day," Jake lied as he wiped his greasy hands.

"I don't get much company here, and since my Suzy died a year or so ago it can get a little lonely you know."

"Well come on in and I'll show you the progress. There's still a helluva lot of work to do, but I was kinda expecting that. Especially since she hasn't flown in so many years."   Jake wanted to get him thinking about airplanes and not his deceased wife. "You look like a pilot to me! What do you fly?"

Hamish perked up. "From time to time I'll fly a little Piper Cub. I shouldn't really. My medical was revoked years ago." As he spoke he fondly stroked the plane's Hartzell propeller. "Back in World War II I flew Spitfires with a fighter squadron stationed at Biggin Hill. Those were some exciting yet terrifying days." Hamish's eyes grew distant in remembrance.

"Why don't you have a seat, there's a lawn chair over there. Soda?" Jake didn't wait for an answer, handed him a cold diet Sprite and sat down on an old 10-gallon paint can.

"Thank you." Hamish took the Sprite, pulled the rickety old lawn chair a little closer and got comfortable. He reached into his back pocket pulled out a silver flask. "May I offer you a taste of my finest single blend scotch?"

"Had to quit it. Unfortunately."

"I respect a man that knows his limits," Hamish said with a very dignified hand salute.

Jake pulled out his pack of Camel lights and offered one to Hamish.

"Thanks, but I quit over thirty years ago."

"I respect that. But speaking quite frankly. There's no way in hell it's gonna kill ya now!" Jake said as he tore of the filter and lit up. "Please continue," Jake loved hearing stories from the old timers. The old man took a deep breath, "Oh there really isn't much to tell. It's a long time ago now. It was an electrifying time to live! There was so much going on. You lived every single day to the fullest, simply because it could easily be your last. In fact I gave a few fellow pilots their last day. I'm certain their thoughts were very similar to ours, just in a different language. But they had the same fears, and desires to return to their families, girlfriends..." Hamish stroked Ambers' ears..."dogs."

"But then in the blink of an eye it's your turn. My squadron was returning from a mission escorting bombers over Germany. We were over France and heading back from an uneventful sortie. The setting sun was in our eyes. I can still remember that gorgeous colorful sunset to this day, but that's all. None of us saw them coming, they descended upon us blasting. My Spitfire burst into flames, and to make matters worse a huge bullet from a Messerschmitt ripped through my thigh. I honestly have no idea how I made it out," Hamish stopped talking momentarily as the images rolled by in his brain.

"What happened next?" Jake asked, feeling like a kid.

"Two of us were gunned down that afternoon. My wingman wasn't as lucky, he went in with his plane. When I set down my wounded leg snapped, I can't describe the excruciating pain."

Jake winced and scrunched his face as the imaginary pain went through his own thigh.

"Somehow I gathered my chute and rolled myself into the marsh on the edge of a canal. All night I could hear the krauts looking for me, I was lucky they didn't have dogs. The freezing water and the buoyancy helped ease the pain of my broken leg. Luck smiled in my direction one more time, the French farmers who found me the following morning were part of the Resistance. A family nursed me for months, they had no medicine to offer, except for red wine. I drank gallons of it. As you can imagine I haven't touched a drop since!"

Hamish took another long swig from his flask. Jake took the opportunity to light up another Camel.

"Despite my closeness to the coast and the English Channel, there was no way to make it back to England to continue fighting the war. My leg was so messed up, as you can see, I've never been able to walk without limping. So I wound up staying for a year and a half, part of '44 and '45 till the war ended. I farmed along side my French family. Wonderful people."

"When the war ended I went back home only to find that my fiancée had given up waiting for me and had married my best friend. When I visited them she was already pregnant. Really can't blame them."

"Oh man that sucks!" The words just seem to pop out of Jake's mouth.

"So at twenty three years of age I decided to make my way to America. Land of opportunity is how the Americans I had met described it. They spoke of its grandeur, I just had to see it for myself. After all, I figured, if I don't like it I could always return to England.

"My original idea was to be a crop duster, or something airplane related. That's what I knew how to do. Bad thing is every other pilot had the same idea. So I joined a flying circus and started making my way out West. I worked primarily as a wing walker," Hamish said this very matter of fact. "And let me tell you, wing walking with the limp left over from my fighting days was no easy feat!"

"No way, you can't be serious! You're pulling my leg, aren't you?" Jake said astonished.

"I wouldn't do that." Protested Hamish. "I'm telling you the God's honest truth. I was a wing walker!"

"All right, I believe you. Please go on," Jake was riveted.

"Well, the circus made it out to Las Vegas. It was a very different town back then. There was the main strip in town, which doesn't look like todays in the least. I was at the newest and swankiest casino, the Flamingo, when this gorgeous cocktail waitress waltzes up to me and asks me if I want a drink. I didn't want a drink, I wanted to marry her! She had these long, long perfect legs. She wasn't your typical blonde bimbo type. This brunette was not only beautiful, she was classy, oozing sensuality and finesse. Her Italian accent was intoxicating, it just drove me over the edge. I was completely and utterly obsessed. I can see her lovely dark brown eyes, her full expressive eyebrows, her full lush lips; a natural deep red you have never seen before." Hamish took another swig from his flask. "To this day the hair on the back of my neck stands on end just thinking about her. And then, after mustering enough courage, I gave her my finest British accented pickup line, and that was the beginning of a wonderful relationship."

"Holy shit Hamish! You've got to tell me that pick up line. I'm gonna have to use it!"

"You are probably not going to believe it, but I don't remember. In any case, Suzy or Susana, in those days, wanted to stay in Vegas. She loved the

desert and the lights. I had no option but to move
here. In hindsight I'm glad I did, Suzy was a wonderful
woman, a great friend and companion, a wonderful
mother. I wouldn't trade my life with her for anything.
But now I miss her terribly."

     Jake could see his eyes water as he
reminisced. Hamish continued. "It might sound silly
but in all honesty I felt like killing myself when she
died. I just couldn't see how I could possibly go on
without her. It's not like we talked incessantly, it's not
like we were together all the time, but there was this
incredible connection. Just being near each other was
enough. She was absolutely amazing!" His words
were far from loud and explosive, but they carried all
the weight of his old heart.

     "From the way you describe her she sounds like
a wonderful person," Jake said sympathetically.

     "There is one thing I am sorry about. I would've
liked to continue what had started out to be a pretty
adventurous life. Now that I'm old, I realize how full I
felt during those war years.   Sure it was very
frightening at times, but it was also very exhilarating. I
wish I could have continued them. Really, I shouldn't
complain, there are people in this world who have
never had a really truly exhilarating day in their
mundane life. Anyway, I've been rambling on like an
old man for way too long." Hamish stood to leave.

     The sun had long since set and the night
started to chill.

     "No, no. Please, stay. I haven't been this
fascinated in a long, long time." Jake extracted
another smoke from his flight jacket and lit it with a
deep draw. "Tell me more."

"No. Enough about me.   How about you? What's your story? Why did you want to fly?" Hamish was truly interested and it showed.

"It's hard to say. I always wanted to fly. As far back as I can remember I've wanted to fly. When I was a little boy I used to make yokes out of Lego blocks and play for hours on end. I have no idea where that came from, especially since I had never been in an airplane. You know, it's when you think about things like this that you wonder about reincarnation. Could I have been a pilot in a past life and the desires of my previous life spilled over into this one? Is there any possibility that I might be your old wingman in a new body?" Jake philosophized.

Hamish declared.   "Are you sure you're not sneaking some hooch when I'm not looking?"

"Come on Hamish!   It's never crossed your mind? Not even in the slightest?" Jake gave his best incredulous look. "Very well. Tell me Mr. Hamish, fighter-pilot-and one-line-picker-upper extraordinaire. Why did you become a pilot?"

"I'm sorry to put a dent in your very interesting theories," Hamish replied with a hint of sarcasm, "but the war had started and I thought there was a certain romance and pizzazz, plus a great way to pick up lovely ladies at the local pub by saying I was a pilot. Honestly not much more than that!" Hamish said truthfully and very matter of fact. "Now I must get to bed. An old man like me needs his beauty rest," he labored arm and leg as he got up with a big grunt. "This is what you have to look forward to, Jake. Make use of every remaining instant of your life to the fullest with whatever satisfies you the most.   Let nothing stand in your way. Whatever it is, do not let anything or anyone stop you. If you don't heed these words you will always regret it later." Hamish walked into the darkness without saying goodbye.

After the morning ritual it was back to work with the aggravation of a convenience store burrito gnawing at his gut. The oil that drained from the pan was thick as molasses and smelled awful, probably from the bacteria festering in it. He drained the fuel tanks of the gas or water, who knows what else? There was no way anyone in his right mind would trust 10-year-old avgas.

At long last she was nearing the much-anticipated first flight, well not her first flight and not his, but certainly their first flight together. She still didn't look very nice, but the paint would have to wait. It probably would have been easier to just go ahead and strip her then and there, in Podunk, Nevada, paint her and fly her back with her new numbers. Most business people in California would agree that the state's EPA, OSHA and every other agency seemed to be hell bent on closing as many businesses as they possibly could. So painting was becoming an incredible pain in the ass. Anyone else would think the country, and the states for that matter were being run by the three stooges.

One solid week of ten-hour workdays was all it took. Every moving part was lubed and re-torqued. New tires, bearings and brakes. New battery, new magnetos and harness. Every square inch of aluminum was checked for corrosion. Every cable and pulley was checked and re-tensioned, the cleaning

alone took a couple of days. She was ready to fly.
Again.

Jake turned the engine over without engaging
the magnetos long enough for the oil pressure to raise
and pre-lube the engine. As he engaged the mags the
engine roared to life, coughing a few times and
billowing an enormous cloud of smoke, which quickly
enveloped the whole plane. Those years of oil
seeping through the rings burned away quickly. Jake
kept a close eye on the oil pressure in case it dropped,
fortunately it remained steady. He pulled the mixture
to shut her down, the engine missed once and kept
running. Better check the mixture setting. Once he
reset it and checked for oil leaks it would be time for a
run up and a flight around the patch.

A flashing M on the GPS interrupted Jake's
thoughts. Forty miles out of Hermosillo. Time to
check in since they do have radar coverage in the
area. Jake's Spanish was poor, and most controllers
speak English but he might as well start practicing
now. "Xtra Alpha Tango Alpha Papa nine thousand
five hundred, 40 miles northwest on the 204 radial
from Hermosillo VOR."

"TAP what is your departure point and
destination?"

"Departure point is Charlie Romeo Quebec –
Palomar, California. Destination Mike Mike Charlie
November, I mean Nectar," Jake corrected himself.
"Ciudad Obregon."

"TAP report when 40 miles from Hermosillo."

"TAP willco."

Way, way off to the East a very slight hue of
sun from the upcoming day started its assent. It

wouldn't be long before the temperature started to rise and the beautiful features of the earth became visible once again. He would revel in the clear water of the Sea of Cortez and the little islands that dot its mass.

Jake checked his engine gauges, everything was functioning properly. The AiResearch turbo charger could provide full power at this altitude, it would come in handy with the density altitude of the Mexican Sierra.

The willing old Cessna 185 joyfully taxied onto the departure end of the 3,400 foot active runway 24 on a crisp clear Nevada morning. Hamish stood by the runway with a cup of steaming tea in one hand while clutching himself tightly with the other to keep warm. Jake had already announced his departure intentions on Unicom frequency 122.8, words, which would never be heard by a living soul.

He eased the throttle to its stop. The TIO-540 Lycoming responded immediately, the runway whizzed by, tail up, rotation speed, and the wheels gently released their grip from the concrete. Freedom enveloped Jake as he departed, relief would wait until he had some more altitude. Amber had remained in the truck sleeping, oblivious to the whole affair. Overall, it was pretty uneventful, which is what you want out of a first flight.

The rest of the now sweltering day was consumed by repacking all his tools and miscellaneous stuff back into the old beat up Toyota 4x4 pickup. With almost 400,000 miles on the odometer it was showing it's age. Either its ride was getting harsher or Jake was getting softer. At a maximum speed of 50 mph, he knew from experience that it would take him almost 9 hours to get home, not in the least something to look forward to. Since the old Pioneer Supertuner III had given up on him a few years back he had bought a portable CD player which was supposed to be skip resistant. At least it kept him somewhat entertained during those long hours fish spotting.

As Jake left Las Vegas on his way towards LA he compared the traffic heading south versus the traffic heading north. Having forgotten what day it was he declared to Amber. "It must be getting close to the weekend. Look at all those people heading to Sin City to give away all their hard earned cash. Shit, they might as well just give it to us!"

Amber looked at him inquisitively with her intense blue and brown marbled eyes almost as if she could understand what he was saying. As quickly as she looked up she gave herself a quick scratch behind her ear and again rested her chin on the lowered window and allowed her cheeks to flail about in the hot desert wind. By the time they arrived at their 'beach house' it was all Jake could do to stay awake. He promptly fell asleep in front of yet another rerun of Seinfeld, and an almost full O'Douls on the coffee table.

Again, the radio interrupted his thoughts and brought him to the present.

"Tango Alpha Papa report present position." The controller sounded a little annoyed.
Jake studied his KLN89B GPS hit nearest and selected VOR. "TAP is 44 miles on the 200 degree radial."

"Next time when I instruct you to report at a certain point be sure you do so.   Contact Ciudad Obregon tower."

"TAP going to Ciudad Obregon Tower," Jake said politely. 'These guys like to dish out a little crap whenever they get a chance. But then I wouldn't want to be controlling traffic at this time in the morning either.' He mumbled to himself.

Jake switched over to 118.30, reported in with Ciudad Obregon Tower and commenced his 21-minute descent towards the small town. And left his mind to it's habitual daydreaming.

Getting back to Echo Bay Airport in Overton, Nevada to pick up the 185 was a helluva lot easier than the drive. Jake got a ride with his old friend Ron in his sleek twin turbo Lancair 4, with a cruise of 270 knots TAS they arrived in just over an hour. What an awesome work of art!

Hamish saw the beautiful bird taxi up and rushed out to gawk and as always offer a top off. Not only was it the only thing that kept him busy, it was also an important chunk of his income. Ron realized this fact, even though he really didn't want fill his gas-guzzler, and especially not at $2.56 a gallon. Call it business – fellow pilot charity.

"I guess this airplane is too fancy to carry Amber?" Hamish said half joking.

Ron quickly replied in defense. "Not really, my dog Ginger is sleeping in the back seat."   Ginger hearing her name peered out the door and barked.

Jake added. "Amber just seemed reluctant to come along today so I let her stay at home."

"Well be sure to give her a good pat and a biscuit from me." Hamish said.

"I'll be happy to do so," Jake said with a smile. There are few things an animal lover likes more than someone who sends good wishes to their pet.

"Ron, I'm not in the habit of asking people for favors. But would you mind very much if I sat in your plane?" Hamish looked longingly at the plush interior.

"Even better. How about if we go for a quick blast around the patch?"

"Please don't toy with an old man!" Hamish said excitedly.

After 20 minutes of yanking and banking Hamish was absolutely and entirely spent. "That was the most fun I have had in years!" He said with the joy of a boy who'd just gotten laid.

Jake said his farewells to Hamish, promising to visit soon. The Cessna launched a few minutes before the Lancair. Ron ripped by the old Cessna like a rocket, and Jake arrived at Palomar a full hour after the speed machine.

"Ciudad Obregon Tower Tango Alpha Papa is 5nm to the Northwest, 2,500, landing."

"TAP cleared to land 31, left traffic."

"TAP cleared to land," Jake repeated only the essential.

Straight down the runway, the winds were calm. Patchy morning fog rose from the farmers' fields that surrounded the airport. Amber didn't even stir as the enormous tundra tires touched down on the perfect 7,546 foot cement runway. In a split second a rabbit appeared out of nowhere, a dog on its heels and closing in quickly. Jake shoved the throttle to the stop, held it and yanked back. In one fluid motion he pulled back to idle and greased her in on the remaining 5,000 feet.

Reverting back to his familiar English Jake commented: "Obregon Tower there was a dog on the runway. I'm going to taxi back to make sure I didn't hit him."

"What was that?" The controller replied, half asleep and having missed the whole gyration. Jake repeated the request and was cleared to do whatever he wanted.

A very young soldier with an AK47 assault rifle, which appeared to be larger than him, walked lazily towards the plane. Once the polished Hartzell three-blade propeller had come to a stop he approached the left door.

The dark skinned young man with black lazy eyes asked in a shy voice. "I need to get some information from you, Señor," he needed name, address, pilot's license number, departure point, time enroute, tach time on the airplane and finally passengers on board. Jake slowly shook his head and rolled his eyes, 'was he blind also?'

"Where is the customs building?" Jake asked.

The soldier pointed to the freshly painted little building with no lights on. "No one is there yet. But immigration is open in the terminal building."

Jake walked over to the modern edifice. He found an older man sitting with his eyes closed behind an even older sickly green desk, dressed in a recently pressed uniform with its collar turned up and his arms clutched around his body in a futile attempt to shield himself from the early morning cold. A small styrofoam cup of instant coffee steamed before him. Jake gently knocked on the door jamb feeling a little awkward about waking the man up.

The official slowly peered through one eye and in a thick sleepy voice said. "Si? What can I do for you Señor?"

"I need to get a tourist card."

"You are not on a commercial flight. So you are flying your own plane?"

"Yes sir that is correct."

"Please fill the tourist card out and pay $15 dollars to the cashier. Oh, wait a second. She isn't here yet," he quickly glanced at his old Timex. "She won't be long, maybe an hour mas o menos. You will have to wait."

"Can't I just pay you?"

"Oh no Señor. Mexico doesn't work that way anymore." The official said somewhat indignant.

"Well can I go get some breakfast then?" Jake inquired.

"Sorry, but you will have to stay within the protected portion of the airport until you clear customs and immigration."

"Shall I clear customs while I wait for the cashier to arrive?"

"No. You must clear immigration first, Señor." The immigration officer said with slight irritation as if everybody should know this obvious fact.

Jake was starting to get irritated but knew it wouldn't help in the least. "I'll go wait in my airplane for an hour or so."

The official behind the old green desk nodded his approval, huddled up again, sipped his coffee, and pretended he could immediately fall back into a deep, unmolested sleep.

Jake walked back to the plane and took Amber for a short walk.   Carcasses of old beat up drug running planes littered the edge of the parking ramp. What a terrible shame, Jake thought. As he walked back to the plane he flagged down the gas truck.

"Buenos dias, Señor!" The driver said with a smile and much too joyfully for this time of the morning.

"Could you fill up the Cessna over there?" Jake pointed in the general direction of the plane.

"Well I would be happy to Señor, but the lady cashier for fuel purchases isn't here yet, so I can't."

Jake gritted his teeth, and remained calm. It wasn't this guy's fault, and it wouldn't help to get upset at him. "Do you know what time she will return?"

The smiling man inspected his watch. "Maybe an hour. I'll come back as soon as she arrives, okay?"

"Sure," Jake said smiling on the outside, absolute exasperation on the inside. As he got back in the plane having achieved nothing, he closed the door and announced to Amber. "We're not in Kansas anymore, Toto," as he pushed his seat back as far as it would go and lit a smoke. He glanced through sleepy half closed eyes for the arrival of the airport personnel.

Even a couple of years after they split up he still missed her. Not always, but sometimes he had a deep yearning to hold her hand, caress her long silky blonde hair, or feel her familiar warm body cupped within his frame on a cold December night. She would breathe heavily as she always did when she slept.

Her face serene and beautiful in the comfort of his grasp and warmth of their bed. Now, Evelyn and Jake were best of friends.

They had been to the same schools in Huntington Beach. Same classes until Jake flunked his junior year in high school. It wasn't so much that high school was difficult academically. It was just hard to balance surfing, partying, picking up babes and studying all at the same time.

Jake was a handsome, tanned, smooth and easy going young man, his body honed by hours and hours of surfing. His kind light green eyes striking and inviting. He had no problem attracting girl friends.

Evelyn Myers had always been there, since kindergarten. She hadn't really noticed him, but he had definitely noticed her. At thirteen or so when he finally caught her attention, she thought he was a jerk. Well, a cute jerk, but a jerk just the same. But then she promptly fell victim to his silly style and smooth charm. It was always a hot – cold relationship, but at sixteen he became her first lover, and she became his first love. In the following years they were only briefly separated while she was in college and dental school at U-Mass. As soon as she graduated she moved back to Southern California and joined her father's practice.

Much to Dr. Myers' dismay, Jake and Evelyn married the following year. He didn't like the young man, he was the word 'slacker' personified. He wasn't good enough for his little princess, she deserved so much better than that 'surf bum'. And what a terrible career choice: pilot! Dr. Myers was elated, even though he said how sorry he was, when things didn't work out between the couple.

Neither Evelyn nor Jake could put a finger on the fundamental issue that made them, mostly her, decide they were actually terminally incompatible. Maybe it was Jake's risk taking, maybe he was too adventurous. Worst of all he didn't want children. 'Why bring kids into this fucked up world? Look at all the problems. The discord among all the people on the planet. Everyone wanting to push their beliefs on everyone else. They are right, everyone else is wrong. If everyone surfed they would have a different outlook on life. There'd be fewer problems in this world. Bringing a kid into this mess is irresponsible'. When Evelyn finally told him she thought it best to split up, he didn't really fight it. In the bottom of his heart he knew it was the right thing to do.

It was, and always had been Jake's assessment, that Evelyn was a truly wonderful and caring person. He wished the best for her. She had not yet found the man of her dreams, and in her perception, time was running out. He could almost feel her soft long blonde hair cascading over her sensual shoulders, down her creamy back almost reaching her firm round butt. She had the body of a goddess and a wonderful disposition to go with it. But she didn't want change. She wanted the stability her father lived with.

A loud hiss and squeak announced the arrival of the fuel truck. Amber looked up and gave her typical low-level warning growl. Three attendants leisurely got out of the truck and started the fueling process. One methodically placed four orange cones around the airplane. Meanwhile a second attendant grounded the plane and set the fuel counter to zeros, even though it was already at zeros. The third fellow ceremoniously dispatched the 100 to 120 low lead. Jake chuckled to himself.

"Beautiful day for flying! Where are you going today?" The grounding guy inquired.

"I'm on my way to Durango." Short sentences were within the limits of Jake's high school Spanish.

"Oh.." The attendant looked to the distance longingly. "I wish I was going to Durango. My Carmen lives in Durango. Most beautiful girl you have ever seen." His heart spoke with deep sentiment, his dick even more so.

"If you want a ride to Durango to visit your Carmen, I can give you a ride," Jake offered.

"Señor piloto, that is so nice of you to offer. But I have to stay and work. You see, it is the cone guy's first day on the job and I have to make sure he doesn't screw up. Very soon I will be moved up to being in charge of filling the airplanes!" He said with obvious excitement. "You are our first customer of the day, Señor. I know that if the first customer is nice like you the rest of the day will be good."

Jake smiled and gave him three-dollar bills, maybe he was being bullshitted, maybe not.
The young man took the money and crossed himself with the notes in his hand. "May God repay you."

The nice attendant informed Jake where the gas bill should be paid. Again they asked for all his personal and aircraft information one more time. Then it was off to immigration.

Jake retrieved the tourist card he had already filled out and paid the cashier who seem extremely put out at being bothered with taking money before having the chance to socialize with the other airport personnel. She stamped it twice, tossed it on the counter, and before Jake could say boo she had already turned and was gone.

"Here is the payment receipt from the cashier," he gently informed the immigration officer who was sleeping again.

"Yes, yes," he said, pretending he was just on an extended blink. "Now Mr," he read Jake's last name but couldn't pronounce it. "Now Mister what is the purpose of your visit?"

"I'm just touring around the country for a few months, that's all."

"Ahhh, really," he scratched his chin with his left index and thumb. "Would you mind informing me why you are flying an aircraft of Mexican registry and you also have a Mexican Commercial pilots license? Are you sure you aren't here to work?" The immigration officer inspected Jake's passport page by page as if there was some additional secret compartment to be found.

"A friend in Durango will be keeping the plane when I leave Mexico in six months or so, and he told me I needed a Mexican pilot's license to fly a Mexican registered plane. And since I am a commercial pilot in the US they gave me a Mexican commercial license," Jake lied smoothly hoping the official would not know the licensing rules.

The official closely inspected the license. Compared something to the passport. Then quickly picked up the tourist card. He studied Jake intently. Jake felt extremely uncomfortable.

"Very well. I will grant you a four-month stay. If you need more time to continue your visit of our beautiful country, you will have to request an extension at any one of our international airports. Durango is an international airport in case you were going to ask. Now please go to customs, they will inspect your aeroplane," he swooshed is hand in dismissal.

"Can you tell me where customs is?"

"Other end of the building. Go outside to your left, past the guard shack and it is to the rear," Jake thanked him as he made for the door. As he took the long walk to customs he asked himself if they could possibly make it anymore difficult.

"Buenos dias. I need to clear customs," Jake announced to the man behind the desk and the plaque that said in both Spanish and English. "Aduana/Customs."

Even though it wasn't a particularly cold day, the customs man was bundled up with a scarf and heavy jacket. He shivered noticeably as he smoked a cigarette.

"Are you flying the Cessna just outside?" He pointed in the general direction of Jake's plane with the smoldering cigarette in his yellowed fingertips.

"Yes sir, I am the pilot of the Cessna."

"Why didn't you come in earlier?" The customs official said accusingly.

"I checked but you weren't here," Jake said as nicely as he could, although he was starting to feel like

strangling somebody. He retrieved a cigarette and lit
it.

"Really?" The official said in feigned disbelief.
"I'm sorry but there is no smoking in public buildings,"
the officer said as he took a long drag. "Do you have
anything to declare?" He looked at him intently,
analyzing Jake's initial reaction.

"No. Just my clothes and other personal items,"
Jake said very matter of fact, continuing to smoke.

"Any guns or ammunition?"

"No! Not at all," Jake said with the best
expression of horrified he could muster as he lied
through his teeth. "I thought they were illegal in
Mexico?"

"They are! That is why I am asking!" The
official said with exasperation. "Very well, we must fill
out this form, and this one, and finally this one, and
then you must pay for your flight plan, use of airspace
and finally your airport fees," he simultaneously fed the
first form into the antique manual Olivetti, standard
issue, typewriter.

"Name?"

"Jake Henry McInnes," Jake came back quickly.

The official looked up from the typewriter in total
displeasure. "One letter at a time please," he
clenched his teeth. Jake spelled his name to match
the rate at which the officer typed, which if you'd had
to guess, you'd have sworn it was his first day making
the contraption work. After a long fifteen minutes the
official ceremoniously extracted the form, ripping it
diagonally in the process. Once it was repaired with
clear tape he instructed Jake where to sign.

"Have you been working here very long?" Jake asked truly interested.

"Almost fifteen years!" He announced with pride. He vigorously stamped all three copies of the form with as many different stamps. "Okay, you rrready to go!" He announced as if he had just broken some kind of personal record.

"Thank you very much," Jake said almost incredulous at the spectacle.

The flight plan took almost as long as the other two events combined. By the time Jake left the building he was short four smokes and a hell of a lot of patience. "No wonder Mexico is in the shape it's in!" Jake mumbled to Amber as he got in the plane. Amber barely opened one eye in acknowledgement.

Once again, the freshly painted 185 slipped from the earths mighty grasp and gracefully climbed skyward. As the altitude increased Jake's sanity returned in kind. Amber nuzzled him from the co-pilot's side. He gave her a nice long belly scratch as he flew with his left hand, feeling a little jealous of the peace of mind that she had, and he lacked.

The beautiful and impressive Sierra Madre Oriental slowly appeared and reached skyward before him. A continuation of the American Rockies some of the elevations between Ciudad Obregon and Durango are over 9,500 feet in areas and it feels like they are reaching up to grab you. Omar had already described the beautiful, yet extremely unforgiving mountains and canyons. Canyons so deep the bottoms were obscured from sunlight. The tops so jagged with rocks and cactus they offered no place to land. Jake thought about these words as he searched for suitable landing spots.

As a matter of procedure he always timed and made note of the heading to a potential emergency landing spot as he flew along. Just in case. 'Well, there is nothing here. Maybe a little ahead there will be something,' Jake thought as he looked at his engine gauges.

The Cessna's big turbo charged Lycoming engine suddenly started running rough. In two instants it quit altogether. Holy shit! Jake said out loud. Amber sat up straight, sensing the danger. Jake ran down the emergency list. Jake's thoughts materialized. 'Best glide. Squawk 7700. Try to contact Ciudad Obregon Tower, approach, whatever. Nothing. Dead silence.
Not a good choice of words. Contact 121.5 emergency frequency. No luck. Try to restart. No luck.'

"Amber get in the back!" Jake shouts. Amber obeys. She knows he isn't joking.

'There! There's a dirt road! Wait.... It's tiny.. It's on the side of a mountain and everywhere else is covered with trees. There is a straight part.' He points a finger instinctively at what he is looking at even though he is the only one there. 'What the fuck happened? Fly the plane, fly the plane.' He reminds himself. 'Try to restart the engine.' Still no luck. 'All right. Concentrate on landing this hunk-a-junk, it isn't gonna start.'

Is that bitch Karma punishing me for something? Evelyn would probably think so. Was it because he had 'borrowed' this plane? Or was it simply because he forgot something or put something together incorrectly. Open the door! You don't want it stuck so you can't get out when this piece of shit impacts.

No doubt this was going to be a harsh landing, with only one chance. That one chance was only a few seconds away. He slowed the plane, the stall strips did their job. Jake had his sink rate dialed in. 'Oh shit! Down draft!' The 185 buffeted towards an imminent stall. He eased the nose and she kept flying, now he was too low. 'Maybe I won't be able to salvage the plane. As long as Amber and I live to see another day.' Jake didn't think about his family, didn't think about much else. All he saw was Evelyn smiling. The type of big genuine smile she had after he had told her a good joke. It was warm and inviting.

Chapter 2.
Where's the Gringo?

A light warm breeze rustled around the dry brush which patiently awaited the next rainy season. Summer was still better than half a year away. A very fine dust was forced up, irritating the eyes and causing allergy-like symptoms. It was typical of the arid semi-desertic environment surrounding Durango. Four bush pilots, wearing their stereotypical Ray-Bans, along with two mechanics stood on the ramp waiting. They shielded their eyes with each in-coming gust as in a strangely choreographed line dance.

"Omar, what time did you say the Gringo was going to arrive?"

"Pancho, how many times do I have to tell you not to refer to the Americanos that way? They find it offensive." Omar shook his head in disapproval.

"You know I don't mean anything by it. Everybody calls them Gringos."

"His name is Jake. Call him Jake."

"Yaik? What kind of name is that? It's not a Christian name is it? I've never heard of a St. Yaik." Pancho turned to the others. "How 'bout you guys?"

They all motioned negatively.

"You idiot!   You haven't heard of Jacob –
Jacobo. Why am I letting you pull me into this dumb
conversation? Just call the man Jake!"

They all shrugged their shoulders in unison and
nodded affirmatively.

"So back to my original question. What time is
Yaik supposed to arrive?"

"I called Ciudad Obregon and they said he left
three hours ago so he should be here any minute now.
He probably had some headwinds, or something,"
Omar said as he searched the distant skies.

They continued to loiter about intently listening
for any transmission on the handheld radio, which was
tuned to the tower frequency 118.10

The boys gave Omar a hard time about the
185. No one around these parts flew a taildragger so
it was fair game. As in every instance when more than
one pilot is present, the hangar flying starts and tales
of misadventure, emergencies, botched landings and
all sorts of strange occurrences are embellished a little
more with each new telling. Of course they had all
heard each other's stories a hundred times before.
They were looking forward to hearing new stories, and
even better, laying their old stories on someone who
hadn't heard them before.   So they wouldn't
immediately be challenged and unequivocally
informed that they were full of shit. - 'It didn't happen
like that you lying turd!'

Four hours, thirty-five minutes. The wait wasn't
sitting well with Omar. His brother Enrique had died
scarcely two years ago in an airplane accident. His
gut was starting to knot up, a sensation he was too

familiar with. That horrible sick sensation of disbelief when he was told his little brother hadn't made it. What made matters worse was the fact that he had taught his brother to fly and supposedly to avoid the pitfalls in aviation, common mistakes, human error. Had he not been clear? In some strange way was it his fault for not teaching him properly? Or was it just a simple unforgivable slip up, like anybody else. These questions were the most troublesome and enduring.

'Maybe I should have met up with him in California, or Ciudad Obregon?' Omar reflected on his choices. 'I really didn't give him much information, except for the customs procedures and flight plans. After all we were going to be flying together for the first few months to get him up to speed on Mexico bush flying.'

"All right guys he is two hours late. We need to organize a search party," Omar announced.

"Give him another 15 minutes," Pancho said lazily.

"No! Sometimes 15 minutes can be the difference between life and death. If he is down, and God willing alive, in a country he doesn't know, that is not something I would want to face. Now, get on your phones and start calling everyone to get down here. The four of us can get going now, and contact whoever you can on our regular frequency. Don't forget to monitor 121.5 on your second comm. just in case he's transmitting."

Within half an hour the original four were airborne and another half dozen who had been enroute back to Durango had joined the search. The direct route from Ciudad Obregon was well known to them all and they divided it up while they flew. Omar searched the farthest from Durango, after all, his plane was slightly faster and would consume the most fuel. It was only fair, this little venture was going to be an added expense for everyone. Today for you, tomorrow for me. That was the attitude. Pilots are a brotherhood, but bush pilots are an extremely tight knit brotherhood. Paying well over three dollars a gallon of avgas all for someone else's hide was a good demonstration of their commitment to one another.

The afternoon made its inevitable transition through dusk. Long shadows changed the temperatures from mild to cold in a matter of minutes especially since it was winter. The latitude may be south of the Tropic of Cancer, but the altitude accounts for the chill. If Jake was alive and had in fact made it safely, he would most likely be spending a very cold night in the middle of nowhere, in a foreign land. Omar admired the guts it would take to just up and leave the comfort and stability of your homeland. He certainly wouldn't do such a thing. But Americans are different, they are very mobile. They don't seem to mind uprooting themselves, even if there are children involved and moving across a vast country for the sake of a new job and possibilities; leaving their friends and family behind. Most Mexicans wouldn't do it. Well maybe, if you are a Chilango. (Term of disrespect for Mexico City residents).

'Where the hell is he? What could have happened?' Omar thought as he keyed the mike to check on any progress. "Boys, has anybody had any luck?"

Thirteen negative answers were transmitted through the airwaves.

"You don't think he got side tracked and went visiting Copper Canyon or something like that?" Pancho queried.

"No. He knew there would be plenty of time to check all that out later. Besides, I told him I would be waiting for his arrival."

Once the flotilla of planes descended upon their base after nightfall the pilots made plans for the following day. With charts spread out over coffee tables in the cafeteria they mapped out the sectors each pilot would take the next day. Two said they simply could not afford to lose a day of revenue, which would also include a day of added expenses. A couple of others said their bosses wouldn't allow them to use their planes for 'non-revenue activities'. That left eight airplanes for the search. "Make sure you bring a friend or family member, maybe even two, the more people we have looking out the windows the better."

Omar made his way home through the rush hour traffic. As he opened the door to his comfortable little house the aroma of a warm spicy meal filled his senses. He just then realized how hungry he was. Little eight-year-old Guadalupe ran to him with open arms, his wife Alejandra peered around the corner with a smile and a nod motioning him to come in. "I guess you didn't find him yet," she half asked, half stated.

"No luck yet. But I'm sure we will be lucky tomorrow," Omar replied as he poured himself an Herradura Añejo. "What concerns me the most is, that just as in my brother's case, if he were alive and the plane wasn't a total wreck, he could transmit to an airliner or any plane he might see and we would get to him in no time, but we've heard nothing. Usually if someone has an emergency we can pick them up in a matter of hours, if they are alive."

"Come and sit down, have some dinner." Alejandra nudged him and gave him a light peck on his stubble-covered cheek.

"Let me relax a moment with my tequila. Give me 20 minutes and I'll be ready." Omar plopped down on the couch and reflected on the day. What would he have done had he been faced with the same predicament? He took a long easy sip from the snifter. Maybe the comm. was inoperative?   If it was inoperative that meant the plane was destroyed. He didn't want to think about the implications. Maybe the fuel tank breached upon landing, and there had been a fire. He could've gotten out before the plane was consumed. Maybe's, "what if's" and "if only's" filled his mind until the third tequila in 30 minutes soothed and numbed his thoughts. Dinner was good, slightly over cooked, but that was his own fault. Also he was saddened to think that Jake should have been there to share it with him.

After a restless night, Omar was at the airport by 4:30am. Everyone would be showing up soon, in cases like this no one ran on Mexican time. The gas crew was already there and ready even though they weren't supposed to start until 7am, but in these situations everyone pulled together, everyone huddling as the temperature neared freezing. They filled the eight planes and Omar paid the bill for all.

"Roberto, I thought your boss wasn't going to let you use the plane?"

"Fuck him! If he doesn't understand that this is the way it works, then he can fire me! Let's go."

Nine Cessna's took to the early morning sky just as the sun was peeking up from the East. As promised, each pilot brought at least one more set of eyes. They all hoped for a successful short day, but most knew it was going to be a long one. It was very tiring to fly the plane and carefully scour every inch of land. Omar flew through the canyons and valleys, the sun was up and brilliant. His deep brown eyes inspected every possibility from behind the protection of his sunglasses. He mapped out the grid within the sector he chose and flew it methodically. As the land whizzed by his mind wandered back to the days when he had taught his younger brother to fly.

Omar Carrillo y Salas was nine years old when his brother was born in 1971. Anybody that knew anything about kids was positive that this one was going to be a handful. He was. Regardless, Omar always enjoyed taking care of him. He took him everywhere, especially flying, a passion they shared. When Enrique was nine he could fly the plane, navigate to perfection, and fly an instrument approach to minimums. He still couldn't land because he couldn't reach the rudder pedals. By 16 he could land and take off from some of the shortest, most treacherous strips in the Sierra. Not only did he love to fly but he loved the admiration and respect his older brother got as Capitán Carrillo. His nice new car, fancy clothes, a better house than his own parents, and the most beautiful fiancée he had ever seen. Well maybe he wasn't ready for the commitment of a wife, but everything else would suit him fine.

On his 18th birthday Enrique received his private pilot's license, instrument and commercial. The two brothers worked together from that moment on. From the get go, he was never happy about the scheduling, particularly because most bush piloting operations start very early in the morning in an attempt to avoid the lack of performance airplanes experience on normal hot days. Density altitude and a cowboy attitude had already killed a great many pilots. Another very valid reason for flying in the cool mornings is the smoothness. As the day warms up, the canyon walls heat unevenly, winds pick up and turbulence will just about knock your fillings out. If you are negotiating a tight little canyon, walls on either side and you're getting buffeted around to the point where you're not really in control, as they say "shit happens". It had always been Omar's policy never to canyon fly in the afternoons unless it was imperative, such as someone's life being at stake.

Enrique and his new found income had a tight social calendar. When you're 18 and you have more money in your pocket than you have ever had before, it's hard to keep focused on work. Especially when there are so many lovely señoritas who like the idea of marrying a dashing young Capitán. Needless to say, it wasn't the marrying part Enrique was interested in, just the benefits.

It was quite common for Enrique to go straight to work after a long night of partying. He was good about the 8-hour bottle to throttle rule and made sure not to drink too much. There was very little he could do about the dead tired part though and fatigue is usually accompanied by bad decisions.

Omar smiled and chuckled as he reminisced. In hindsight, it was funny, but when it happened he was pissed off beyond belief. An old Indian couple had paid their hard earned pesos to be flown back to their tiny little village up in the mountains, about 340nm to the Northeast of Durango. A place called Bataquitos. Enrique, after a night on the town, flew them 250nm to the Southwest of Durango and left them in a little fishing village on the Pacific called Barquitos. These old folks had never flown in their lives and had no idea they were heading in the wrong direction. You would have thought the ocean in front of them would have made them realize they were in the wrong spot in time to demand to be taken to the correct destination. Who knows what they may have been thinking. But when they showed up a week later at the Durango Airport, they were not very happy campers.

Once Omar had given them a full refund and flown them free of charge to their village he decided it was time to teach his younger sibling a lesson. Enrique would no longer have the benefit of flying a well-maintained aircraft and the protection of his brother. Now he was the low man on the totem pole with the worst scheduling and the worst locations. No more cargo and supplies (cargo and supplies don't bitch and throw up) just people who were nervous and usually not too happy to be flying. It was not unusual that if one passenger lost their cookies, the stench alone would get another one going. On days with a lot of turbulence it would become a regular barfarama in the back of the little Cessna 206. Good thing you can open the window in flight.

Omar reflected solemnly. Did that beat up, poorly maintained plane have anything to do with his brother's death? Or was it, as the company reported, his brother's fault for flying into the clouds without the proper flight instruments.

A bright reflection caught his attention. Was it a signal from a mirror? Omar made a sharp bank and dropped the nose of the plane, forgetting he had passengers in the back.

"Daaaaad!" Guadalupe screamed at him.

"Sorry. I forgot you guys were back there. You've been so quiet."

As he came around again he realized the source of the reflection was a small puddle of water reflecting the sun skyward. "Damn. Where the hell is the gringo!" Omar said under breath.

The standard bantering and harassment back and forth over the company frequency was non-existent. Worst of all no news of finding Jake came either. It wasn't a good sign. Everyone knew that if there were no results today the outcome would probably be as grim as so many times before. Bush piloting was a hazardous job and everyone in the business knew it, no matter the perspective or twist you put on it. This event was a large dose of bad luck. Airplane engines, when properly maintained are extremely reliable, even more so than automobile or truck engines. Omar had over 15,000 hours of flight time and never had an engine out. Sure, there were a few very rough running engines, but he always managed to return to the field before they ceased altogether.

Omar's thoughts turned to anger. This was to be the big break he had been waiting for. Finally he would be his own boss. Finally he was going to call the shots. 'Was life, karma or what ever greater power testing me? Again? Am I destined to live my life as a grunt? No. I say fuck destiny and karma or whatever!' The thoughts whirled around as his eyes dashed back and forth in search of the plane.

As the 210 over flew a large granite cliff, images of the final moments of terror that must have filled his younger brother's mind came rushing into his own. Horrible thoughts permeated his soul with less frequency, as time tends to heal all. Images of the mangled wreck, which was once a 206 reduced to the size of an incinerated garbage can, now only came to mind twice a day. Omar wasn't looking forward to the prospect of finding his partner's plane in similar condition. But then, Omar thought, it wouldn't be. It was very different to slam head first into a mountainside obscured by clouds, than making an emergency landing with the pristine conditions, which had prevailed yesterday.

Omar wasn't looking forward to looking at death's ugly face again. Enrique and Jake were close in age and this not only opened the recent and barely healing wounds, but also rubbed salt in them. What would the newspapers speculate this time? With Enrique's death they had accused him of being a drug runner. His airplane shot down in an attempt to get him to land and hand over his load. Every pilot is a suspect.

Newspapers, and the media in general know
that horror, mayhem and misery sell.   Alarma,
Mexico's colorful version of the National Enquirer
published the story in graphic and extremely gory
detail, or at least their twisted version of it on page 5.
Page 1 was taken up by a 15-year-old girl who had
given birth to a baby with a wooden leg. The title of
the article covering Enrique's fatal crash announced:
'Drug runner shot down. – Slams into mountain side.'
The first sentence of the article continued: 'Millions of
dollars worth of drugs burn, adding another victory to
the federales' fight against the underworld.'

There was a day, it popped into his mind as if it
happened yesterday, when Omar and Enrique were
having a nice lunch at El Marlin in Tepic, Nayarit, best
seafood restaurant ever.   The two brothers enjoyed
the nice warm weather, the Mariachi band played
slow, rich and as never before the chef out did himself
with the Huachingo a la Veracruzana.

A high-ranking military man had marched up to
the table, his two goon/soldier bodyguards behind him.
Assault rifles at the ready.

"You the Carrillo brothers?" Even though it was
a question, it sounded more like a statement.

"Yes, who wants to know?" Enrique came back
before Omar could swallow the delectable red snapper
he was savoring

"Yes Sir, that is us. What can we do for you?"
Omar said diplomatically, in an attempt to counteract
any animosity caused by his brother's testy reply.

The uniformed man glared an instant longer in
Enrique's direction to emphasize, without doubt his
displeasure at such insolence.   He focused his

attention on Omar. "I would like to talk with you." Before he could be invited to sit, he was already seated.

"You two stand over there and make sure we are not disturbed! Oh, and get me a tequila and coke," he directed.

"Si, mi General." The henchman snapped to attention and left.

The General continued, "I have heard that you two are the finest pilots in this region," he waited a few instants to dramatize his words. "I have been informed that you can get in and out of airstrips other pilots wouldn't dare go," he did not wait for their affirmation or denial. He continued the monologue he was used to delivering. "I need some help in the Sierra from time to time." The younger, bulkier of the soldiers placed a drink in front of him and waited for the General to taste it. He lifted the tall glass reverently. Sipped it slowly. Sloshed it around his mouth as if he were a sommelier. "Ahhh! What is this shit!" He spat the liquid on the floor. "I want the good tequila! And make it stronger!" He threw the rest of the drink on the floor. "Tell that idiot at the bar that you will be pouring my drinks. You know how I want my drinks!"

El Marlin, fortunately, was almost empty. It was too early for the dinner crowd and too late for the lunch crowd. Don Valenciano came over to address the problem, and in a very low and humble voice requested, "Is there a problem, General?"

"Yes there is a fucking problem! Your bartender deserves to be shot! He doesn't even know how to mix a drink. You should fire his ass!"

"I'm terribly sorry. I will personally prepare your drinks while you are here."

"Very well. Now bring me some food," he didn't wait for an answer. "Anything! Just make sure it's the best of whatever you have." The General turned back to the two brothers and continued pleasantly but firmly. "As I was saying before I was so rudely interrupted, I require some help from time to time. We have some drug busts in the middle of absolutely nowhere and we need good pilots to fly the confiscated narcotics out."

"I thought the military was burning the drugs right on the site where you find them?" Enrique inquired. Omar quickly stomped on his foot under the table. "Hey, watch out for the new boots!" Enrique scowled his brother.

El General gave a harsh look at Enrique and turned his attention back to Omar. "Not that I have to explain my actions to anyone, but I am a reasonable man and I understand an upstanding citizen may have certain apprehensions," he explained in a patronizing tone. "We have to get the drugs to a safe location so they can be analyzed, inventoried and their incineration cataloged by the American DEA. It is part of the deal our federal government has negotiated in exchange for the money the Americanos put up for our drug interdiction program."

"If you are worried about getting into tight areas why don't you haul the drugs out with your military helicopters. They can land in much tighter locations than any bush pilot ever could." Enrique quickly asked, heedless of his brother's warnings and stomping feet.

"You have a lot of questions, young man. May your life be long enough to have them all answered. I will indulge your curiosity. Our helicopters and their pilots are stretched to the limit, they are working overtime and beyond maintenance specifications. We are using them almost exclusively for the initial attack on illegal drug depots. That is why we need civilian operators to pick up the slack in the system. Not only will you be helping your country and the youth of many nations, but we also realize the danger involved in such operations and are willing to pay very handsomely to the few we choose."

"With all due respect, General," Omar inquired cautiously, "why would it be dangerous if whoever decided to fly these missions would be flying for the military and most likely with an escort on board?"

"This is a fine question," the General said, turning to face Enrique. "That is the proper manner and inflection one should use when asking a question. You should learn from your brother.

"Yes. In fact, most of the time there will be a soldier or DEA advisor on board when narcotics are transported. However, the danger we refer to comes in landing on some very difficult terrain and from the fact that you are carrying millions of dollars worth of a substance the dealers would love to get back. Furthermore, they are extremely pissed off at the fact that you have their product in the first place."

"Let's pretend momentarily that we are interested. How much does it pay?" Omar inquired.

"Four thousand an hour," the General said flatly. He raised his glass and took a long swig from his ice cold drink.

"That's not much money considering the danger and the fact that I am presently charging passengers and cargo four thousand an hour for ordinary flights," Omar stated.

The General laughed out loud. "That's four thousand US dollars my friend! We are not speaking of pesos, my dear piloto!"

Omar's eyes widened in astonishment, his mouth fell open. Enrique remained cool, and asked. "When will you have some work for us?"

"Right now, in fact," was the rapid reply.

"Whoa, whoa," Omar said quickly. "Sorry, General, my brother gets a little over enthusiastic sometimes. I don't have my own airplane and he certainly doesn't either. So I can't see how we can possibly be of help."

"For you two, I will make special arrangements. I will see that you use one of the many confiscated drug runner airplanes. Later on we will find a crashed plane and switch the tail numbers, re-issue papers and you can keep it. How does that sound?" His face was frozen in a permanent sneer. It was obvious to most that this man had very little happiness in his soul.

"Well, it sounds very tempting, but to be very honest with you, even if I had an airplane of my own I don't think I could bankroll the expenses of running it," Omar said lying with a straight face. "I can't imagine the army pays very quickly. It would probably take over 90 days to get any money back. I'd be bust in a week." Omar was looking at any excuse that would nicely and politely get himself and Enrique out of a potentially sticky situation.

"Money will not be a problem Mr. Carrillo. You will be paid in cash on the spot when you deliver each shipment," the General said with a dismissive motion of his hand.

"Cash? With all the respect your rank deserves, General, wouldn't you agree that cash is a strange form of payment when you are dealing with the government and drugs?"

"The CIA is the one paying and they can pay however they please. I don't particularly care as long as they are not paying with my money!"

"CIA? I thought you said DEA in the beginning? Who is involved in this operation, the DEA or the CIA?" Omar inquired pleasantly.

"What's the difference to you, as long as you are paid for the services rendered? I don't know why it would matter to you. But if it makes you happy, it's the DEA." The General was starting to sound slightly irritated.

"I sincerely appreciate your more than generous offer, but I would like some time to think about it. I have made commitments to my boss and I'm not in the habit of breaking my promises. Is there a contract I could go over so we are aware of the terms of our business relationship?" Omar asked, fully knowing the answer.

"Let's not insult each other's intelligence, Mr. Carrillo. You know as well as I, that the DEA doesn't make contracts in this type of operation. Here is my card," he said as he placed it in front of the brothers. It had an olive green background and two phone numbers in gold ink – no name. "If you are interested, and you should be, give me a call. I seriously doubt that either of you have ever made four thousand U.S. Dollars for an hour's work! Now I must leave. Good day gentlemen." The General stood abruptly and left. As he walked towards the restaurant's main entrance he shouted at the proprietor. "Don't charge those boys a single peso. Put it on my tab." And he loudly slapped his 9mm automatic Browning, which rested at his side, protected by its black leather holster.

The proprietor came over to the Omar and Enrique. "What tab? He doesn't have a tab!" he protested.

"Don't worry, Don Valenciano, we will pay our bill. Now how about if you sit down with us and have a tequila. I certainly could use one about now," Omar stated, relieved that the interview was over.

Don Valenciano left to get the tequila. "It sounds like a hell of an opportunity, Omar!" Enrique said excitedly, imagining the dollar bills floating around him.

"Yes indeed, it does sound like a fantastic opportunity."   Omar   waited   a   second   before continuing.... "to get a bullet in the back of your head! What the fuck are you thinking, Enrique?"

"What!?" Enrique said in exasperation, raising his shoulders and hands at the same time. "It seems like a perfectly legitimate proposition."

"You know, Enrique, sometimes I wonder about you. You really don't think there is something fishy about his proposition?"

A distant crackle, barely audible came over the radio of the 210 interrupting his memories. "Omar I just received some news on the missing plane," Omar tried transmitting with no luck, obviously out of range or below the necessary altitude. He quickly turned the Cessna around and climbed a few thousand feet in order to get better reception.

"A military helicopter spotted the plane on the side of a mountain near El Manzano at around 15:30." That's all he said, that is all he knew.

They were getting low on fuel. Omar made a quick mental calculation. He wouldn't be able to make it there and back, furthermore he wouldn't be able to make it back before nightfall. It would be better to go back in the morning with full tanks, smooth air and a mechanic. He only hoped his new partner wasn't already dead.

He knew this night would pass even slower than the previous one, especially while dwelling on the uncertainty of whether or not Jake had managed to survive. The helicopter pilot said the plane didn't look damaged so he assumed that the pilot was well, even though there was no sign of him. Omar's vision was bleary, his body ached from the incessant tension. Tequila soothed, Alejandra warmed, he slept.

The clearest blue sky. A bright sun and crisp light breeze typical of the high desert. Omar stood next to runway 21. It was Enrique's 16th birthday, it was a Sunday so there was no traffic in the vicinity of the international airport.   With only 10 or so commercial flights a day the first wasn't scheduled to arrive for several hours. They had the airport to themselves.

Enrique had not been allowed to log most of the hundreds of hours he had already flown. Today he would be allowed to fly solo – legally. It would have been very easy to make this an inconsequential event due to his experience, but that would be cheating him out of one of the most precious memories any pilot possesses, ranked right up there with getting laid for the first time.

The little 172's engine spooled up to as close to full power as one would get a that altitude. It gently bounced its way down the uneven runway. Enrique lifted off early and stayed in ground effect demonstrating a perfect soft field departure. He wagged the wings as he passed his brother on the ground. Omar smiled and laughed out loud. Enrique pulled the plane skyward as he neared the end of the runway. The Cessna shot up, and up, and with each additional foot slowed at an increasing rate. 'What the hell is he doing? Push the nose over!' He shouted as he ran. His leaden legs would not respond. In horror he watched as the plane snapped inverted in a full stall and spin. It's nose pointed straight down. It did two complete 360's before it hit the ground with a loud explosion.

Omar screamed, "No!" as he launched out of bed, sweating profusely and fighting for breath.

"It's all right Omar." Alejandra's voice soothing. "You had another nightmare."

"Yeah," he mumbled, vivid images still fresh in his mind. He glanced at the alarm clock. 3am. Too early to get up, but who wants to sleep if those dreams await you. A nice cup of coffee and a shower sounded much more appealing.

The mechanic and Omar made good time to the latitude and longitude reported by the government chopper, and as advertised it was right where they said it would be. From this distance it looked to be in good shape, but that wasn't saying much, from 50 yards and going 85mph just about anything could look good.

Omar found a place to land, it would be tight but it was do-able. He over flew the relatively smooth yet slightly rutted old field. He could land, but taking off would be another question entirely. A few quick calculations and he committed to the spot. It wasn't his best landing but as they say, any landing you walk away from is a good landing!

An old man appeared from nowhere, hobbling towards them with the assistance of an old branch which served as a cane. It was worn smooth and shiny from many years of use and it was clearly as much a part of his outfit as the typical Huichol garb, loose fitting clothes, button shirt, baggy pants which ended just below the knee and a bright red woven belt around his waist. He wore the standard well-worn leather huaraches needlessly protecting his equally leathery feet.

"Buenos dias, Capitanes! I guess you have come for the airplane on the hill?" he asked, giving them a big, virtually toothless smile.

"Yes, that's correct. Do you know where the pilot of the plane may be?" Omar inquired voicing his primary concern.

"No. But a I was told he just took some of his things out of the plane and started walking towards Durango with his dog. Do you think he knows how far Durango is from here?" The old man asked as he took a long drag from his hand rolled cigarette. He was hunched over so he had to look up from the top of his eyes at the strangers. Despite his thick gray hair, the deep-set wrinkles, an obvious sign of his age, his eyes told of a young and vibrant heart.

Omar knew that the question was rhetorical so he didn't bother to answer. "Does someone around here have a pickup to take us up to the plane?"

The old Huichol smiled again, and gave a little chuckle. "No, no vehicles around here, Señor Capitán. But I would be willing to take you myself with my cart and burro." All of a sudden the old man's face became apprehensive. "Have you boys had breakfast yet? It's a long hard ride up there." He didn't wait for an answer. "My Petra will make us some breakfast, please follow me," and scurried off in the direction of his little house before they had time to say a word.

They approached the tiny adobe and wood cabin, smoke slowly rose from the chimney. Omar absorbed the pretty rustic scene in the middle of the little valley full of trees.

"Petra, make some breakfast for these boys, they look hungry. And cook up some meat," he spoke in his native Huichol. He turned to his guests. "Please have a seat close to the fire. My wife will make us breakfast," he announced with pride, "today we will have some beef!"

"That's really not necessary, Señor. Beans, tortillas and chile will do just fine." Omar knew this old man and his wife probably hadn't eaten beef in weeks, since it was reserved for special occasions only.

"Nonsense. We never have important visitors in these parts. I want to treat my guests with the honor and respect they deserve." His words where final.

Old Petra always soaked the corn kernels she would need for the entire week, then she would crush them into a masa by hand, on the same metate her mother had used for decades before. This morning she would prepare her special tortillas which had just a taste of beans in the middle and were cooked over an open wood stove called a 'comal'.

An hour later, bulging with steak, eggs, beans and Petra's wonderful hand made tortillas, all washed down with strong cowboy coffee spiced with cinnamon and molasses, they made their slow bumpy progress in a rough wooden cart up the first valley, and sometime in the afternoon towards the second.

"Get comfortable, friends we have many hours ahead of us," the old man announced happily. "We would've made better time but there was a pretty good rain storm last night."

Omar gave the mechanic a filthy look, which was returned in kind. 'Comfortable', Omar thought, 'exactly how do you get comfortable while you are being bounced around on a solid wooden deck?'

Coming down the other side of the hill was another experience altogether. In some spots it was so steep the old man used a manual hand brake connected directly to the wheels since the poor little burro couldn't manage to stop the load himself.

"How do you get up this hill if the poor little burro can't even get down it?" the mechanic asked.

"Oh, that's very easy!" the old man declared. "We all have to get off and hike up. The burro can manage just fine as long as we are not in the cart."

"Hopefully I'll be flying back and you guys can do the hiking!" Omar said with a coy smile on his face.

The mechanic glared back at him knowing that he wasn't joking.

The old Huichol Indian kept them entertained with a large repertoire of stories about life in the Sierras. Feast or famine and it seemed that the harsh latter prevailed most of the time.

He couldn't remember how long ago it was exactly since he married, nor could he remember how old he was at the time, but he guessed maybe 15 or 16. He had built the chozita, the little cabin they had breakfast in for his new bride. By Omar's estimation that would make it 60 years or so. It had no electricity, no running water, none of the modern conveniences, but as far as the old man was concerned they where completely unnecessary anyway. He had seen electricity and running water in Durango once. Stayed in a hotel. He hadn't been impressed.

"I feel sorry for the people who live in the city, they seem so busy and hurried. When I was in Durango I had to look in every direction at the same time so I wouldn't be run over by a person or worse, a bus. And the noise! How can anyone live with that constant roar! I was there for two days and two nights, I barely slept a wink. Once in the big city is enough for me. I would never go back." The old man stated firmly. "Sure, I realize my life may seem simple and mundane to you city folk, and it probably looks uncomfortable and deprived, but as I look back on my long life I can truly tell you that I would not trade my quiet little life among my beautiful mountains and valleys, with the woman I have loved for anything I have seen elsewhere," he continued. "As long as you young men can say the same thing when you are my ripe old age then you can declare to the world that you have lived your life successfully!"

"Has your wife been to the city?" Omar asked truly interested.

"No, my Petra has never been to the city. When I got back and told her about it she didn't want to go. In fact she never learned Spanish. Her first language is Tepehuano, and since she met me she learned to speak Huichol. Do you have children?" The old Indian inquired.

"Yes I have a wonderful little daughter. She is eight now and growing up very quickly," Omar responded.

"Yes, I have seven. That is why I fly whenever I can. I'm hoping God might take pity on my wretched soul and take me away from the horrible bunch once and for all!" The mechanic replied with a straight face.

"What makes you think God wants you? Hell, the devil probably doesn't want you!" Omar said with a laugh.

"Please, please! No more talk of the devil. It will bring us bad luck." The old man said with urgency.

"Do you have children?" Omar asked trying to return to a more pleasant subject.

"My sons don't visit much anymore. They live in a big town, Santiago Papasquiaro. It's big, but not nearly as big as Durango. It's sad because the few times that they have visited they can barely talk to their mother anymore. They've forgotten almost all their Huichol. It's a sad thing for us. It is a beautiful heritage that is being lost, but I don't want to complain to them. If I did they might not want to visit again."

After a long and arduous seven hours it became very obvious that they were not going to be flying out this evening even if the airplane could be fixed very quickly. Also, there was no doubt that it was going to be cold.

As if their guide could sense their thoughts he said, "There is a tiny cabin up ahead.   The lumberjacks use it from time to time and travelers are welcome to shelter there. If it is empty and it usually is, we will sleep there out of the cold wind and we can light a fire in the chimney. Don't worry it'll be nice and warm."

"How far to the..?" The mechanic didn't get the word "plane" out of his mouth because at that moment it came into sight. It sat out on a point, with just enough room for a cart and burro to get by. A middle-aged man stood up, shotgun in hand. He immediately recognized the old man and lowered the weapon. They spoke in Huichol. Omar and the mechanic were left out.

"This is my nephew. He was making his way up the hill when he saw the plane landing on the straight away over there," he pointed in the same direction as the nephew had pointed moments earlier.

The mechanic and Omar looked at the make shift runway and touchdown spot in amazement. "If that doesn't have anything to do with beginner's luck then this Yaik is one of the best pilots I've ever seen. Didn't you tell me he has never done any bush flying?"

Omar nodded in amazement, and thought. 'How could he possibly have landed on such a tight, uneven slope? And the only damage seemed to be on the wing tip. Either Jake is a very talented pilot or this is certainly the reason why so many Alaska bush pilots favor this plane.'

As they inspected the plane, which was perched precariously on the edge, the mechanic said. "I'm glad the storm that rolled through here last night didn't blow it over the edge."

"My nephew was just telling me that a couple of times in the night it started moving around very violently like it was going to take-off. So he filled the plane up with rocks."

Omar quickly peered into the plane to see a huge pile of rocks littering the plane's interior.

"My nephew says that the Gringo promised him fifty American dollars a day to take care of the plane." The old man translated from Huichol and seemed embarrassed by the request.

"No problem, I'll pay him," Omar offered.

It was too late to do much more than a cursory inspection. However, one of the first things the mechanic did was sump the fuel tanks. "Omar! You've got to see this! There's a ton of water in these tanks. I'll bet Yaik forgot to check the fuel after he was filled up in Obregon," he continued sumping until no more water was present.

"But why would the contamination suddenly affect the engine, and not before? He was at least an hour and change into the flight when he made it to this point," Omar asked.

"He probably didn't switch tanks for that hour, and when he did the water contaminated fuel from the wing which was filled first came rushing in and made the engine quit," the mechanic theorized.

"We'll have to wait 'til morning to test her. It's much too late to do anything now."

"I was sure we would be spending the night so I asked my wife to pack some extra blankets and some food. It's not much but it's better than going to bed on an empty stomach," said the old indian.

The old Huichol found the cabin and started a fire in the make shift chimney. The temperature was well below freezing outside and not much higher inside the drafty little hut. They huddled around the fire. One half of them was a little too warm and the other half not exposed to the fire was freezing cold. All three enjoyed the beef jerky, chilies, tortillas and beans. Tequila, instead of the old man's normal cheaper Mezcal, warmed their innards, or maybe just numbed them very efficiently.

"I see you pilots flying over from time to time. Way above my head. I enjoy watching the eagles and other birds fly around so effortlessly when I'm taking a break. I dream, and I wonder what it might feel like. But then I think, if God meant for us to fly he would have given us wings."

"Well he didn't give us wheels and we drive all the time!" Omar came back with a smile. "And he gave us a brain with the capacity to develop such machines. So why not!"

"That is very true. Would you mind taking me up for a ride one day? I would love to see this beautiful land from the perspective of the eagles, and a few lucky pilots."

"Absolutely! One of the things we enjoy the most, as pilots, is to be able to share the wonderful experience we know not everyone is able to see. And

I don't mean flying in a commercial jet at 35,000 feet, where everything looks flat and featureless. But down low, through the canyons, or just above. It is an extraordinary sensation!"

As night drew on it got even colder and the jug of tequila emptier. After a few hours of story telling their eyes were heavy with sleep. But the topic they kept returning to was covered: Where was the gringo? And what would it be like to be in an unknown country, with little knowledge of the people or the language?

They all slept the hard deep sleep of the dead tired.

Smoke! Omar awoke with a jolt. Don Ramiro was warming some water over the open fire for the morning coffee. He noticed the man jump out of bed from the corner of his eye. "Buenos dias capitán. How did you sleep?" He asked with a thick still sleepy voice.

As he rubbed his head and yawned, "You don't want to know. Every single muscle in my body aches from clutching myself against the cold, and staying in one position all night. I didn't want to move because every time I did a shot of ice cold air would race through any opening in the blanket." Omar shivered as he spoke.

The old man handed him a tin cup with steaming coffee. "This will help warm you."

Omar huddled close to the fire and held his cold hands around the tin. He took a careful sip so as not to burn his mouth, "Oh man that's good coffee! A little early for the tequila though."

"It helps cut the cold. Drink up."

The mechanic continued to snore loudly, as he had all night, oblivious to the freezing temperatures.

"And then you have this donkey snoring all damn night," Omar said as he kicked his leg in retaliation, just a little harder than friendly.

"What? Give me a few more minutes to sleep."

"All right but we're leaving now," Omar lied and smiled at the old man.

The mechanic jumped up, quickly studying his surroundings. "You're not leaving! You're not even ready."

"Well we will be soon. Let's have some coffee first, along with a couple of cinnamon tortillas Don Ramiro's wife made."

The mechanic sipped the warm brew. "Man that's good!"

"No wonder your wife left you! You snore like a damn calf pining for its mama!"

By 7 am the morning sun started warming the day as they made their way back to the plane. It didn't take very long to thoroughly check her, and determine that the only real damage was to the wing tip. When it hit the side of the hill it had peeled back and deformed the aileron slightly. The mechanic declared it wasn't something to be worried about, since the hinges were solid and intact. Now it was simply a question of whether or not she would start. The water had been drained from the tanks and the mechanic bled all the fuel lines all the way up to the fuel injector. But how much still remained in the system?

It was a good thing Jake had sprung for the new battery since they turned it over a good five minutes before it actually caught, but once it did the big Lycoming purred effortlessly. Omar let it run for a good 20 minutes before convincing himself that it wouldn't quit as he was flying back to Durango.

'Jake had landed on a steep uphill, this fact, in combination with a stout headwind meant that the 185 would be off the ground in a matter of a few feet. Well sorta.' Omar made mental calculations. Now if he could figure out how to takeoff in a taildragger everything would be all right.

"Omar!" The mechanic shouted over the roar of the engine. "How about I fly back to Durango with you?"

"No, I don't think it's a good idea. She sounds fine now. But there are no guarantees," Omar shouted.

"I know there are no guarantees, but I don't think my ass will take another beating like yesterday. If it's the same to you I'll take my chances with you."

"No! I'll be back for you tomorrow morning in the Centurion," he closed the window and waved goodbye.

Omar eased the power in while holding the brakes. He let her roll slightly as he released the brakes, she was at full static and roaring. The tail came up instantly and Omar danced on the rudder pedals trying to keep her straight as she bounced over the gravel and ruts. In no time she was off. Only one thought crossed his mind as she climbed into the sunny day.

'Now I have to land this thing!'

Chapter 3.
A Long Walk.

Jake sat there staring into oblivion. Fleeting thoughts meandered randomly through his mind, and as quickly as they came they were gone. It took him several minutes to pry his fingers from the yoke and actually begin to breathe again. Amber licked his face, maybe in appreciation, maybe in apprehension. A man came into focus some twenty yards away, he slowly materialized from behind the protection of a large rock at the side of the trail. The Mexican Indian stared wide-eyed from a safe distance, after all he had never seen such a contraption up close and had no idea what would follow such a spectacle.

Jake extended his arm to turn off the master and alternator switch but was shaking so violently he had to steady his hand with the panel. Slowly he opened the door, and remembered all the things he should have been done before touchdown. 'I'm not going to scold myself too hard. Amber and I are alive, and the plane doesn't look too bad.'

"Buenos dias, Señor," Jake beckoned at the man behind a rock. "Venga."

As the man approached Jake lit a smoke using his free hand to steady himself and took a long deep drag.

"Buenos dias." The Indian replied sheepishly as he approached.

Jake moved half way, Amber trailing him. "How can I get to Durango?" Jake asked in Spanish.

The Indian regarded him thoughtfully. "I didn't know airplanes stopped wherever they wanted to ask directions."

"Well they don't. I had engine problems," Jake said hoping that 'el engin-o' meant engine in Spanish. "Can you tell me how to get to get to Durango?"

"You have to get to the main road first. Twice a day there is a bus, it will take you to the highway and then you can take the bus right to Durango."

"How far is the main road?"

"Oh not far. Just go straight. Don't make any turns, and don't go down any smaller trails. Most of them aren't as nice as this one so you'll probably get lost." The Huichol Indian nodded to himself and mentally retraced the route. "There are plenty of streams along the way so you should be all right for water."

"Can I pay you to stay here and take care of the plane?" Jake asked hopefully.

"No. I must get to my uncle's house to make a delivery."

"I would be willing to pay you thirty dollars a day for your help."

"How much is that in Pesos?"

Jake made a quick mental calculation. "About three hundred, más o menos."

"I suppose I might be able to stay a few days if you paid me five hundred a day," the man negotiated.

"Very well five hundred pesos a day it is! I will be back as soon as possible." Jake shook the man's calloused hand to seal the agreement.

Jake quickly repacked a few essentials in his backpack, including the .45 Colt Peacemaker his father had given him. He also took a small Ziplock with Amber's dog food and the two energy bars he always carried in the plane.

Amber was bouncing back and forth growling and barking ferociously down the steep mountain side. Jake went over to see what she was so excited about, and was horrified to see a huge rattlesnake coiled and ready to strike. "Amber!" he yelled loudly and watched with relief as she reluctantly turned away, obedient as always. Jake continued to look down towards the bottom of the precipice as the snake slowly slithered away to safety and he silently thanked that somebody 'up there' for being on his side once again.

They started walking along the rugged trail avoiding the huge boulders littering their path. Wind rustled pleasantly through the trees, bringing with it a heavy scent of pine, which helped soothe the troubled thoughts, which were replaying the event over and over in an endless loop. 'Could I have done anything different?' As much as he recognized that those self-doubting thoughts were probably normal and permeated most people's minds at one time or another, he still couldn't shake them off. The breeze was warm and dry and did nothing to cool him or Amber. Jake wondered if she also had the same nagging headache, most likely due to dehydration. It was important to find water. Soon. How could he have forgotten to fill his canteen? He had always made a habit of filling his canteen, if nothing else to make sure Amber had water.

Jake's progress slowed as the day wore on, as shock and weariness combined to numb his mind and weighed down his feet. The only souvenir they took was the fine layer of dust that covered them. Dust that coated his mouth and throat, making him lick his lips to moisten them and long for some cool fresh water. As the sun fell behind the mountain ridge above them, to their right, it started to cool noticeably. It was time to look for a place to spend the night, to sleep. Jake knew full well that at this altitude and time of year he would need to collect enough firewood to last him through the night before he could let himself think about resting.

Just as Jake was giving up any hope of water Amber suddenly loped ahead a hundred yards or so and took a long sloppy drink from a little creek. He caught up at a slightly accelerated pace and joined her. It was the best thing he had tasted in a very long time. 'This little gully will do well for the night', Jake thought as he visually scouted the area still on all fours drinking next to Amber.

The two traveling partners huddled together and stayed as close to the fire as they dared. Thankfully it was a virtually windless night, it was cold enough without also having to contend with the chill of the wind. Jake tried to concentrate on the fantastic, unspoiled spectacle provided by the unimpeded view of the stars, but his troubled mind persisted with the 'what if' ponderings and iterations.

It was too late to go back now. Or was it? Was it too late to make amends with Evelyn? Did he want to? In any case, would she want him back? Jake visualized the fun times on the beach in the middle of summer; in the middle of nowhere. Nothing to worry about but when they'd sleep, eat, or make love. During the first few years of deep love and lust everything seemed so easy, so magical. But then reality and life had stepped in and the memories returned and reminded him of the seemingly endless succession of difficulties they would have to overcome in order to make the marriage last.

There was no animosity, they would always be friends. They had different interests, and unfortunately, different objectives. Evelyn was very content to be a homebody, movies, cooking and gardening were her preferred weekend pastimes. She was really never passionate about anything in particular. It was hard for her to relate to Jake's limitless passion and desire for flying and adventure.

Evelyn had tried just about every hobby and sport imaginable, horse riding, gym, yoga, cycling, aerobics, even flying. The list was endless, and after trying all of them she had given up trying new things and simply stuck with what she did best. She wasn't all that keen on dentistry either, but it was certainly a hell of a good living.

Jake felt he had been supportive of her endeavors, but now in hindsight he wondered if there was anything else he could have done. He had loved her deeply then, and still did. He just wasn't going to give up his passion to endlessly search for hers. Then of course there was the crowning problem: children.

Evelyn desperately wanted a family. Most likely a
reflection of her strong family ties, which were in direct
contrast to Jake's.

'I realize how incompatible we are. So why am
I always thinking of her?' The dilemma continually
nagged at him, and he eventually came to the
unsatisfactory conclusion, 'It must be one of those
can't live with her, can't live without her, cases.
Anyway it's time to get some rest I just have to get her
out of my head. Tomorrow will be tough enough
without adding a sleepless night to the equation.' Jake
got as comfortable as he could on the hard packed dirt
and got as close as he dared to the camp fire, his
backpack serving as a pillow. Amber volunteered to
snuggle up to his back with her warm wooly coat
shielding him from the cold. For a while she kept her
nose and ears high, sniffing and listening for intruders
until she could no longer help herself from falling into a
deep bunny-chasing sleep.

Morning rays cut through the forest and
underlying bushes surrounding the camp, and caught
Jake directly in the eye. He started to wake, surprised
at how well he had slept. His eyes refused to open but
he slowly coaxed them with a rub. 'Where's Amber?'
He thought.

"Buenos dias." Came a voice from behind.

Jake nearly jumped out of his skin, his hand
instinctively going for his gun. The owner of the voice
came into focus, he raised a tin cup toward Jake.
"Café?" He enquired.

Jake still bewildered stood staring at him a
while his brain did it's best to assess the situation.
The stranger looked 50 or 60, faint Indian features but

no Indian garb. He wore a thick US military jacket underneath a Mexican poncho.

The stranger politely and slowly repeated his inquiry without getting up, obviously enjoying the fire. "Buenos dias Señor. ¿Gusta un café?"

He was surprised to notice that Amber was sitting close to the man as if she had known him for years. She got up and marched over to Jake to say good morning. Jake accepted the cup of coffee, still bewildered, and took a sip of the steaming rich brew. It was hot, thick and strong. As it made it's way through his system he began to feel almost human again.

"Gracias," Jake mumbled as he wondered how this stranger had come into his camp without stirring Amber. Without waking him. Hell he had obviously been here a while. The fire was raging and the coffee was brewed. With some difficulty Jake carefully constructed a sentence in Spanish in his mind before saying out loud. "¿Cuanto tiempo te llevo alla?" (How long can I take you there?)

The newcomer pondered what the Americano really meant to say. "Oh!" Finally it occurred to him, and with a smile in almost perfect English responded. "An hour or so. You have a wonderful dog. She is very happy with you."

Jake was shocked and dumbfounded. "You speak English!" He exclaimed the obvious.

The man enjoyed Jake's astonished expression and smiled. "Indeed. You are a long way from nowhere and honestly don't look very well prepared. What are you doing out here?"

"I don't mean to be rude but do you have any food you might be willing to share with me? I haven't eaten in 24 hours," Jake responded.

"Sure, absolutely. I have some beef jerky, beans and tortillas in the pack on my burro over there," he pointed in the direction of the animal which grazed contentedly, its pack off to one side propped against a pine tree. "Did you sleep well? You looked almost comatose when I arrived."

Jake stared in amazement at the burro a while longer before answering. "I slept unbelievably well. I'm still surprised you didn't wake me, or for that matter; Amber."

"I was trying to be quiet." The man spoke as he prepared the food.

Amber was by his side. Not only for the company and to be petted, but drawn by the delicious smell coming off the grill.

"I don't think I've smelled anything that good in my life!" Jake proclaimed as he was handed two tacos. He scarfed them down so fast that his taste buds didn't have a chance to sense the flavor. The subsequent five he savored more slowly.

"So what's your story?" Asked his new companion.

Jake gave him the sanitized version as they digested their meal, and then began packing for the hike ahead.

"I'm heading towards the main road that leads to Durango so we can travel together if you like."

"Yeah, that would be great." Jake was appreciated the company and even more so with someone who actually knew the way. Not to mention that he also spoke English.

"So now that you know my story. What's yours? What are you doing out in the middle of nowhere? Fully supplied. And why do you speak such good English?"

"It's a long story but I'm guessing we have enough time since we'll be walking for a couple of days yet. I was born in Punta Arenas on the North Western corner of Costa Rica. Beautiful place, with some of the best fishing in the world. My father was a fisherman, and a drunk. A violent drunk. My mother was scared to death of him, she was completely subjugated by him. I was a meek little eight year old and really couldn't do anything about it, even though I beat myself up for years wondering if I could have. My older brother was killed in a bar fight and that left me to take the brunt of my father's punishment. Needless to say, this didn't sit very well with me."

The morning started to give way to the afternoon and the heat rose steadily. Dense trees gave only minimal relief from the blazing sun. Eagles soared effortlessly on the strong thermal columns radiating off the harsh rock of the canyons, their massive yet graceful wings bearing them aloft without the need of a single flap. The distant drone of a single engine airplane in the distance hummed tantalizingly beyond reach.

"When I was about that age, eight, that is, I was working at the old Marina on the south side of town. I'd do odd jobs for the turistas on their big fancy yachts, or help out during the fishing high season. Sometime in the Spring of 1959 this beautiful 73' sailboat made port, 'Escapade'. I remember it vividly, even though I was so young. She had a gleaming black bow, teak decks and a very stylish wheel house towards the rear."

"'Escapade' was owned by a wealthy American couple who were traveling around the world. In fact they had really only just started. They had stopped along their way down the coast at Mazatlán, which is not very far from here. If you had a plane," he added with a big grin.

"Not funny," Jake said sincerely and kept on walking.

Amber had long ago stopped sniffing at everything along the way and was concentrating on the hike.

"'Escapade' sailed on to Puerto Vallarta, Acapulco, then on to Guatemala, and soon arrived at Punta Arenas. Their plan was to sail around the cape at Tierra del Fuego and then travel up the Eastern coast of South America, through the Caribbean, across the Atlantic to the Canary Islands, Morocco, Casablanca, Spain, Suez Channel, anyway, you get the picture. One hell of a trip."

"How did they make their money?" Jake inquired. After all one always wonders how other people manage to make the fortune they have been unable to amass themselves.

"He wasn't an old man really." His friend replied. "Fifty or so at the time. He had just sold a nationwide chain of dry cleaning stores he had started when he dropped out of high school. The Burrards stayed in Costa Rica for a few months and we became very attached. So much so that one day they asked me if I would like them to adopt me. They were such kind wonderful people and I loved being with them so I immediately said yes, but of course they still had my parents to contend with. And that, of course, was an entirely different story."

"Myles and Lynette Burrard invited my parents to the yacht for dinner. My parents were extremely apprehensive about the situation, but accepted. We were dirt poor, they felt so out of place. As usual, my father drank heavily before going to boost his confidence."

"This doesn't sound like it is going in a very good direction," Jake offered.

"Oh you can't imagine. Not only did my father unequivocally say no, but he got into a very ugly fight with Myles. Once he'd calmed down a little he did mention that there was perhaps the possibility of the Burrards buying me!"

"You can't be serious!" Jake exclaimed.

"Myles said that was entirely out of the question, and reminded my father that I would have the best possible college education and upbringing. Again, my father flatly refused and that seemed to be the last of my hopes. A week later the 'Escapade' was leaving. I knew it was my only chance to change my life, and get away from the cycle of poverty that I was trapped in. So I stowed away in the tiny supply room of the yacht with six gallons of water and three comic books. I knew the boat very well by then and knew exactly where to hide. In my young mind it was obvious that I would have to remain undetected a period of time sufficient to make taking me back home a huge obstacle and almost impossible."

Afternoon winds started to pick up blowing dust and sand into their eyes and mouths. Jake was sweating profusely and the grime stuck to him, scratching his face each time he wiped it with his arm. It wasn't a pleasure cruise, but the scenery before him made up for some of the hardship of the forced hike and his companion's story helped divert his attention from the discomfort.

"The hardest part about hiding was staying still and quiet for such a long time, and of course the problem of going to the bathroom. But I knew my whole future was tethered to my effort to survive for those few days, so I endured. I read the 3 comic books so many times that I still know them by heart. Would you like to hear a few passages?"

"No, that's all right. I believe you, just keep going." Jake replied.

"After three weeks I finally came up on deck for the first time. It was late at night and I was starting to feel pretty sick. Lynette was at the helm while Myles slept before his watch. She was so shocked to see me that she fainted. Unfortunately she hit her head as she fell and it knocked her out. I felt awful! I raced down stairs to wake Myles, and damn near gave him a heart attack!

"Once they had overcome the initial shock, they were just happy to have me back with them and we had lots of fun during the first weeks. There was also enormous tension while they couldn't decide what was the right thing to do with me. I stayed up nights listening to them going back and forth, why I should stay, why I should be returned. The final decision was reached as we traversed the Straight of Magellan, between Tierra del Fuego and Chile. Finally we opted to use democracy as they say and the Burrards wanted me to stay. We automatically gave my parents a vote against simply because it seemed like the right thing to do. Although I honestly believe that my family was probably feeling some measure of relief that there was one less mouth to feed. Finally my own vote broke the tie in favor of staying. Strangely, I was born in Punta Arenas, Costa Rica; and in a sense, I was born again off the coast of Punta Arenas, Chile."

"That's one helluva story! You should write a book one day," Jake said in admiration. "I have to hand it to you. You certainly took control of your destiny at a really early age. You didn't like what you saw as your imminent future and you changed it. There aren't too many people with the guts to do that at any age. It seems to me that most people will shuffle along, dragging themselves day after day living a life they despise. Sure they'll bitch and moan but they won't actually do anything about it," Jake commented.

"Well, we continued to travel around the world and eventually made it back to California. My new parents pretty much snuck me in, which isn't very difficult since there are so many nooks and crannies on a sailboat, and I was just a skinny little boy then. I could fit just about anywhere.

"The Burrards managed to get me into a school despite the fact I had no papers. They even hired private tutors so I could catch up with the other kids of my age. Those years were so much fun, school in the morning, surfing in the afternoon. Sta. Barbara was a dream come true. Had I known how good it would be

I'd have been willing to hide on that yacht for a whole year before coming out!

"My new family spent a small fortune trying to find a way to adopt me legally. But it was an extremely difficult process, and after three years we were no farther ahead than before. It was very disappointing.

"A few days before my fifteenth birthday I was studying in my room when the police knocked on the front door. I was afraid to open the door since I was sure they were there to take me away, but the news was much worse than that. Myles and Lynette had just been involved in a terrible head-on collision on Highway 1. A drunk driver lost control of his pickup and jumped the median, for them it was over in a brief instant."

"That's terrible," Jake offered, thinking how trite that sounded, but nothing else came to mind.

"The local Department of Child Services immediately put me in foster care until they could figure out what to do with me. I had no papers, adoption or personal. To them I didn't really even exist. My adopted parents had no relatives. No brothers, sisters, cousins, absolutely no one who could corroborate our relationship. I was treated like a hobo.

"After little more than a year of being shuffled around, back and forth an attorney who had been handling my adoption informed me that the State of California was seizing all my parents' assets since they didn't have a legitimate heir, and furthermore, they intended to deport me back to Costa Rica."

"That sounds like the typical government bullshit. Fuck your constituents as often as possible," Jake commented acidly.

"Needless to say I wasn't much in favor of their plan to deport me so I took a few belongings which would remind me the most of my parents, and escaped across the border to Mexico. I made my way down to Cabo San Lucas and worked the sport fishers until I could figure out how to come back to the US.

"Over time I became disillusioned with the system that had screwed me and my parents, so I decided to stay in Mexico. The way I look at it, the Mexican authorities are pretty blatant about their intentions to screw you wherever and whenever they can. The American government seems to fuck you with a smile. You don't even know what hit you before they have left you destitute." His statement was unemotional and to the point.

"That is one of the most amazing stories I have ever heard. You really should consider writing a book," Jake said for the second time.

"I wouldn't know where to start. Anyway, the shadows are getting long and we have a good six hours till we get to the main trail that runs through the Sierra, so it wouldn't be a bad idea if we made camp here. There's a creek and a little logging shack up ahead, people share it freely as they transit the area. We could use the hour or so of sunlight to collect firewood and try hunting a couple of rabbits or something else for dinner."

Pinus Pseudostrobus, intermixed with Durangensis, towered over them and continued on as far as Jake could see in the gradually diminishing daylight. A distant canyon wall shone brilliantly in pink and gold, "I never imagined Mexico to look like this. I thought it was nothing but desert and cactus!" Jake shouted.

No more than fifteen minutes later Jake saw a beautiful young doe nibbling at the tender underbrush. Not being a hunter himself he could not imagine shooting such an innocent looking animal, but just in case he threw a rock in her direction to spook her to safety. He thought he hadn't been seen when a voice came from close by, "Don't worry. There is no sense in killing such a large animal. We are only two and we certainly can't carry the rest with us. Also, if you keep shouting we'll be going to bed hungry!" His traveling companion said with a hint of irritation in his voice. He continued to search for their supper.

With a great deal of interest Jake observed the man from a distance. He had his slingshot pulled back and poised. A few seconds after he released he reached down and lifted up the biggest rattlesnake Jake had ever seen. The man noticed he was being watched, and lifting the dead limp creature above him and shouted victoriously, "I got dinner!" Mother earth had provided once again just as she had since time immemorial.

'Yeah.' Jake said to himself, dreading his next meal.

Flames performed their primeval dance eerily illuminating the surrounding forest and the rickety old logging cabin. Small ring shaped medallions had been placed on skewers made of small branches, and placed around the fire. The rattlesnake hissed for the last time as the little body fat it had dripped onto the red-hot coals below. It smelled delicious. Amber drooled profusely and even Jake's stomach seemed to agree with her, even though his mind didn't.

The man took the first bite and as he joyously masticated he stated: "I've traveled all over this wonderful rich country. So many cultures have tried to rape and pillage her and she just keeps on giving. Presidents come, steal and leave. And she keeps giving. Her diversity is amazing! It's just a shame the government is so corrupt. If there is a hell I am sure it will be filled with politicians and lawyers from every country! But I'd bet the majority of them will be speaking Spanish!"

Jake held a skewer and stared at his next meal. His stomach ached from its own emptiness and longed for some food. Jake's brain tried to coax his hand to raise the meat to his mouth. He removed one medallion, blew on it to make sure it wasn't to hot and fed it to Amber. She took it gently as she always did, but after two bites she swallowed it and immediately begged for more.

"Are you going to give it all to Amber?"

"No. I just wanted to give her a little bit is all," Jake justified himself.

He took the next medallion and gave it a quick sniff. It smelled great, and his stomach growled for food. Jake took a small tentative bite and savored the meat. It tasted almost identical to chicken, but better. But then again that might have been the hunger.

"So what do you think? Do you like it?"

"It wonderful," Jake said as he slipped a second piece into his mouth.

A branch cracked near by and they were startled when Amber started to bark urgently, growling and insistently advising of potential danger.

"¡Buenas noches!" Came a man's voice from the dark forest, trepidation clear in his voice.

"Buenas noches!" The two travelers responded in unison watching as a Mexican Indian man approached cautiously and inquired. "¿Puedo compartir la cabaña?" (May I share the cabin?)

Jake looked at his guide to see if this was acceptable, after all he was ignorant of the ways of this land. "Of course!" was the shouted response. "If you are hungry we have a nice big rattlesnake cooking, so come and join us."

The man approached with a sincere smile. "And I have chorizo, tamales, chile and tortillas. Oh and mezcal of course. So we have a feast to share!" His wrinkled face showed his jovial disposition.

Jake was always fascinated by the stories and lives of those that shared a different background to his own. It didn't really matter what education a person had, Jake had always found that after a certain age, experience in the school of hard knocks provided most people with a good number of fascinating stories to tell. He always thought that it would be a great idea to write them down one day.

The three men huddled around the fire, told stories, ate and drank plentifully. Jake shared his American cigarettes, which were considered a special treat and swapped stories and a few jokes late into the night. Amber was the first to fall a sleep snuggling up to Jake's side. The three companions quickly followed her example. A long day of walking followed by a good meal washed down with mezcal will knock out even the toughest mountain men.

A loud crack and bang walloped through the forest. Jake was up in a flash to witness the second lighting strike which hit even closer to the cabin. Amber was not happy, and looked at her master for protection. Brilliant wires ripped and danced through the dark menacing clouds illuminating the canyons below. Jake watched the spectacle from the doorway of the tiny choza as the two other men slept deeply. Sheets of torrential ran started to pound the surrounding forest in a ferocious attempt to wipe the earth clean. Jake was taken, dreaming of the millennia of ancestors who had watched similar spectacles in worried wonder and absolute awe. The nights chill and his thoughts gave him goose bumps.

"It is rare that it rains during this time of year," the Indian said just behind him.

Jake jumped out of his skin.

"Sorry. I didn't mean to startle you."

"Don't worry my mind was wandering."

"Our Gods are trying to tell us something," the Indian said as he absorbed the view. "Unfortunately we have become deaf to their wise words, and only listen to ourselves and the god of others. We had our own Gods, but when the Spanish came they brought us their God, and since they were able to conquer us, their God became the correct and only God. Do you suppose it would have been any different if we had conquered them?"

Jake didn't know what to answer. But he supposed that the overall outcome probably wouldn't have been very different.

The storm raged on all night, the shack leaked like a sieve.   Despite managing to keep the fire burning and staying close to Amber, Jake only slept a wink or two, the cold dampness streamed through every little crack cutting into him like a knife.

With utmost reluctance the sun crawled above the far Eastern horizon exposing a fresh clear morning.   Well-defined puffy clouds lingered lazily as the only testament to last night's storm.   After breakfast the travelers who had shared a few hours of one another's existence said their goodbyes and farewells to the Indian.

They walked in silence for a good three hours. Even Amber wasn't very interested in smelling around, she simply kept pace next to Jake. Puddles remained on the trail and the mud slowed their pace slightly, but to a lesser extent than either traveler had silently anticipated.

"Feeling any better?"   Jake inquired as he stopped and cupped his hands around his Zippo to light another cigarette.

"A little better. Maybe a few more hours and I'll be as good as new." his companion replied but looked pretty green in the face.

They resumed their slow, methodical march in silence, each man lost in his own thoughts. A light breeze gently whispered through the thick forest but was entirely ignored by the weary travelers.

"So Jake. Since we still have some time to kill, let me ask you something."

"When ever somebody leads up to a question that way I know for certain it's going to be trouble," Jake stated flatly.

With a smile he continued. "So what are you really escaping from? Did you do something or someone? Am I going to see you on 'America's Most Wanted'? What's your story Jake? There's got to be more to it than your personal quest for fame and fortune."

Jake thought for a moment and measured his words. "I'll answer your questions in a different order. No, I doubt very much you will see me on 'America's Most Wanted'. And no, I didn't do anything to anyone."

"Boy this sounds like it's going to be a boring story," his friend interrupted.

"Let me finish!" Said Jake. "Now for the biggy. What am I escaping from? I guess I'm escaping the mundane, the everyday drudgery. I'm looking for a little adventure. You know, a little Indiana Jones."

"Shit, I didn't realize bush flying was that exciting!" Exclaimed his friend with a big helping of sarcasm.

"Well I'll let you be the judge of that. I left three days ago and I'm here. In the middle of nowhere with the likes of you. Which I may add is not particularly where I wanted to be. My airplane stranded on the side of a mountain. Call me crazy but that seems a little adventurous. Wouldn't you agree?"

"I suppose you are right. It's just no Indiana Jones if you know what I mean." The man persisted. "So that's it! You're looking for love in all the wrong places, or for that matter any other Country & Western song saga?"

"That is the last thing on my mind! Long-term relationships seem to go against my nature. I may however be interested in a few short-term relations though. Possibly with some lovely, and did I mention shapely young señorita.   Long flowing, shiny black hair, deep dark eyes…"

"Hey! Wake up!" He gave Jake a good shove, "I don't want the gory details."

"You asked. Besides this story has two options. Take it or leave it," Jake informed him at the same time while smiling at the obscure memory of the waitress that first mentioned those words. He was having breakfast in Bishop, CA. and the overweight waitress was hell bent on giving everybody the hardest ribbing any one person had ever received.

"Getting back to your sad story.   Have you found what you are looking for, whatever that may be?"

"I honestly don't really know specifically what I am searching for.   Maybe it's not one thing in particular. But a series of things which when placed all together the whole seems to make sense. If I'm lucky I might become aware of these things as I travel through life and collect them down its bouncy, pothole-ridden Mexican road."   Jake kicked a stone to punctuate the end of his thought.

"If you are lucky my friend, you will uncover these things. And more importantly, hopefully you'll have the wisdom to notice them and collect them as you go."

As the day warmed the scent of the pine forest weighed heavily in the thin mountain air. No sounds permeated the clear serene silence. Only their own footfalls, accompanied by the occasional tumbling rock dislodged by the donkey's hooves broke the ultimate quiet.

Another hour slowly ticked by. Jake wanted to continue the conversation but nothing relevant came to mind. He reveled in the magnificence of the surroundings. A hawk rose effortlessly on the afternoon thermals methodically scouring the landscape in search of its next meal, its loud shrills announcing its lethal presence.

"How long have you been visiting these mountains?" Jake asked as he lit the tenth cigarette of the day.

"Must be twenty years at least," he thought a moment making a quick mental calculation comparing significant dates with the question. "Yeah. Twenty years. Things haven't changed much up here. Unlike down there. I guess that's why I like it so much. It's one constant in an ever-changing world."

"I've heard that there are a lot of Indian burial sites left undisturbed in these mountains."

"There are a few left. Most have been looted. I have found quite a few but I never touch, and much less take anything. The more inaccessible they are the greater the chance they will be left alone. And alone is how they should remain. Some years ago I was hiking through some canyons just North of here. I was about to descend into a ravine when I heard two airplanes, Cessna's I think, but then what do I know about airplanes? Anyway, at first I thought they were simply fooling around until they got a little closer. That's when I heard machine gun fire. The chasing plane was firing on the one in front. I have no idea why, but I imagine drugs had something to do with it.

The airplane which was trying to get away was hit or simply didn't turn fast enough because it impacted the mountain side with a huge explosion."

"Did you go check it out?" Jake asked.

"Are you shitting me? Hell no! There was absolutely no way anybody could survive such an impact and also I couldn't be sure that the killers weren't keeping an eye on the area. No way did I want to become involved with that situation."

"That poor guy. It must have been a terrifying few last moments," Jake observed.

"Well, Jake, this is the main road." His friend pointed to the hard packed dirt and loose rock trail, which may have been scarcely a foot wider than the one they had just traveled. He looked at Jake's expression of total disbelief and laughed. "What where you expecting, a freeway?"

"Well, no. I just... Well, I was expecting a road," Jake said as he gestured at the dirt before him.

"Jake this is a road. It's a 'dirt' road."

"I gather."

"Trucks come by on a regular basis picking up passengers. It's not like they have a regular schedule or anything, just in case that is what you were expecting. There is no formal bus stop, pole, hut or otherwise. You just wait, and wave your hand like this," he motioned with slight lateral nonchalant hand motion. "Please don't do the 'jumping jack please stop' deal because they'll think you're out of your mind."

"Ok, ok, I think I got it. How's this?" Jake imitated his trainer's suave motions.

"It's all right I guess. You need to practice, but you'll get it," he said with his now trademark sarcasm.

"Where are you going from here?"

"Oh, I don't know," he looked this way and that, pondering the possibilities. "I think I'll head back the way we came. I saw a canyon back there that looked interesting. So Jake, it was great traveling with you. I'm sure we will meet again one day," he knelt down to Amber and gave her a good pat and a little shake. "It was nice meeting you too. Take care of the Gringo!" He gave her a little kiss on the top of her head.

Amber didn't know what to make of him.

"Take care! I hope you find your keys!" Jake shouted from a distance.

He didn't turn, either because he didn't hear or didn't want to acknowledge the silly comment.

Jake and Amber waited until well after nightfall. He rested his tired body against a big gnarled old oak tree and was just dozing when the noise of grinding and scraping could be heard in the distance. He watched the painfully slow approach of an old 60's Ford two ton bellowing thick blue smoke behind and grunting with every rut.

He performed the gesture as he had been instructed and obtained the intended result. Jake handed the driver a couple of dollars and jumped in the back. The thirteen other passengers looked a little surprised to see a gringo and his dog climbing on board, but their surprise didn't last long, except for one staring little boy who probably thought he was looking at some kind of alien. "Buenas noches," Jake said with a smile. A few responded. Others were too tired or just not interested.

It was going to be a long night, and a very long ride.

Chapter 4.

Learning to Fly.

Gleaming marble floors lay before him. They accentuated just how filthy he really felt. Jake stared momentarily at the pristine and empty interior of Durango's International Airport. The lack of travelers, people dropping off or picking up made it obvious that no flights were due to arrive or depart for a while. Jake debated for a few seconds whether he should soil the clean interior. After almost six days of hiking dirt roads and being bounced around on a flat bed he was certain there was a cloud of dust in his wake. Seven days of growth on his face and the rattiest clothes he had ever worn were not the best presentation but he quickly realized he was beyond caring.

He approached an attendant behind one of the airline counters. Her initial smile quickly gave way to what could best be described as 'mild horror', her grimace probably matched Jake's potent odor.

"I'm looking for Capt. Carrillo. Do you know where I can find him?" Jake inquired in English, because he was just too tired to try speaking Spanish.

And anybody who works in an international airport should speak English. Or at least that was his belief at that moment.

"Capt. Carrillo knows you?"   She asked in astonishment.

"Was that the question I asked? Let me repeat the question," Jake enunciated each and every syllable nice and slow. "Do – you – know…"

Not wanting him to finish his slow mockery, she cut him short. "Capt. Carrillo is probably at his hangar. Straight through those doors, walk a hundred meters, he will be in the first hangar."

"Thank you," Jake said flatly.

The cowl was off the Centurion 210. Omar was pointing at something by the firewall and explaining animatedly to the mechanic.   Much to Jake's astonishment, sitting proud and tall next to the 210 was his 185; last seen precariously balanced on a ledge in the middle of nowhere.

"So you broke your plane again!?"   Jake shouted across the hangar.

Omar turned quickly. "Where the hell have you been?" He protested. "I was starting to think you were kidnapped by a bunch of nymphomaniacs!"

"Well, in case you weren't aware. It's a long walk to Durango."

"If you had stayed with your plane you would've been here days ago."

"I just couldn't imagine how you would be able to find me. So I started to walk almost immediately," Jake said with a shrug.

"Hopefully there won't be a next time. But if there is. Stay with your plane and use your radio!"

Omar went to shake his partners hand but stopped short. "Holy shit! You smell awful! There's a shower next to the office right over there." Omar pointed to the office. "Why don't you freshen up and then we'll get something to eat."

Jake felt much more alive and part of the civilized world once he had scrubbed off the thick coat of grime. Clean clothes, shaved and a little Aramis aftershave he had found in the medicine cabinet, he was more than ready for a nice medium rare steak with a baked potato, including all the fixings of course.

As they ate Omar sipped an ice cold Pacifico. Jake had lemonade and told Omar about his long hike in the unforgiving Sierra Madre Occidental and its beautiful sights.

"You are very lucky, Jake. That was a helluva landing you made," Omar commented. "Next time I would suggest you check for water in the fuel," he paused and continued to razz him. "Did you miss the class when the teacher mentioned that?"

Jake couldn't believe he had forgotten something so basic and refrained from commenting. Instead he tried to move the subject away from himself, "have you ever had an engine out?"

"No. I've had a few close calls where I've made a precautionary landing on a highway but no complete failures, and I hope to maintain my record."

Jake ordered a rare steak for Amber before they left. He cut it into small chunks so she might savor it a bit at a time. It was her reward for being such great company during their ordeal and the fact that she had to wait outside, hungry.

"So when do we start?" Jake asked eagerly.

"How about I show you around town this afternoon. Take it easy, and we'll start tomorrow. I have a flight in the morning down to Guadalajara and then over to Ciudad Guzmán. It has nothing to do with bush flying but that's all right. It'll get you used to the never-ending bureaucracy of filling out forms so you can just take off. In that respect, American pilots have it so good."

Durango's afternoon temperature was perfect. Just right for jeans and short sleeves. The new partners dreamed of their future in aviation.

"Have you given notice to your boss?"

"I've been working solo for about a month, a hired gun. So far, so good. Tomorrow we'll be flying the 210. It'll help you get up to speed on the procedures, takeoffs and landings," Omar informed his partner as they sipped espressos next to the plaza.

"When are we going to do some bush flying?" Jake asked anxiously.

"Man, you are so wound up. Maybe you shouldn't have any more espressos. Tomorrow is spoken for. Day after tomorrow we will be working all day on your soft field takeoffs and landings, as well as precision landings. Friday we have a short regular route for passengers and cargo. We'll fly to Otinapa, then to El Salto, over to Milpillas, on down to Guacamayita, then Alchihuites and back home. After a day of flying like that you are going to be so tired you won't be able to see straight."

"We'll see," Jake said with confidence.

"In a few weeks, once you've got the basic bush flying techniques down, we'll transition to the 185 and

you can teach me the finer points of flying that plane,"
Omar concluded with enthusiasm

"Deal!"

Durango is a nice, yet plain working city, which
got its start back in 1563 when Captain Fransisco de
Ibarra settled the area as a beach head to further
conquer the contigious areas and exploitation of the
possible gold reserves in the region. When the
Spanish arrived they believed the hill just in sight of an
Indian settlement was made entirely of gold. The
Spanish conquistadors, many of them from the
Basque region, quickly developed the necessary
infrastructure to exploit the riches. A bustling little
Durango was well under way when the Spanish
discovered their mistake, realizing there was little or
no gold in the hill. They decided to stay anyway.

Both partners agreed that it wouldn't be a very
good idea to stay up too late, even though they were
supposed to be celebrating their new venture and the
eve of their first day of operations as Aces Aviación
SA de CV. Their first day of flying was going to
generate revenue, a great way to start a new
business.

"If you can successfully make the emergency
landing you pulled off in the 185 on that hill side you
won't have any problem flying around here. Now let's
get some sleep. We have a long day tomorrow."

After the sleepless nights on the trail and the
uncomfortably hard surfaces, combined with the day's
events, Jake was exhausted. The hot chocolate he
ordered from room service warmed his soul and eased
his senses.

A fine, cool day, devoid of clouds greeted the sound of the 210's engine as its throttle was mashed against the firewall. The maxed out plane slowly gathered momentum down the long runway. Temperature in their favor, it expedited the climb to their cruising altitude of 11,500 feet. It would be a short flight, only an hour and a half.

Landing at Guadalajara's International Airport was just like any American Class Charlie. The biggest difference between one and the other was the bureaucracy to get out of there. Ciudad Guzman was another hour and forty-five. Unfortunately not as uneventful as the first leg. One of the passengers, unused to bouncing around in some light thermals, blew chunks early on in the flight. The stench didn't stick around for long since he got most in the bag and that was quickly expelled through a window. Overall not a bad day for their first day of business. At the end of the day the partners had a good excuse for a little celebration.

The following day was reserved for training. "Are you ready for a workout?" Omar inquired with a mischievous smile.

"What do you mean by 'workout'? Jake replied with hesitation.

"You don't expect this to be easy, do you?

"Well, I…" Jake stumbled for words. "I don't particularly expect it to be 'that' difficult."

"It's good you have confidence in your skills. Just don't get pissed off when you realize it isn't as easy as you may have thought," Omar informed his partner. He knew all too well how pilots with a certain amount of experience feel about their abilities. "Today we will work on soft field take offs and short landings. As you know, the plane is full of fuel and has 800lbs of lead shot in the passenger compartment to simulate the gold cargo we will be transporting. The 210 is going to stall at 64 knots, even with the STOL kit, so I want to fly the approach at exactly 70 knots, full flaps and plenty of power. You want to hang the plane on the engine."

Jake nodded as he recorded Omar's instructions.

"The landing strip at the mine is 2,300 feet long, 28 feet wide and 8,500' msl so your touch down mark is going to be exactly the point where the runway numbers end. Also, you have to be on the center line. No excuses. If you are off, you are in the ditch. Got it?"

"Got it!" Jake replied firmly, sure of his skills.

"Now. On take off I want you to position the nose wheel on the end of the numbers. Hold your brakes. Power to full static and let go of the brakes. Pull back all the way on the yoke until you break ground then back off slightly as you come into ground effect. Build a little speed and start your climb at Vy. Do you have any questions?" Omar inquired.

"Where are we having lunch?" Jake asked cockily.

"Let's see if you want lunch first!" Omar retorted.

The old but superbly maintained Centurion 210 lazily taxied to the run up area and then on to the active runway. Jake stomped hard on the brakes to hold back the powerful Continental engine.

"Ok, go!" Omar instructed.

The departure was textbook perfect. But Omar really didn't expect any problem there, especially on a nice paved runway. 'Wait 'til he hears the rocks and debris slamming into the fuselage... that'll get his attention.' Omar thought. 'Now for the fun. Landing is always the hardest part.'

Jake smiled as he approached for his first landing. He was following Omar's instruction to a 'T'. It was a vision of beauty. 'The 210 is such an easy plane to fly', he thought. Just at the moment he was supposed to touch down, she continued floating well past the numbers and finally touched down 40' beyond the intended spot.

"Fuck!" Jake exclaimed as he motioned with his fist.

"That's why you have to hang her on the nose. If you use that technique she won't float at all."

Ten approaches and departures later Jake was absolutely wiped. "Let's have a light lunch. Go over the morning's practice and then we'll go to a nice easy dirt strip up in the mountains for your first taste of real bush flying."

Even though it was a nice cool winter day, the afternoon offered a smorgasbord of turbulence, not bad enough to make things dangerous, but enough to make things interesting.

"There's the strip we'll be using." Omar pointed out the window. "The elevation is 7,200 feet, the length of the runway is 2,200 feet and the width is around 40 feet. It's a nice even strip to break you in. Just fly the way you did this morning. Or even better, as you did when you landed on that mountainside a week ago, and you'll do fine."

Jake searched the area at which Omar was pointing. Once he located the tiny uneven strip he made some quick mental notes and calculations and gulped hard. His motions became jerky, his knuckles white from the tension.

"Are you thinking about making that yoke part of your hand. Would you like me to fly the first approach so you can see how it's done?"

"Yeah. That would be great. I've got myself pretty worked up over here," Jake said swallowing his pride.

Omar took the controls with the ease of a pilot who had been doing this type of flying for most of his adult life. He explained every move he made clearly and concisely. The 210 landed firmly yet gracefully and stopped well before the midway point.

"Show off!" Jake said with a smile.

"Ready for the departure?"

Jake maneuvered the plane, getting it as close to the beginning of the strip as he could and remembering the old adage, "There is nothing more useless than the runway behind you and the altitude above you." Full static power, release the brakes. Just as they started barreling down the strip Omar yanked the power to idle.

"What the fuck are you doin'?" Jake said loudly, irritation clear in his voice.

"It's the little mistakes that kill you. Please be more careful next time."

Still pissed off Jake inquired. "What?!"

"Flaps, Jake. You didn't set any flaps. Set yourself up into a calm and collected rhythm. Don't ever rush yourself, or allow anybody to rush you. If you always use your rhythm, it's very unlikely you will forget something."

The rest of the afternoon went well. Jake was getting the hang of it. A couple of weeks of practice and he'd be ready to solo. But for now he was absolutely wiped. Tomorrow was for real. They would be flying paying passengers and cargo out to the middle of nowhere. Jake was about to start doing the flying and the work he had come here to do.

The next day, Omar and Jake didn't bother to inform the old man and his grandson that this was Jake's introductory paying bush piloting flight. The customers probably couldn't hear over the roar of the engine, but just in case Omar gave directions in English.

"All right Jake. Start your descent into this canyon just ahead." Omar pointed just to the right of the windshield. "You need to be nice and low. Hug the left side of the canyon and get ready for a quick right at the end of the canyon. Then another quick descending left turn directly to the strip. It's straight ahead half a mile. Because of your altitude you're going to need full flaps as you turn out of the canyon, or you won't make it. Oh, one more thing. There's a church on short final. I prefer to go over it and dive. Other pilots prefer to slip around it. Since you have to come down immediately after the cupola you have to be on the verge of a power on stall so you don't pick up too much speed on your way down and find yourself going off the end of the runway. Any questions?"

"You've got to be joking." Jake came back.

"No!" Omar said with a smile.

"I got most of it, but coach me as we progress on the approach."

"Don't worry, Jake, this is an easy approach. You already have a good feel for the plane," Omar said, as he looked out the window at a herd of cows being wrangled by a young lad on a burro.

Jake looked over at his partner to make sure he wasn't joking. Omar wasn't very good at keeping a straight face, and on this occasion he didn't have to.

It was a silky smooth day, not a ripple in the sky. The little boy in the back was around eight years old and was flying for the first time. He absorbed everything in absolute wonder and fascination. His sudden ambition to become a pilot seemed so out of reach that he had already vowed that he would never mention it to another living soul.

"Now that you are in the canyon you need to get really close to the left wall." Omar pointed vigorously as he spoke. "Start slowing her up, and give me the first notch of flaps."

"Got it," Jake said as he turned the yoke to the left.

"A little closer Jake. You don't want to have to pull too hard on your turn."

Jake did as he was instructed. He concentrated harder than he had in all his flying years. There was a scarce twenty five feet between the plane and the unforgiving canyon wall, and it appeared to be a hell of a lot closer than that. He saw his turn coming and started easing right with some good backpressure on the controls.

Omar spoke softly, but with a hint of urgency. "Unless you want to impact the canyon wall you are going to have to pull and turn a lot harder."

Jake knew his passengers where not going to enjoy this. He pulled hard and heard a little grunt from behind.

"Harder!" Omar instructed and put his hand under the yoke and pulled. "Like that."

"Ok." Was Jake's only response, his adrenaline pumping. The plane buffeted lightly signaling the onset of a stall.

"Looking good. Now wings level and turning back to left. Get your flaps in. Gear down."

Jake did as he was told, he re-trimmed.

"Go ahead and put in the rest of your flaps," Omar said calmly.

Suddenly, just as promised the church came into view, and Jake remembered how close a half-mile looks as you approach at 70 knots.

"Slow her up some more," Omar instructed.

Jake pulled lightly on the yoke. The stall horn sounded off in protest. The top of the church whizzed by a few feet under the landing gear.

"Push the nose over and slip her a little. Power off!" Omar instructed with a little more urgency.

"Holy shit! That's the strip!?" Jake exclaimed as he saw the tiny makeshift runway ahead.

"What where you expecting? LAX?" Omar said with a smile.

Jake didn't bother to respond. It wasn't necessary, and there wasn't enough time anyway. The tires made solid contact with the ground and bounced slightly. Jake went light on the brakes.

Omar hit the flap switch to the up position and stomped on the brakes. The 210 came to a full stop a scarce three feet from the end of the strip.

"Nice job Jake. Just next time don't forget to use your brakes!"

Jake simply nodded slowly as he pried his fingers from the yoke. "This is like learning to fly all over again," Jake mumbled under his breath. Remembering he had paying passengers in the back he looked over his shoulder and was surprised to find them calm as could be. They were collecting their things in preparation to deplane, completely oblivious to the fact that Jake was drenched in sweat and totally spent.

They unloaded the precious cargo, fifteen cases of Tequila the local grocer had ordered in preparation for the coming fiestas. A couple of lumberjacks rushed to the plane, anxious to get the spare parts they desperately needed to continue working, and make the money they required to feed their families.

In less than five minutes the Centurion 210 was ready to blast down the strip with its two new passengers on board. American fly fishermen in search of the perfect secret spot, were the fish are huge, fight like hell and never stop biting. Omar instructed in Spanish in the hopes that the two anglers wouldn't understand.

"Make sure you are at the very beginning of the strip. You want to take advantage of the entire strip available to you. One notch of flaps, hold the brakes hard and pour on the coals. Get the nose light and into ground effect."

Jake did as he was instructed and the 210 was airborne faster than he thought possible even though they were at 7,200 feet msl and the day was already getting pretty warm.

"Hey Buddy, don't worry about us back here. Do all the steep turns and maneuvers you like!" The chubby guy on the left said smiling. His friend to his right was not so happy about the suggestion.

The flight to Infiernillo was only 45 minutes. Jake had offered them a little sight seeing in an attempt to get them to spend a few more of their dollars with someone who needed them. Unfortunately the two anglers were hell bent to get down to fishing at Mexico's premier Large Mouth Bass lake.

By the end of the day Jake was completely wiped. The level of concentration required to land on those short narrow strips was more than he had ever imagined. He realized that it was simply a matter of practice, eventually he would master this particular type of flying, after all, anything is possible, it just wasn't going to happen over night.

Over the next few weeks, Jake's bush flying skills improved dramatically and the decision was made to start using the 185. After all it was the company plane, and it was a lot cheaper to operate than the lease back payment due for the use of the 210. Omar picked up on the peculiarities of the taildragger very quickly. He also began to realize why it is the preferred workhorse of bush pilots around the world. Omar mentioned over and over that he could kick himself for not trying one years ago.

By spring Jake was in his fifth month and had accumulated over seven hundred hours of bush flying. He had mastered some of the more challenging strips around the Sierra. It was very demanding work, but the flying was fun and Mexico was a new and exciting experience. Every day offered something new to learn and see. So far, he was finding the adventure he sought and in general was happy with his decision to come down. Only one thing was lacking in his life. Evelyn.

Jake's mind often wandered as he flew, especially on the long hauls with smooth skies. Was it Evelyn that he missed, or was it the comfort of just having someone you trust entirely to hold quietly at the end of a long tiring day? He wasn't sure.

The 185 performed its intended job flawlessly and the partners were seriously considering purchasing a second plane. Minera San Patricio wanted to sell the partners the 210 Omar had flown for them for some five years. That plane had always hauled the gold shipments between the mine and Durango, but now that Aces Aviación always used the 185 there wasn't much sense in keeping it. The partners didn't want this inferior aircraft and had set their sights on an even loftier aircraft than the 185. Omar was working several potential contracts and the need of a big turbine powered Cessna Caravan seemed to be the ideal match for the job. It also happened to be their mutual dream plane.

Instead of a lifting eight hundred to nine hundred pounds twice a week, the 185 would carry around twelve hundred pounds every four days. This meant fewer trips, and lower costs. Each load was valued at around four and a half million dollars and regardless of the fact that Jake was Omar's partner, the owners of Minera San Patricio didn't want the gringo picking up their gold. "What if he just flies off to El Norte?" they would ask Omar.

Since Jake began bush flying he never passed up on the opportunity to hone his precision short field landings, and even Durango International's 9,511 foot runway was no exception. In fact he landed so short it was easier to make a 180 and go back to the feeder taxiway than taxi to the first exit. Life was good.

After putting the plane to bed for the night he walked into the office to find Omar talking with Don Epifanio Lopez (the fourth), the eldest son of Don Epifanio Lopez (the third), owner of Minera San Patricio. Omar didn't look happy and Jake theorized they had finally requested a price reduction. He only heard Don Epifanio say 'sorry' as he shook Omar's hand and left.

"That didn't sound very good," Jake offered.

"You can't imagine just how bad that really was," Omar said, as he slowly shook his head. "The mine is closing."

"What? Why? Those guys are making money like it was going out of style! We are moving around twenty seven million dollars a month for them!" Jake shouted.

"I'm sorry Jake. I should have told you sooner. But honestly I really didn't think the problems at the mine would come to a head in the explosive manner they have," Omar tried to clarify.

"What do you mean? What problems are you talking about?" Jake queried and tried hard to keep his cool.

"The mine has been in litigation for almost ten years now, and since it has been so long I just kinda didn't think about it much any more. Furthermore, I didn't want to bother you with the subject since you have enough going on dealing with a new culture, a new type of flying, and everything else."

"Omar! Cut the shit! What the hell is going on?" Jake asked entirely exasperated.

"In short, the mine is closing, along with eighty percent of our revenue," Omar said as calmly as he could.

Jake stood silently, absorbing the news and trying not to explode. 'I guess we are simply not supposed to have any fun during our life time,' Jake thought. Amber sat next to Jake and leaned on his leg. She knew something wasn't right and it was her way of letting him know she was there for him.

Omar continued, "The history of the gold mine started over a hundred years ago. It all began when two young Cora Indians, who also happened to be best friends, were out hunting. Not for sport, but to feed their young families. These two young men, nineteen at the time, had spent most of their childhood together and had spent just about every waking hour together. They shared one rifle and only had enough money for a couple of shells each. The two friends lived in a tiny little village way out in the Sierra. In fact, it is so inaccessible we can't even come close to landing a plane any where near there."

"I hope this is the introduction as to why we are losing our business," Jake interrupted.

Omar didn't skip a beat. "The two friends were tracking a mountain goat on very steep and inaccessible land. The previous year's harvest had been terrible and food was very scarce, so the goat was certainly a godsend. During the chase Epifanio Lopez saw an unusual glitter between some rocks. It stopped him in his tracks. Ignoring their hunger Epifanio and Adalberto Rosas stopped to investigate. Their curiosity would pay off. It turns out that the glitter in the big rock came from a thick vein of gold running through it."

"This sounds like it's going to be a long story. Do you want a beer? Because I'm havin' a soda," Jake said as Omar took a breath to continue.

"Sure. It'll relax me if nothing else," Omar resumed. "Epifanio and Adalberto had a pretty good idea of what they had found, and immediately swore one another to secrecy. As soon as they could, they made the long trek to Durango where the rock was picked apart and it's contents extracted and purified. Gold! The exchange house tried to get the information out of the two men. They told no one. Not even their wives." Omar took a long swig from his beer and continued. "With the reassurance that what they had found was in fact gold, and knowing they had no money to go and buy the property, the two friends went back to their site on weekends and any spare time to clandestinely dig and pick at the mountain until they had enough to purchase the site from the government. The federal government was more than happy to sell such a desolate piece of land to a couple of dumb Indians who didn't know any better for just pennies an acre. And so, Minería Santa Lucia was born."

"Years and decades passed. Epifanio and Adalberto became extremely wealthy. They diversified into lumber and trading. They remained the best of friends until they both died at a ripe old age. In fact they died within just a year of one another." Omar took a sip of beer. Jake lit another cigarette and drained the rest of his orange Fanta. "However, as is quite common among the children of wealthy parents, who didn't have to struggle for food or money during their lifetime, they tend to find ways to create problems for themselves and others. Soon after the two old men died, envy and greed started to develop in the minds of Epifanio Lopez's and Adalberto Rosas' boys. I suppose the vast wealth they inherited didn't seem as enormous when divided between fifteen offspring."

"That's insane!" Jake exclaimed. "I don't know what the profit margins are on a gold mine, but if we are transporting twenty seven million dollars a month, there's got to be a large chunk of change left after costs."

"The Lopez boys were the first to start claiming they had more rights to the mine than the Rosas. They claimed that their father discovered the first rock when the two friends were out hunting. The feuding escalated to new heights. Board meetings were all out brawls. Guns were laid out on the conference table. The two families truly despised one another."

"Since neither family wanted to sell out, and no one could decide on an independent manager each thought to be impartial, the conclusion was to split up

the mine.   The old Santa Lucia mine was closed.
Years of geological surveys and analyses were
conducted at an exorbitant cost in order to determine
exactly how the mountain should be split.   As you
already know, the Rosas got the northwest half, and
the Lopez got the southeastern half."

"That is so stupid!" Jake said as he shook his
head. Amber looked up from her comfortable position
on the rug.

"Well, you'd think that once they had divided the
mine all the problems would be solved. No! Not by a
long shot.   Now the two families had no bond, and
therefore no reason to be even slightly civil to one
another.   The fighting was rampant, to the extent of
shooting at one another."

"I can't believe you didn't think this wasn't worth
mentioning!" Jake said.

"It happened such a long time ago, and things
have calmed down, somewhat," Omar offered.

"All right. Go on."

"After a few decades or so the sons grew a little
older, wiser, and richer.   They finally calmed down.
Unfortunately along comes generation number three of
wild hotheads and the shit starts hitting the fan all over
again. To make matters worse about fifteen or twenty
years ago, the Lopez' mine started to dry up." Omar
cracked himself a fresh beer, taking a long gulp.

Jake also took advantage of the little break to
get himself a cold Coke out of the fridge and lit another
smoke.

"As it turns out," Omar continued, "the
geological survey can only tell so much, and especially
with the technology from yesteryear. So the Lopez'

decided to start drilling through the mountain and into the Rosas' side. This worked fine and dandy, since the foreman of the Rosas' mine was getting payola to advise the Lopez family which way they shouldn't head and furthermore steer the operation he was in charge of away from the Lopez dig. Well sure as shit, one fine day two shafts finally met, and all hell broke loose."

"Holy cow! And when did you say all this happened?" Jake asked.

"About ten or twelve years ago. Everyone was a little more civilized by then, so instead of resorting to bullets they started suing the hell out of one another. The Lopez family filed a lawsuit claiming the original contract was bogus, and furthermore that the original geological survey was tampered with. In essence they wanted the contract, which split the mine declared null and void. The Rosas' contention is a lot simpler, the Lopez' had been stealing their birthright for years." Omar sipped his beer and continued. "All this made for what seemed like an unending succession of lawsuits, injunctions, expert testimony, appeals, payoffs, scandals and everything else you might imagine. But finally, just over a month ago the grand jury declared unequivocally in favor of the Rosas, and awarded them reparations of over one hundred million dollars!"

"Omar I can't believe you never told me all this!"

"In order to ensure compliance with the ruling, the army is going to the mine tomorrow to ensure a smooth transition to the Rosas." Omar took the last swig from the bottle and tossed it into the trash can.

"I can't believe you didn't tell me! Even as a matter of general interest or idle chit chat," Jake protested for the third time.

"With all the legal mumbo jumbo having gone on for so many years, I guess I just figured it would go on forever," Omar explained apologetically.

"Now what the hell do you suppose we are going to do? How can we pay for the lease on the 210?" Jake questioned the biggest bill first.

"I wouldn't worry about the 210. It'll probably be transferred to the Rosas so no more payments will be due. I'm a lot more concerned about how we are going to stay busy enough to pay ourselves."

"We better get out and start drumming up some new business, that would be my opinion," Jake offered.

"The problem is our field is pretty limited and until now we really haven't had to compete very seriously. We are probably going to have to start carrying more passengers and supplies to smaller mining operations and logging outfits. It's not great business, but we might be able to squeak by."

"This might be a dumb question, but I'll ask it anyway. Is there any chance the Rosas would consider hiring our services?" asked Jake hopefully.

"Not a chance in hell. We are viewed as the enemy, and in any case, they already have a fleet of their own planes and pilots. It's a class operation. Brand new turbocharged Cessna 206's."

"This is really not good Omar!"

"There are three or four strips no one wants to fly into because they are so treacherous to get in and out of that most pilots refuse to go," Omar offered.

"Not exactly the niche market I had in mind, but if it helps us to stay afloat, so be it," Jake said with little enthusiasm.

"There is one last gold run for the Lopez', but it's not the standard pickup I've been doing all these years really," Omar hesitated slightly as he said this, and Jake picked up on it immediately.

"Cut to the chase Omar. What's up?"

"As I said before, the army is due in tomorrow morning to enforce the federal judgment. They are on their way through the Sierra as we speak. As you can imagine there is still an important amount of gold in different stages of process at the mine and ready to be picked up. The Lopez' want us to fly in and get it," Omar concluded.

Jake gave a little quirky smile, "You're fuckin' with me?"

"No! I'm totally serious," Omar replied.

"You mean we are supposed to fly in there in spite of a potential barrage of gunfire from the army? Sounds like an excellent way to get killed if you want my opinion!"

"I thought you said you wanted adventure in your life!" Omar retorted.

"Sorry, but I think you are confusing adventure with certain death. In my culture we consider them two very different things."

"The army probably won't even arrive until late morning, and by then we'll be gone. If they are already there we'll simply over fly the place and get the hell out of there. Deal?" Omar asked hopefully.

"Just one more question. Isn't this called stealing in most countries?" Jake inquired.

"As I see it, until the army shows up to take possession who's to say what is already there and what is not," Omar justified.

"All right, I'll do it. Just one last problem, I've never flown into the strip at the mine, and secondly, I'm not used to the kind of weight you're talking about," Jake protested.

"Piece of cake. You've flown into tougher strips than this one. It's almost like an international airport in comparison!"

"Who the hell are you trying to fool? Name one international airport which is 2,300 feet long, 28 feet wide and at an 8,500 foot elevation?" Jake waited a few seconds for the answer. "Exactly what I thought!"

"Details! I'm telling you it's no big deal," Omar tried to soothe his partner.

"All right," Jake affirmed. "What weight did you say you usually take off with? Was it around 800 pounds of cargo?"

"That's about right, only tomorrow we'll probably be carrying a little more than that."

"Great," Jake said sarcastically. "Would you like to tell me how much this little joy ride pays?"

The airport was quieter than usual that morning. Many operators had cut back their flights during the past few months due to a general slow down in the economy. As it turned out Mexico's president, who had been in office for over three years, seemed to be hell bent on doing more damage than good. At least back when the corrupt PRI was in power people had jobs.

Aces Aviación's two pilots flew their planes in loose formation due north/northwest towards Minería

San Patricio. Jake speculated on what may lie ahead. 'Would the army already be there? Would they be willing to shoot them down? Don't be silly!' He told himself.

Omar's voice crackled over the silent airways, "Taildragger, follow me through the canyon. It's no big deal. Just fly the approach as you have been doing and everything will be fine," they had agreed not to use names over the frequency on the odd chance that someone may be monitoring it.

His partner's boost worked. Jake already felt pretty good about his ability to get an airplane down safely on a tiny piece of earth, but Omar's words reassured him just the same.

Omar landed the Centurion 210 with the practiced ease of thousands of landings on this familiar strip and quickly taxied off the active, making room for Jake, who was hot on his tail. His landing was also picture perfect. "Nice job," came the comment over the radio. He taxied next to the other Cessna and shut down.

The gold mine was deathly silent. Its regular hustle and bustle of trucks and materials were gone. The Lopez' had put up over a decade of fighting before finally being forced to give in. Any further battle would've meant confronting the army and that, they concluded, would be a complete waste of money. Money, which from now on, would not be quite as plentiful as before.

"Teofilo!" Omar shouted in no particular direction. The last superintendent was probably hiding before the army showed up. Teofilo peered from the shack/office/home, which he had inhabited for the past twenty-five years. His hair and face showed he had been fast asleep moments ago. Omar greeted him as he had done for the past fifteen years.   .

The three men quickly split the load of gold bullion and precipitate between the two planes. The 185 would haul 1,200 pounds while the 210 would depart with 1,000 pounds. San Patricio's bullion was around 90% pure and required further processing in Durango to achieve the desired ninety nine point nine percent purity to be ready for market. The precipitate was around thirty percent pure but was still worth retrieving. The Lopez family certainly didn't want the Rosas getting their grubby hands on it.

As Jake, Omar and Teofilo were struggling with the last barrel of precipitate they became aware of the distant sound of the grinding gears of a large truck. Most likely a military truck. Startled, Omar and Teofilo dropped their portion of the weight leaving Jake to manage. The two hundred pound barrel caught him square on his big toe.

"Fuck!" Was all he managed to utter under his breath. The other two turned back instantly to help get the barrel off Jake's foot.

"Let's get the hell out of here! Come on Teofilo," Omar shouted anxiously as he ran towards his plane.

"No way am I getting into one of those things! I know my way around here. They won't be able to catch me. Take care Omar! Hasta la vista!" Teofilo turned and ran.

"Wait, Teo, catch!" Omar tossed a 30 pound gold ingot towards Teofilo. Omar knew that even though Teo had worked for almost 40 years at the mine he would receive no pension from the mining company. He would have to make do with the miserable pittance provided by the government.

Teofilo picked up the heavy bar from the dusty well-trodden ground, smiled appreciatively at his friend and ran.

Jake didn't wait a second longer and fired up the 185. He quickly taxied his plane before Omar even had a chance to get in his. As he positioned himself at the very edge of the tiny strip, he firewalled the throttle. When the tach came to full static he released the brakes and leaned forward, his mind and body willing the plane to take off sooner.

The 185 lethargically lumbered down the dirt strip at a less than acceptable rate. Jake's heartbeat at a frantic pace, adrenaline raced through every vein in his body. It surely didn't look good. He made a quick mental calculation of the distance to the end of the strip vs. the developing speed to achieve rotation and flight. 'Hopefully,' he thought. Jake knew the stall speed would be higher since he was well over max. gross. The tail was up, but she still felt very heavy. "Just a little more!" Jake said out loud as he grit his teeth. 'You don't have any more!' was the answer that popped into his mind.

Incredibly at the very last second and last couple of feet of runway the 185 hit a little bump on the strip and was launched into flight and over the edge of the cliff. Just in case Jake pushed the nose over and flew deeper into the canyon. The windshield filled with the fast approaching valley floor. 'She can fly!' Jake thought as he slowly pulled back on the yoke and started his slow climb out of the canyon.

Omar watched as the scene unfolded and cringed.

Two trucks were upon him and one was already directly on the strip before he had a chance to start his takeoff roll. 'Now what?' His brain screamed.

Men started jumping from the military truck, assault rifles in hand. Omar didn't hesitate. He gunned the engine, even though the strip was out of the question. If nothing else, he would make them work for their pay. The big question was: Where to go? The access road from the mine up to the airstrip was pretty wide. Possibly just enough for the wings to squeeze by, but then again, maybe not. He had never given it much thought, but then he hadn't had to until now.

A huge dust ball arose behind the plane blowing into the eyes of the pursuing soldiers and slowing them, just enough for Omar to stay ahead. The 210 barely made it down the access road and on to the main mine road. This road would usually be a traffic jam of trucks moving back and forth with loads of ore. It was wide enough for two trucks side by side and then some. He was too close to the bottom of the incline so he would have to make it up the hill at least two hundred yards and turn around. With a nice downhill grade Omar was certain he'd get her off the ground in no time.

As Omar maneuvered in the only wide spot, dragging the left brake to sharpen the turn, the first military truck was half way down the access road and quickly heading towards his makeshift runway. The engine roared in response and quickly picked up speed. Stones dinged the leading edge of the horizontal stabilizer. The large Dina military truck was just turning onto the strip. There wasn't enough time or room to stop. He knew he would either crash into the side of the vehicle or jump the front of the solid mass ahead.

Omar quickly opted for the unknown prize behind door #2. The 210 came off the ground with a scarce six inches to spare cleared the truck with a tremendous roar, as the driver flattened himself behind the wheel, arms clutched over his head, eyes and teeth clenched, praying loudly to anyone that might be listening. After clearing the large truck, Omar eased the backpressure on the yoke and followed the contour of the makeshift strip in ground effect until he had gathered enough airspeed to slowly commence his climb. At that moment holes started appearing in the windshield and quickly glancing back Omar could see the soldiers firing at him. The rear window was also riddled with holes. Omar ducked slightly and continued to fly the plane as he frantically searched for the nearest available canyon in which to take cover. The corner was cut a little too soon and he muscled the plane just in time to prevent smashing into the rocky wall.

Omar sat up straight again. At least he was out of the line of fire. He got on the radio to Jake. "Taildragger are you on frequency?"

"I'm up," Jake responded quickly.

"That was an interesting departure! What the hell happened? You took forever to get off the ground." Omar commented.

"I'm a little embarrassed to admit it."

Omar thought momentarily, and made his conclusion. "Flaps?"

"Yup," Jake said no more.

"How long have you been flying?" Omar asked sarcastically.

"I'm doing a fine job beating myself up. I don't really need your help," Jake retorted.

As Omar flew the plane, he performed his usual scan around the panel, and immediately noticed how low the fuel gauge was. A quick glance out the window showed a contrail of fuel dispersed in the slipstream and atomized into the atmosphere.

"Taildragger?" Omar requested over the comm. still avoiding the mention of Jake's name, just in case anyone may be monitoring the frequency.

"Yeah," Jake responded.

"I have a bit of a problem here. As I departed the mine someone was using me for target practice. The left tank was punctured and I only have gas from the right tank remaining. I'm definitely not going to make Durango."

"What's your fuel status?" Jake asked.

"It looks like I've got around an eighth of a tank remaining. I'll burn whatever is in the left tank and then switch to the right, which seems to be fine," Omar continued. "I think I can make 'La Purísima." You should continue to the rendezvous point and then on to Durango for fuel."

"Isn't there an easier strip than 'La Purísima'? Why would you pick one of the toughest strips in the Sierra for an emergency landing?"

"Because I like the taco stand that's next to the church," Omar said with a chuckle.

"I hate to tell you, my friend, but you are full of shit! I'll fly ahead at full power and buzz the town for you. By the time you arrive on an economy setting the soccer field should be cleared of goal posts for your landing," Jake offered.

Just as Omar was approaching on a higher than normal final, his engine coughed once, farted twice and quit altogether. He deadsticked the 210 in for a flawless landing.

While Omar waited for Jake's return from Durango he took advantage of the time to visit with some old friends. They barbecued some fresh venison and ate it with fresh homemade pico de gallo salsa and beans. Omar headed back to the plane for a short siesta and then it was time to fuel the plane. Jake and Omar siphoned fuel from the 185 into the 210's right tank.

The Lopez brothers had been waiting for their shipment when Jake arrived, and they were still waiting for the rest of their shipment when Omar landed in his crippled bird.

"Thank you for your help in this matter Capt. Omar." Epifanio Lopez said ceremoniously and with a patronizing back handed wave. "You have served my family well over the years, and in appreciation I am not going to charge you for the money you owe me for the airplane lease during the last month." Epifanio showed a crooked smile as he extracted the time sheet from his coat pocket and tore it up with great fanfare.

Jake made a quick mental calculation of the number of hours owed. He whispered to Omar. "That is around five or six hundred dollars! He's got to be kidding!"

"With all due respect, Don Epifanio. Jake and I put ourselves in a great deal of danger today. I don't mean to be ungrateful, but I sincerely believe that being shot at is worth a great deal more than five or six hundred dollars," Omar stated.

The older man stood there momentarily glaring back and forth at the two partners, a stony tight-lipped expression on his mean face. It felt like an hour transpired before anyone spoke. It appeared that everyone present knew that whoever spoke first conceded.

Epifanio slowly began nodding, "Very well. But I will give you a choice. I will give each of you a ten-ounce ingot, but in doing so we will forever cut all ties. We no longer know one another. We will never again acknowledge one another. On the other hand, if you accept my original offer with due gratitude, we shall remain friends, and as friends, if you ever need a favor, an investor, a reference, or anything else for that matter, you will always be able to count on me. Now, the decision is yours."

Omar and Jake looked at one another momentarily. Jake spoke first. "I'll take the ingot, thank you very much, I have enough friends."

Mr. Lopez didn't even bother looking at the gringo. He had expected such a crass response from a foreigner, "How about you, Capt. Carrillo? What is your decision?"

"Don Epifanio, you know how much I value your friendship and any good reference you may give me.

But at this particular moment with the shape the economy is in, I have a family…"

"Say no more, Capitán. I understand. Just remember our agreement. I fully understand your predicament, but the rules of your decision stand." Without shaking hands Mr. Lopez turned to one of his goons, spoke briefly, then walked to his big black Mercedes and drove away. The big burly goon handed each an ingot and he also was gone.

In a consolidated attempt to make the little money they had collected from the last gold run, the two partners of Aces Aviación took immediate pay cuts and put their big expansion plans on ice. Business was slow for everyone. They might just manage to stay afloat but it would be very lean times, and they both knew it.

Jake moped around the office as the weeks slowly ticked by. Omar frantically pitched new customers with absolutely no luck. A stationary overcast hung over the entire region for weeks on end mimicking Jake's state of mind. Tomorrow, as long as the weather didn't turn too ugly, Aces Aviación would make its weekly flight to La Esperanza. This would be Jake's first flight as PIC to what every pilot in the state of Durango called the most dangerous and difficult landing strip they had ever seen. The operative word was 'seen' since no one dared attempt it.

The Cessna 185 bounced around in the unstable air of the Sierras. Jake in the left seat struggled to maintain wings level. As they approached from the north, Omar explained the approach one more time.

"You fly the approach and I'll take it on final. I'll talk you through it, so don't worry. This is by far the most challenging landing you will ever make, other than the forced landing you made when you were moving to Mexico. But, as long as you know what you are doing it really is no big deal," Omar said this with the utmost confidence.

The tiny mining town called 'La Esperanza' has clung precariously to the side of the mountain for almost 500 years. The 185 buzzed it for the second time advising the residents and more importantly, the airstrip crew, that a plane intended to land in a few minutes.

Located on a 20 degree sloped ledge on the side of a mountain deep in the Mexican Sierra Madre Occidental, the little town ends abruptly with a 1,500 foot precipice. The other end of the town faced a direct ascent to the 10,000 foot summit of the mountain. It's a strange place to live, but then humans will go wherever the money is, and in this case Omar and Jake were proving the point.

There was the option of driving up the mountain, but the trail was mostly fit for only the most daring of mountain goats and took a good three days of the harshest driving one could possibly imagine. Jake's eyes got wider and wider as the mountain side got closer and closer. Nothing but village filled the windshield. Jake swallowed hard. "No chance of going around here!"

"Going around is for sissies!" Omar exclaimed, not believing his own words. "Aim for the spot just beyond the cliff's edge. Don't be fooled by the optics of the approach. OK, my plane."

Jake gladly released the controls. The patch of dirt he recognized as the touch down zone was ridiculously small. Jake couldn't comprehend how this was going to be possible without a tail hook, or a miracle.

"I'm slowing to 70 knots, but we are still descending steadily with constant manifold pressure. Prop is in full." The mountain side approached quickly. "Here's the flare, and full power!" The big Continental roared loudly with the extra fuel being pumped into it. At that instant the huge tundra tires slammed hard absorbing most of the impact, the landing roll was around twenty-five feet. "You have to keep full brakes as well as full power until the boys have a chance to tie us up to the winch," Omar shouted over the engine. "If you don't give her full power the brakes won't hold!"

Two young men flipped a thick nylon rope up over the landing gear. The big electric winch at the top of the hill started turning until the rope was taut. A thumbs up from the landing crew was Omar's cue to pull back the power so they could be hoisted up the slope to the basketball court. "Make sure you keep the power at idle. If you shut the engine off and the rope snaps for some bizarre reason you would be going backwards over that precipice so fast you won't even be able to wave good-bye," Omar said with a smile. "Oh, by the way, do you know why we are being hoisted to a basketball court?" Omar inquired.

Jake thought for a few moments. "Because there's not enough room for a soccer field at La Esperanza?"

"You got it! By the way, don't worry about the departure. It's a lot easier than the landing. All you have to do is not over rotate. If you do, you will smack the empennage," Omar informed his student.

The two sole employees, and just barely at that, of Aces Aviación unloaded the plane with help of the ground crew. As was now the norm, several cases of tequila were off loaded for some fiesta or another. They were ready to depart in less than half an hour and two passengers were allowed to board.

With the engine running Omar inquired. "Do you want to try the departure?"

"Yeah. It can't be too difficult to roll down a hill!" Jake responded.

"I hope you are joking! It's not that easy."

"Just tell me the technique now and then coach me as we go," Jake said with confidence. 'After all, the tough part was landing.' He thought.

"All right, first you want to just inch yourself off the basketball court. In the 210 it feels as if you're going to put your feet through the firewall, but I don't think it's going to be quite so dramatic in this plane. Just remember, with the slope you see before you, once you roll a few meters beyond the edge of the court there is absolutely nothing that could possibly stop you."

Jake nodded his head understandingly.

"Go ahead and do your run up here. Make sure you're ready to go. Don't forget your flaps!" Omar said as he waved his finger in the air, reminding Jake of his previous error at the mine. "Go for full power, get the tail off, and once you hit your airspeed, give very light back pressure. Then she'll just float off,"

Omar spoke with a smile. "How about we come round and do a quick landing while the procedure is still fresh in your mind?" He asked, knowing Jake was not expecting that.

"Yeah, that sounds like a plan," Jake retorted before his brain had a chance to analyze the situation and provide a more sensible answer, such as: "Maybe next time, I'm all full up just now."

The fat tundra tires eased over the edge of the basketball court with a slight thump. Jake applied a little a bit of brake until the tail wheel also cleared.

"Go ahead and give it the coals," Omar calmly instructed.

With the steep angle and the three hundred turbocharged ponies under the cowl, Jake had the tail up in a second or two and was easing back on the yoke a second after that. "Shit! That was the shortest takeoff roll I have ever experienced!" Jake exclaimed.

"Just be careful. If you encounter strong winds from the west, as soon as you clear the protective area of the mountain side you'll encounter some brutal downdrafts. Needless to say that applies to the approach also. Are you ready for the approach?" Omar inquired.

"Am I!? Are you? Would be the best question."

"I'm serious! You might as well start getting used to the more challenging strips if we are going to stay in business."

The air was full of invisible bumps, potholes, divots and the occasional ditch, or at least that is what it felt like. Not an ideal practice situation but certainly a realistic situation. As the day's temperature rose, the bumps would get harsher, not earth shattering, but enough to get your attention.

Jake made his way around the strange pattern and lined himself up for final.

"You are not aiming at the touchdown point," Omar said calmly. "Slow her up a little more."

Wallowing in a downdraft Jake smoothly gave the Cessna a dash of power. The stall horn startled one of the passengers.

"Good. Hold on to this visual. Slow her up again. Okay, now start to hang her on the prop," Omar instructed.

Jake pushed the throttle forward. The engine wound up.

"Good. Looking good," Omar counseled. The sink rate suddenly increased. "Power Jake, more power!"

Jake rammed the remaining throttle to the firewall. 'Oh shit!' Jake didn't have a chance to verbalize his thoughts. He was sure the ledge was going to rip the landing gear off the plane. The big turbocharged Lycoming IO-540 screamed bloody murder at full power, its nose higher than you would think possible.

"Ease off the power!" Omar shouted.

XA-TAP came down in a harsh, bone jarring three-point landing. "Now full power and full brakes! I think we have arrived!" Omar announced with a smile. "Congratulations. That was a very nice piece of air work."

"Nice!? You've got to be shittin' me! I just about ripped the gear off just before I almost collapsed it!" Jake said trying to get his wits back together.

"Don't be so hard on yourself. You did great, and next time you'll do better."

The winch clanged away as the old machine dragged them up the incline to safety. The two Indians stared wide-eyed and less than sure about the trip they were about to embark upon. Omar read their expressions and eased their fears with a few well-chosen words.

Four months passed slowly and frustratingly, as they tend to, when things are not going in the right direction. Business was worse than ever. No one was spared. A general slow down in the economy brought on by the stupidity and lack of action by Mexico's not-so-new president Vicente Fox. Oh yes, according to him everything was fine, 'couldn't be better'. Unemployment was rampant. Mexico's favorable exporting position had been permanently compromised due to an overvalued peso.

Jake vacated his nice apartment just off Avenida Juarez for a cot in the little office attached to the hangar of Aces Aviación. He didn't mind. It was a sacrifice to be endured in order to accomplish future dreams. Furthermore, the smell of avgas and oil made him sleep better. Omar and Alejandra had offered that he stay with them, but Jake insisted he preferred the current arrangements better. And he honestly did. To continue with honesty, his Gulfstream trailer by the beach in Carlsbad also seemed very appealing. Amber didn't particularly care where she lay down for the evening, as long as she was with Jake. 'Dogs are wonderful!' Jake thought as he lay reading a book and caressing her ear with his free hand.

Omar sold his truck and Alejandra's car. She wasn't impressed but knew that it was necessary to survive. Omar was even less impressed since the bus ride to the airport took almost two hours. The old run down buses were an awful sight and smelled worse. Diesel fumes polluted the interior. Omar was amazed they still ran. And to top the whole thing off, the run down vehicle was jammed with so many people that the old suspension could barely take the strain and groaned and protested every inch of the journey.

Aces Aviación was down to its last can of beans, or can of oil to be more precise, and the worried partners had no idea when or where their next one might be coming from. In other words, they had no idea when they might have another flight. The only ones still flying were the majors.

Jake was suddenly given a short reprieve from the monotonous hardship of sitting around with his thumb stuck up his ass waiting for something to happen. Anything, anything to break the desperation and unending frustration of nothing to do. A young, wealthy and very pedant lumberman wanted to go fishing with a customer to Mazatlán in his P210. It delighted and boosted his over inflated ego to have his own personal aircraft and his own personal pilot at his beck and call, an Americano at that. The man would brag to his friends to the point where they could no longer hide their disgust and Jake would be dismissed with the swoosh of the hand and the admonishment, "Remember you are on call 24 hours a day!"

It was a high price to pay, but a weekend in Mazatlán at the Camino Real, along with the opportunity to sign everything he wanted to his room, including the most decadent dinner and massage ever. It was certainly something he couldn't afford himself, and probably wouldn't be able to for sometime to come. For this he was willing to take a little more shit than usual. He would make sure that, on top of a very high hotel bill, the arrogant little bastard paid a hefty PITA (pain in the ass) fee for his haughtiness.

Jake played with the sand between his toes as he sipped on the third virgin piña colada, munched away on shrimp ceviche and tried to concentrate on reading one of Guy Bellamy's novels. The sun was starting its descent to the west and he angled his chaise lounge to the south so the rays wouldn't hit him square in the eye. He knew before he started that his favorite author would again weave a funny and extremely entertaining story, and 'In the Midday Sun' was no exception. But he just couldn't focus. Mounting problems rushed his mind and wouldn't allow him to concentrate, he mulled them over and over with no conclusion, just unending frustration.

He just wanted to relax, enjoy the moment, enjoy the pseudo-vacation of a paid-for weekend in a nice hotel on the beach. Jake hadn't been on a vacation since...hell, he couldn't even remember.

A piña colada with a double shot of vodka would certainly help to dull his troubles. He silently fought the urge. 'Four years clean and sober.' He repeated in his mind. It was the most difficult thing he had ever done, and now more than ever he missed that wonderful flavor, that feeling, and the hiding place a smooth cool cocktail will undoubtedly provide. "Fuck it!" He said out loud. "You only live once, and I'm not having any fun the way my life is going." Jake scoured the beach for a waiter.

As he waited for the ceremonial arrival of the delicious concoction, he vacillated, back and forth on his decision. The tall glass appeared in the middle of his turmoil. Beads of condensation created by the clash of temperatures, the cold contents within the glass and the hot humid Mazatlán climate, created trails down the sides of the hand blown glass. A tiny colorful paper umbrella made a failed attempt at keeping the sun away from the piña colada. A chunk of sweet pineapple on the rim added the final exotic touch to the beverage.

"Señor, Señor!" The waiter said a little louder than usual in an attempt to wake Jake from his trance.

Jake took the ice cold drink from the wooden tray and was surprised by its size and heaviness. He couldn't stop thinking about the wonderful taste and even better effect just ahead. He slowly put the glass to his forehead to cool himself off. As the glass passed his nose he could smell the alcohol. It was like greeting an old and very dear friend. His mouth began to water in expectation and he swallowed hard. The straw was in his lips and he began to draw on it. Just as the poisonous liquid was about to touch his lips a voice interrupted his actions.

"Jake? Jake McInnes? No way! What the hell are you doing in Mazatlán?"

The man's face came into focus slowly since Jake had been reading for a while. A database of faces swooshed by until his dulled CPU made a match. "Len?" he said without certainty.

"Larry! Remember me? I flew the ditch out of North Vegas."

"Oh right! I remember!" Jake lied. "How have you been? Still flying?"

"Do bears shit in the woods?" Larry exclaimed.

Interesting analogy Jake thought sarcastically. "So what are you doin' nowadays? On vacation?" Jake lit a cigarette and casually tipped his piña colada over, the contents quickly absorbed into the dry sand. 'Damn that was close.' He reflected.

"No! I work down here. Great pay and plenty of it!" Larry said with a smile.

The two pilots talked shop for over an hour, exchanging their favorite flying stories and the tales they had heard from undisclosed third parties.

"Tell ya what. I'll buy dinner. There's a great little restaurant in the old section of town that only the locals know about. It's the best!"

Jake had the arrogant bastard's extra cell phone with him so if he if the little shit called he would be available. "Okay, you're on."

The two gringos took a local 'pulmonia' cab and enjoyed the warm evening ride down the costera. Other turistas were doing the same, quietly enjoying the magic, rest and relaxation of a well-deserved vacation. Others, usually within the 18 to twenty-something range, were hooting and hollering and making idiots of themselves. Reinforcing the world's image of the ultimate ugly American.

Jake commiserated about the difficult state of the flying business along with the seemingly endless downward death spiral in which it appeared to be.

"I'm not supposed to be talking to anyone about this," Larry hunched down in his chair, looking from side to side, and having established secrecy from the surrounding tables, he continued, "But we're buddies so it doesn't count.   I've been working with a secret operation for the past four months or so. The work is challenging, plentiful and very well paid.

Getting right down to the important point Jake inquired, "How much is 'very well paid'?"

"$5,000 dollars a day," Larry said with a big smile.

"You've got to be shittin' me! What the hell are you moving?"

"Drugs and cash," he said as he took a big bite of dorado fillet stuffed with seafood and baked in a white wine sauce.

"Are you kidding!?" Jake inquired.

"Oh! Don't worry! It's completely legit. It's a DEA operation," Larry responded after seeing his friend's expression. "And they just might be looking for some extra help."

Chapter 5.

Workin' for the Man.

"No! Absolutely not!" Omar said emphatically.

"Do you have any better ideas? We are in no position to be picky at this particular moment! Business is slow. We can't pay our incoming bills, or the debts we've already incurred." Jake urged his partner.

"Well, no. But just because I don't have any good ideas at the moment doesn't mean we should settle for a bad one!"

"Omar, have you ever made five grand a day? This could jump start our business. We could buy the Caravan on floats and fly 'turistas' around the Caribbean if we wanted," Jake pleaded.

"Jake, I don't care what you say. The money they are offering you is dirty and there is no way you can convince me otherwise. You're going to wind up with a bullet in your head. Besides, I don't want to move to the Caribbean. Durango is my home. My family lives here. My friends live here."

"I was kinda kidding when I mentioned the Caribbean thing. But how about flying tourists around

Los Cabos?   We could take rich folks fishing and diving, maybe camping around the gorgeous Baja Peninsula.   Don't tell me that doesn't sound appealing?" Jake affirmed with excitement.

"Look Jake," Omar said clearly exasperated, "There is absolutely, unequivocally, and certainly no way in hell you are going to convince me. Your life and mine are very different. I have a family and I am completely responsible for them. I don't take that lightly! I can't take the same risks as you. And I won't!"

"But just…"

Omar interrupted him with a firm raised hand, "Please believe me when I say, thank you. Thank you for your effort. But no thank you. I truly appreciate it. Maybe I would react differently if I didn't have a family. I doubt it. Perhaps it would be best if we both took a short break from Aces and get back together when business picks up again."

"I don't want to break up the company, Omar."

"I'm not saying that. I sincerely mean what I said. We can start up where we left off in six months or maybe a year. It's no big deal." Omar tried to put his friend at ease with a genuine smile and a nudge on the shoulder.

Jake stood silent for a moment as he mulled over his partner's words. "Let me think about it. But give this some thought. How about you run Aces, keep the 185 as active as possible. Surely there is enough business so you and Alejandra can make ends meet. When things pick up I'll come back to work."

"Let's both think about it. We don't have to make a decision today."

The following work week, if you could call it that, was somber. Aces could no longer afford to hangar the 185 so she was tied down outside. Seeing her bounce around in the wind bothered the partners no end, but then she had bounced around in the wind for at least a decade back in Nevada. In any case there was nothing they could do about it and hopefully it was temporary.

Jake had negotiated a reduced rate for the office space within the hangar since he would also be covering as caretaker.

"I have thought very seriously about our conversation last week, Jake. As long as your offer still stands I would like to continue running Aces, and as soon as things improve you should come back, join in again, and pick up where we left off."

Omar's partner was not surprised by the decision, and hoped his friend would see the advantages of the proposal. "I'm glad you agree. I'll be leaving for Mazatlán in a few days. Let's make sure we keep in touch."

"Since we don't have any flights for the next few days, I'll be doing some things around the house and probably won't see you before you leave. Just remember, Jake, these are not nice people. If you rub them the wrong way it's almost guaranteed that you'll end up with a bullet in your brain, face down in a shallow grave. Please be very careful, my friend."

"I'll make sure to watch my back, and I'll make sure not to do any rubbing!" Jake smiled.

"Don't be a smart ass!" Omar admonished. "If there is anything you need, any time, anywhere. Just call. I'll be there to help."

The partners shook hands and slapped each other on the shoulder. They parted company without saying another word. Both were saddened that their venture had hit the skids so soon after starting. They'd had such big plans, and for a while things seemed to be progressing so nicely, but then life has a way of keeping one in check.

Jake spent the day packing his few belongings in a duffle bag. Since leaving the US he hadn't spent much time in a single place, and now it would probably be worse. Hotel to hotel, bunk to bunk. There was no sense in weighing himself down with unnecessary stuff. Amber's eyes followed him suspiciously as he moved back and forth. She knew the routine. They would be moving soon, and she wasn't happy about it. She was just getting comfortable with her present surroundings.

Jake noticed her discontent and sat down next to her. Caressing her soft velvety fur comforted both of them. "I'm sorry Amber but this is what has to be done. You're coming with me, so it's not all that bad." Amber's little ears perked up to the words 'coming with'. She lay on her side with her hind leg up, a clear indication that she was ready to have her belly scratched. Jake complied.

Waiting for his ride outside the hangar and former home of Aces Aviación Jake relaxed in the afternoon sun. The baseball cap and Ray Bans kept the bright rays from his eyes. He took in the dusty desertic surroundings and knew he would miss the stark beauty of this place. Jake had learned to fly all over again during his stay. The camaraderie and ribbing among the bush pilots was great. He would miss that also.

A loud monotone buzz came from the big high winged PT6A turbine engine as it taxied up to Jake's siesta area. The big Pilatus Porter, just like the ones used by Air America during the Vietnam War, came to a standstill and with a whoosh the engine slowly spun to a halt.

Jake usually professed 'there is no such thing as an ugly plane, some are just prettier than others'. The Porter sure fit the not so pretty category very well and the faded flat beige and green exterior did nothing to improve its looks.

Larry jumped out of the cockpit, and like a circus magician demonstrating a great trick announced, "How do you like your new ride?"

The plane's new pilot got up from his resting spot and pointed with his index finger. "That?"

"Beautiful, isn't she?" Larry said with a smile.

"I suppose so, if butt ugly is your cup of tea," Jake said with a grimace.

"That's not very nice! The Pilatus Porter is the best bush plane ever built. Have you ever flown one?" Larry queried.

"Can't say I have. But I've heard a lot about them."

"You're in for a pleasant surprise! Ready to go?" Larry asked. He looked at the one duffle bag Jake had in his hand. "You can't be serious? Is that all you've got?"

Jake tossed his bag into the cavernous compartment and helped Amber into the plane. He walked around to the right side and was confronted by Larry. "Where do you think you are going? This is your bird, you're flying it!"

"All right, just let me know what the speeds are."

The take off roll was all of 700 feet and the Porter leapt to the skies at a mere 55 knots. Mr. Pratt and Mr. Whitney hummed away effortlessly under the cowl with 550 derated horsepower which gave the plane a 1,200 feet per minute climb. Jake pulled the throttle back to a cruise-climb setting for the rapid ascent to 20,000 feet. The short flight to Mazatlán was a scarce 40 minutes long.

"Approach the field at 10,000 feet and I'll show you what this ugly bird is capable of."
Jake knew Larry was up to no good but still relinquished the controls to his co-pilot around three miles away from the airport. As soon as the yoke was in his hands Larry pulled the throttle to idle, bled a little speed off and pushed the nose over near vertical. The VSI was pegged at a descent of 5,000 feet per minute.

"Impressive!" Jake said as he looked out the windshield to see a farmer plowing his fields. "Don't you think it's time to level off just in case you want to flare before touching down?"

"Don't worry Jake. With all that power up front we can get real low!" Larry announced.

"We, Kimosabi? How about you do your clowning around on your own time!" Jake said with a little more than apprehension in his voice.

"Okay, okay. Your plane!" Larry let go of the controls way too close to the ground. Jake grabbed at the yoke and hauled back. As the plane came level he added a little power. The PT6 took a little more time than a piston engine to respond but when it did it certainly got your attention.

Mazatlán tower came over the frequency. "XA-BTA what are you doing? Do you need some help?"

"Mazatlán, Bravo Tango Alpha is continuing the straight in approach."

"Nice approach! Clear to land." Came the reply from Mazatlán tower.

Jake jockeyed the Porter like a pro, soft and short, and came to a full stop within 400 feet, "This really is an amazing plane!" he exclaimed.

Larry suggested Jake stay in one of the ritzier hotels in the Zona Dorada, the touristy area of Mazatlán. Jake knew from prior stays in the city that he would prefer to stay in the old section of town, on the south side. He wanted to keep as far away from the turistas as possible. Furthermore, hotel rooms were half the price, and he wasn't on vacation, he was there to save money.

Old town had a certain charm, although it was in desperate need of a thorough facelift. It was authentically Mexican, and devoid of the 'Fancy American Hotel' image. However, since the bulk of the tourist industry had slowly moved to the north end, along with most of the repair funds allotted, it would have to make do with the sparse funds afforded to it.

Even though he felt tired enough to turn in early, Jake tossed and turned most of the sweltering night. His troubled mind fabricated images which haunted his sleep. He realized he would probably be a wreck for the meeting with the General in the morning.

"So, are you ready to meet the man?" Larry asked as Jake got off the elevator.

General Gasdas was staying at his beautiful villa on the south side of town, or 'Old Town' as the locals referred to it. This section of the city was quaint and colonial. There was a swanky residential area on the hills just in sight of old town, which still boasted some of the most exclusive vacation homes of Mexico's rich and famous.

The architecture of the General's villa was entirely colonial. Fortunately the interior decorators he'd hired knew what they were doing and had faithfully preserved the colonial flavor of the interior. The nouveau-riche General left to his own devices would probably have made a complete mess of the décor in a feeble attempt to show off his wealth with appalling bad taste.

Escorted by a uniformed maid, Larry and Jake made their way to the ample veranda, which overlooked a glittering little bay and the Pacific Ocean. They sat down at an ornate wrought iron table; it was covered with a sumptuous array of delicacies. The General paced back and forth talking animatedly on his cell phone.

The two pilots sat silently waiting for their host. Waves a hundred feet below could barely be heard, as they continued their inexorable assault on the shoreline, slowly turning old shells into the fine powdery sand, which covered the beach. Palm trees surrounded the area and rustled lightly in the warm, humid breeze. Jake leaned forward, getting a little closer to Larry. "Are there any more people showing up for this meeting?" He motioned towards the buffet table laid out with enough food to feed an army.

"As far as I know it's only us," Larry answered almost in a whisper.

"He's been on the phone for twenty minutes. Pretty fuckin' rude?" Jake said with irritation in his voice.

"Take it easy Jake. What's the hurry? You're going to be paid very well for your time."

Eventually General Ignacio Gasdas ceremoniously closed the lid on his cell phone and sat down, "So, this is the new pilot?" he said to Larry while inspecting Jake in the same way a farmer might check out cattle.

Wanting to see the General's reaction, Jake thrust out his hand before Larry had a chance for the introduction. "Jake McInnes."

The General continued studying him for a moment longer. His dark, little beady eyes held a cruel intensity Jake had never seen before. As he shook Jake's hand he said, "Are you any good, Jake McInnes?"

"Would I be here if I wasn't any good?" Jake taunted.

Larry jumped in to defuse the tension, "Yes, General, of course he's good! Jake's a great pilot. He just flew the Porter for the first time and it was like he had flown it his whole life!"

"As I said before, are you any good?" Gasdas asked again, still staring at Jake and ignoring Larry's comment.

"What can I say? Yeah, I'm good. Are you a pilot General?" Jake inquired. He didn't know why he was doing it, but he knew he was putting on an attitude of defiance, which would certainly piss off the General.

Gasdas hated the question, and even more hated having to answer it. After all, who was this gringo asking him questions? "No. I'm not a pilot."

"Well, in that case it's going to be kinda difficult to explain why I'm good."

Larry couldn't believe his ears. He would've greatly appreciated falling off the face of the earth at that particular moment, especially since he was the idiot who had introduced Jake.

"Well, we'll find out sooner or later, won't we?" The General said with a Machiavellian little smile, and turned to Larry, "Have you explained the operations to Mr. Jake?"

"Yes Sir," Larry replied quickly as he chewed on a piece of lobster.

"Do you have any questions about the operation, Señor Jake?"

"No General, I don't at the moment. But I will probably have a few as I get started," Jake replied.

"Very well. I only have one small item to cover before you can start. Do I have your full attention?" The General paused. Jake and Larry put down their cutlery. He looked straight at Jake. His eyes were cold, emotionless pools of darkness. Jake fought the shiver that crept up his back, "Be warned Sr. McInnes. We are running a very secret and sensitive operation with the highest levels of the DEA," the General paused as he sipped some coffee. Jake took advantage of the break to light a cigarette. "You'll be transporting millions and millions of dollars in cash and drugs. Do not get any stupid ideas. It would be extremely unhealthy for you. We don't fuck around with trials and due process. If we discover any anomalies with your shipments, you will pay the price. Do you understand?"

Jake had just taken a long drag as the question was posed, so his affirmative answer was enveloped in a cloud of smoke.

"Very well, Señores. I have appointments to attend to. Help yourselves to brunch. I will talk to you in a week." The General turned and left without further ado.

When enough distance lay between the pilots and the General, Jake commented sarcastically, "Nice pleasant fella, just loaded with old fashioned charm!"

"Careful, Jake." Larry raised his eyebrows and pointed his index finger to his ear and made a circular motion with the same finger, "Do I make myself clear?"

"Clear as can be, Larry."

Warm, moist, salty air blew through the cab's open windows and filled Jake's lungs. Despite the General's reassurance that the operation was completely legitimate, he had his doubts. But really all he needed was six months or so. Then he would have enough money to fulfill some dreams. Which dreams exactly, were yet to be determined but he was sure that by focusing on these dreams he would have a better chance of remaining sane.

The big olive green Pilatus Porter was in the hangar. Amber slept patiently in the back. The flight plan filed was vague and involved sightseeing.

Cruising altitude was quickly reached with Jake at the controls.

"So, Larry.   What do you know about the General?"

"It's not a great idea to be asking questions about the General," Larry replied with a serious look on his face.

"That's why I'm asking you as we fly along. I doubt anybody can hear our conversation."

"Really not much is known or talked about when it comes to General Ignacio Gasdas Sanchez. As you can imagine it's not a very healthy topic of conversation, since no one wants to draw attention to themselves, especially if word got back to the General.

"Doesn't surprise me after the little I saw this morning," Jake interjected.

"I've been flying for the operation for just over a year and I've pieced together a few tidbits of information.   He was born in one of the shittier neighborhoods in Mexico City.   A real pit, open sewers, you would have to see it to believe it.   Just think Karachi."

"I think I get the picture," Jake assured him. "Haven't been to Karachi, but I think there is a universal understanding."

"Anyhow, he was kid number 11 of 16. Haven't heard anything about his parents, or family so I can't elaborate. Unless you want me to fabricate. And I'm pretty good at that," Larry said with a shitty grin on his face.

"That's all right. But how does a poor kid from the barrio get to be General in what seems to be a pretty short period of time?"

"The way I heard it, one fateful night as he was running with the wrong crowd of street kids they came across a rival gang rolling some poor son of a bitch. The problem was, the gang doing the beating up was on Ignacio's gang's turf. To make a long story short a big fight ensued over the prey. Finally the offending gang was expelled, the victim thought he was being rescued, not realizing he was going to get some more of the same."

Jake interrupted. "And exactly how does this relate to the General's story?"

"This is where fate smiled on the young Gasdas. For some reason he felt bad for the man lying on the ground and convinced the gang to leave him alone. Why he did this is a total mystery, because rumor has it he was a real violent little sack of shit. Not that he has changed much. As it turned out this fella was a colonel in the army and in gratitude he starts a friendship with the young hoodlum. He probably had the notion of changing the young Gasdas around to being a productive citizen or something like that. Anyway the Colonel gets Gasdas into the military academy and onto officers' training. Spots in the military college are extremely hard to come by and usually reserved for the elite of the established military institution. However, the Colonel is now a General with no kids and packs some influence. Young Ignacio thrives at the college and rapidly moves up the ranks. He kisses the right asses, gives the right favors, marries the right girl, and the rest is history."

As Larry finished the story they approached their intended landing spot. The location was a half hour south, south-east of Tepic, Nayarit. They dipped in over the tall ridge top and deep into the valley to a short grassy field on the crest of a hill. A little boy cleared the cattle off the landing strip for the incoming airplane. Jake slowed to a ridiculously slow 55 knots on the approach and came to a stop a scarce 500 feet after touch down. They taxied the other 500 feet of the make shift strip and turned the plane around in preparation for departure.

"So what's the deal?" Jake said feeling very uneasy since he couldn't see anybody around. "What are we here for?"

"Don't get your panties in a wad. They'll be here in a minute. Remember, we are in Mexico." Larry reached over and killed the engine. The PT6 slowly wound to a stop.

"So who are "they" anyway?" Jake inquired.

Just as the words had left his mouth ten dirty rag tag soldiers appeared from the forest carrying between them the first five of twenty duffle bags. They made their way to the plane in single file preceded by a man in a slightly cleaner uniform.

"Oh, great, it's that asshole Lieutenant Perez. Now there's a guy with a chip on his shoulder. He's got a real nasty reputation for beating on his troops. I guess I better introduce you to the jerk, he might take it as an insult otherwise," Larry said as he jumped out of the high cockpit. Jake followed suit. Amber stayed behind panting and inspecting the surrounding area.

"Tardes." Short for 'buenas tardes' was offered by the point man Lieutenant Perez said with little enthusiasm, "We will be returning with you to Mazatlán."

"No one told me we would have passengers," Larry stated matter-of-fact.

"Well, I'm telling you now, gringo. Are you going to make a big issue of it?"

"No, I'm just saying I wasn't advised. We need to plan these things so we know how much fuel to carry. These aircraft can't lift an infinite amount you know," Larry said coolly as he did his best to contain his irritation.

The soldiers where loading the last round of duffle bags when one of the younger and smaller of them dropped his end, spilling its contents all over the ground. The perfectly wrapped bricks of bright white heroin hit the soft ground with no breakage. Good thing because at twenty thousand dollars a kilo it would be very hard to explain the loss. Painted on the middle of each brick was a finely detailed red dragon and what looked like Chinese characters.

"Hey! Watch out!" Lieutenant Perez shouted. "That stuff is worth more than your miserable life, you idiot!" He shouted at the man while pistol-whipping him.

"Take it easy, man. Nothing broke, there's no problem," Jake interjected before his brain had a chance to stop his mouth.

"Who are you anyway?" The lieutenant yelled as he pointed his gun at Jake.   "It's none of your damn business gringo. So just back off."

Larry raised his hands, as if he was surrendering. "You're right, you're right. Take it easy. The guy is new to this."

Perez slowly lowered his weapon and gave the young soldier one more light whack as if to show he was boss.

Jake walked away and had a smoke. Hopefully he would feel a little calmer before the return flight. Larry immediately called for him. It was time to leave. He reached the plane at the same time as the Lieutenant.

"So, you are the new pilot," he said, stating more than asking. "Are you any good?"

Jake's blood began to boil. He could feel his cheeks grow hot. The General was one thing but this stupid little dipstick was another. Larry quickly cut in to defuse the situation, "Yeah, of course he's good. Do you think the General would have personally selected him if he weren't?"

Perez looked surprised, "You were selected by the General himself?"

"What did I just say?" Larry asked. "Now, how many kilos do we have?"

"Eight hundred kilos of Southeast Asia's finest," Perez responded. "We caught some stupid runners moving the stuff on burros up from the coast. They didn't know what hit them."

Jake made a quick mental calculation seventeen hundred pounds of smack plus eleven soldiers, two pilots and a dog. That would be around four thousand pounds. He checked the fuel. The Pilatus Porter has a useful load of 4,850 pounds, so no problems there.

The turboprop performed effortlessly and made the take off a non-issue despite the weight being right at the maximum permitted. Jake flew low through the warming canyons, getting enough turbulence to make the passengers and especially Lieutenant Perez just a little more than green in the face. After all if the scumbag barfed who was the one that would have to clean it up? One of the poor ragtag soldiers no doubt and not Perez.

They turned up the coastline and with it came smooth air. Jake absorbed the calm tropical views below and daydreamed about lying on the beach without a single worry. Small fishing villages almost hidden by palm trees, jacarandas and parota, appeared and disappeared fleetingly.

Time stood still, or at least moved very slowly in those remote areas. Men would launch their small fishing boats several hours before day break and be home with a full catch by eight in the morning. It wouldn't net them much money, but then a lot of money wasn't something they were particularly interested in. Their catch would be sold to owner operator, mom & pop fish brokers in their pickups who in turn would take the day's haul to a number of restaurants for the big mark up to the tourist trade in Mazatlán.

Once the catch had been exchanged for cash, the fishermen would tend to their nets and equipment. If nothing needed repair or it was too hot to work, they would sit around under the shade of a palapa playing dominos or cards. Cold beer would be consumed every day as if it were going out of style. Before long the whole process would be repeated. But then, why change the routine, the people were content and it worked.

As Jake studied his gauges to make sure everything was copasetic he wondered 'who had it right'. Those who worked their asses off every single day of their existence amassing enough money to retire somewhat comfortably and then die of a heart attack brought on by the years and years of unending stress derived from the search for their retirement money. Life having whizzed by at such a frantic pace they'd forgotten to enjoy the part they where supposed too: All of it.

Or the absolute contrary, such as the people that lived and fished from those tiny little villages he was flying over. It was probably a combination of both. The harmony of both would be the hardest thing to accomplish. Jake made up his mind, then and there, that would be his objective.

Just as the sun hid behind the faraway waves of a distant portion of the vast Pacific Ocean, he eased back the throttle approaching Mazatlán International. Jake took the Pilatus long, after all what was the point of taxiing most of the 8,859 foot runway. He decided to have some fun. Still in flight he maneuvered onto the taxiway and touched down to a perfect three pointer, beta, and then taxi.

"Nice flying Jake," Larry said. "Only thing is, it's not a good idea to attract attention like that."

"Oh shit! What can I say? I was bored. I bet the tower didn't even notice," Jake came back. "In any case you shouldn't be talking after yesterdays little stunt!"

"Oh, they noticed. They just aren't going to say anything because they know who is responsible for this plane."

As they pulled up to the hangar, a Chevrolet Suburban painted with military livery pulled up close to unload the cargo.

"Where's the smack going?" Jake inquired.

"Don't know, don't care. Only the General and his closest aids have that info," Larry answered as he stared at the duffle bags being unloaded. "We have a flight bright and early so you better get some sleep. Four AM here, all right?"

"Where are we going?"

"Again. Don't know, don't care. I do know we are on a money run, so no one knows until the last moment," Larry stated.

"Well, how much money are we transporting?"

"Jake, would ya stop asking questions. It's not good and I don't have the answers. All right, I'll answer this one. But no more. It usually works out to be around 15 to 20 million dollars." Larry said nonchalantly.

"Are you shittin' me!" Jake said incredulously.

As the radio alarm clock blasted to life with louder than need be Banda music, its um-papa base and shrilling accordion, Jake couldn't hit the snooze button fast enough. Amber didn't look very happy to be awakened by such an awful racket either.

Gratefully, the DJ was talking when the radio sprang to life the second time, sparing Jake the annoying music. So he wouldn't forget to change the station later, he decided to make it his first priority of the day. He wondered if there were any good rock stations. Jake reached over and found his smokes, tore off the filter and sparked one up. Static was replaced by more annoying music, and then came the quick realization that the elevator music station was the only half decent option.

The little hotel in old town was clean, comfortable and cheap. More important, the owner didn't mind dogs in the rooms. In fact she owned five herself. Most of them collected over the years from people who didn't understand that dogs need attention and are not inanimate objects you just feed occasionally.

Jake stumbled towards the bathroom, yawning and scratching his ass with one hand and stretching with the other. A feat accomplished simultaneously. He coughed loudly, phlegm gurgled, he flicked the small remaining cigarette in the toilet and mumbled to himself, "Fuckin' things are going to kill me." Amber ignored him as she was still balled up on the bed.

Morning light was yet to brighten up Mazatlán, and the town would be asleep for hours. A few cars roamed the streets; taxies took the last drunk turistas to their hotels to sleep off the excess tequila slammers ingested the night before.

Larry was performing his walk around as Jake showed up. It was quarter past four. "Beautiful day for a flight around the countryside!" Jake said in his best morning voice.

"Can't tell yet. It's too dark," Larry said with irritation and not seeing any humor in the comment.

"Exactly my point. Do we really have to get going so early?"

"Even by leaving this early we'll be back very late tonight, and that's if all goes well." Larry explained.

"Can I ask where we are going? Or is that one of the questions I'm not supposed to ask?"

"Guadalajara-MMGL, Uruapan-MMPN, Guanajuato-MMGT, Aguascalientes-MMAS, Zacatecas-MMZC, Durango-MMDO, Laredo, Texas-KLRD, then finally back to Mazatlán MMMZ."

"Yikes. That does make for a long day. Have you filed the flight plan?" Jake inquired.

"No. Why don't you do it while I finish up here and get the plane fueled."

On Jake's return two soldier escorts awaited. AK47's slung over their shoulders, 9mm Brownings as side arms, flack jackets and helmets. Larry announced, "Our protection has arrived, we can leave now."

"Larry, I never saw such huge soldiers in Mexico. Where the hell did they get these monsters from?" Jake commented. He walked over to the two. "Hi! My name is Jake. I guess we have a long day ahead," he said with a smile and extended his hand.

The two soldiers simply stared at him like he was a nut job. Their hands remained immobile, one by their side and one on the assault rifle.

"Jake, what the hell are you doing?" Larry asked from the cockpit.

"Just introducing myself."

"They have strict instructions not to talk to one another or to us. We always fly in complete silence," Larry explained.

"What's up with that?"

"The General has this idea that if they don't talk they can't scheme about the best way to swipe all the money we'll be picking up."

Jake studied the two soldiers a moment longer, turned on his heel and made his way to the left seat.

The first leg was easy. MMGL GPS direct. Jake engaged the S-tec 55, pre-selected 17,500 feet put on his O2, kicked back and listened to a CD. He let the equipment do its intended job. As the plane passed through fourteen five Jake turned to Larry, "Do you want to tell the goons to put on their oxygen?"

"Fuck em!" Larry didn't even turn to face Jake when he said the words. He just kept strumming his imaginary guitar. Boston's 'More Than a Feeling' could be heard over the engine noise. Feeling bad for them Jake turned to see how the goons were doing. They were either dead or just out cold. He decided on the latter.

As he would later learn, the pickup procedure was well established and never varied. The copilot would radio before landing on a discreet frequency to ensure the load was waiting and ready. If the transport was not in place or did not answer to the calls, the pilots were instructed to fly on to the next rendezvous point and follow the same procedure.

Once the cargo being picked up was confirmed in place, the land guards had made a thorough sweep of the area, and advice received that the loading zone was sterile, the landing would take place. With the Porter's engine running, the air guards would re-check the zone and check in with the land guards. All armed guards would take their respective positions covering every possible angle of attack. Loading could now take place.

Invariably a black Suburban with dark tinted windows would pull right up to the cargo hold to transfer the cargo to the plane. In the same fashion as the airplane, the ground-based vehicle would also keep its engine running and driver at the ready. The loaders were the last people out of the Suburban and in a very expeditious manner they rapidly transloaded large shrink-wrapped bricks of cash contained within military style duffle bags. A clipboard was then presented to Jake for signing. He reviewed the form and returned it without signing.

"Hey buddy. You're PIC, you sign," Larry informed him.

"I'm not ready to sign for 3.5 million dollars."

"Well, I hate to be the bearer of bad news but it comes with the job."

"How the hell am I to know if there really is three million four hundred and eighty thousand dollars in those bags if I haven't even had the chance to count it?" Jake inquired.

"The seals aren't broken. The bags aren't ripped. Don't worry, as long as you deliver as you received them, you won't have any issues," Larry stated as he listened to his portable CD player in one ear.

In less than ten minutes they were off again, and climbing to 17,500' heading GPS direct Uruapan, Michoacán. Each stop took around ten minutes, and thirty if they needed fuel. Finally after a long day of up down they approached the 30-minute zone marked by ADIZ. Jake reported in to Laredo Approach. They had already flown almost nine hours with five pickups, unfortunately the longest leg back to Mazatlán was still ahead. Jake was really looking for a little shuteye.

The customs agent appeared to be very familiar with the money drops because he didn't fuss in the least. Yet another suburban awaited the unloading, and on this occasion Jake was very happy to see the eighteen million dollars off his rig and signed receipt of delivery 'in condition' as fair exchange.

Level at seventeen five and everything on auto. This was the longest leg of the day, and as long as the winds cooperated they wouldn't have to land for fuel.

As Jake taxied the Porter towards yet another pickup area, a suburban slowly approached, he felt a chill run up and down his spine. Nine million dollars on board were enticing bait for any thief. Images filled his mind and silence prevailed upon shutting down the powerful turbine. Five of the six doors of the Suburban burst open and six men in ski masks, Uzi's and body armour rushed the plane from all sides. Before the two guards had a chance to reach for their weapons their blood intermingled as it splattered the interior of the plane. Larry was next. His Discman still played CCR's 'Who'll Stop the Rain' to his now deaf ears. Jake cringing, tried to make himself smaller. Nothing happened.

Larry slapped him on the back bringing him back to reality.

"What a face! Where the hell where you anyway?" Larry asked.

"I'm just tired. I was half asleep," Jake responded. "Would you mind giving me hand with the flying?"

"You better get used to it buddy. You'll be flying the entire route all by yourself soon enough."

Sitting on the balcony of his hotel room Jake dealt himself another game of solitaire. He counted the days since his last flight. Eight days. He had now been workin' for the man for three months. Three months of flying six or maybe seven times a month. The original impression was that there would be a lot more flying than was actually taking place.

Even though it did take a full day to recover from the eight stop, eighteen-hour day, Jake was always ready to fly again within a couple of days, but the wait for the next flight usually worked out to be at least five. He was bored and a little more than cranky. He smoked another filter less cigarette as he dealt himself his hundredth game of solitaire.

'What to do tonight?' Jake thought momentarily. He knew he needed a change of scenery, but he had already seen all the movies, he was tired of the bars. He'd watched all the obnoxious kids making fools of themselves that he could handle. What Jake really missed was flying with Aces Aviación. Even though a tiny operation, it was his operation.

When there was flying to do, there was usually a lot of it. And it was challenging. The General's idea of planning was to stuff a week's worth of work into a twenty-four hour period. To make matters worse, you were on call 24-7, you never knew when you were going to leave.

But then, Jake really couldn't bitch too much, he was paid promptly in cash upon his return right off the time displayed on the Hobbs meter. For a long day's work the pay could be as much as six thousand dollars. Maybe it was time to take his money and run, after all he had lived frugally and already saved over one hundred sixty thousand. Jake realized that the sum wouldn't go too far. It would be best to stay on until he'd saved a million or so. That way he could put a down payment on a Caravan and fly rich tourists around the Caribbean.

The more Jake saw of the activities he was involved with, the more he became convinced there was no way it was a legitimate operation. He struggled to convince himself that it was legit, but deep down he was certain that it was a crooked deal and it filled him with apprehension. Deep in thought, Jake absent-mindedly petted Amber. Mazatlán's evening activity was unfolding in the street eight stories below his hotel room. A few tourists wandered aimlessly this way and that, looking for entertainment and tales to tell their friends back home, as the locals did their best to avoid them and silently cursed them.

Two gringos dressed in the tourist uniform (shorts, tee shirt, sunglasses, baseball caps and the inevitable camera) stood on the other side of the street. Their legs were as white as white can get. The reason they stood out was simply because they weren't moving. Not only were they standing still, the two men were not browsing and neither were they talking to one another. 'Strange'. Jake thought.

The phone in his room rang loudly. It was one of those old rotary dial phones that became extinct in the late 70's and early 80's. Only a hotel like the Gascóna would have such vintage equipment. Jake knew it could only be one of two people. The General's secretary, who gave him his assignments, or Larry.

He was certainly due for a flight. So it could very well be either.

"Yellow," Jake said on purpose.

"Do you want to grab a bite to eat?" Larry asked.

"Sure, I don't have anything else to do," Jake replied with a yawn brought on by days and days of utter boredom.

The dining room of the Camino Real, all the way on the other end of town, was dead quiet, but then it was the off-season. Only a couple of honeymooners shared the cavernous room. The two lovers kissed, caressed and carried on, making Jake nauseous.

"I don't know how you do it Larry. I'm going stir crazy!" Jake said.

"What are you talking about? I've got a ton of things to do. I golf almost every morning. Sometimes I go fishing. Sometimes I just sleep in because I was lucky picking up a little gringita at the bar," Larry bragged. "Get a life, Jake!"

The storm that had been brewing for hours started to release torrential sheets of rain. Lightning flashed brightly through the dark and angry night sky, thunder accompanied it moments later to reinforce its fury.

"I sure am glad I'm not flying tonight," Jake stated as he looked out the window next to their table.

"Jake, the problem with you is, you just don't know how to take it easy. Relax and enjoy the moment," Larry said as he slouched a little more and took a long sip from his piña colada.

"I suppose you are right. I just feel guilty when I'm not working for some bizarre reason. And nowadays that is most of the time!"

"Well, I would offer to take you fishing tomorrow morning, but both of us can't be out in the middle of the ocean. We could be called at any moment."

Their main courses arrived with the fanfare the most expensive dish on the menu deserved. That was how Larry always ordered. He paid more attention to the price side of the menu than the item itself. And then he would customize it. Jake hated people like that.

Jake had a salad with seared tuna. The fish was caught only a few hours before and was, without a doubt, the most exquisite thing Jake had ever tasted. The two pilots ate in silence. Jake was busy enjoying his meal and the magnificent spectacle nature was providing outside the window. Larry was too intent on stuffing his face with the lobster, steak and crab cakes, (he had ordered the crab cakes instead of the potato) to notice the show outside.

As Jake slowly and methodically savored the perfectly seasoned and seared tuna, he tried to place the reasons why he didn't trust the man sitting across from him. Sure, they were very different people and everyone has their own set of values, desires, needs and ambitions. As long as none of them infringe on your own rights, we should all learn to respect or at least tolerate them. One of the main things that unsettled Jake was the way Larry seldom looked straight at you. His eyes darted back and forth as if searching for his next attacker. When he walked, he always scoured left and right, and then quickly behind him. Jake surmised that if you were so edgy, something must be wrong. But what?

The two pilots finished their meals. Larry had the Crepes Suzette. Most likely because he liked the attention of having the waiter come to his table to make them. Jake had an expresso accompanied by a cigarette and called it good.

"What's troubling you Jake? You seem bothered by something," Larry asked as he merrily chomped away at his crepes. A tiny drip of juice ran from the corner of his mouth.

"Oh, no just day dreaming, is all," Jake lied.

"Don't give me that shit, Jake. You have more on your mind than you're letting on. You've been moping around for days now. What the hell is eating you?"

Jake sucked hard at the last remaining drag from his smoke and without exhaling, drank the last of his sugar-overloaded expresso. As the words came from his mouth he already repented confiding in Larry. Pufflets of smoke belched from his mouth as he spoke. "This operation has been bothering me for some time. To tell you the truth, I have a hard time believing it's above board."

"Not that I'm saying it's legit or not, but seriously, what do you care if it is or isn't? Aren't you making enough loot to really give a shit?" Larry asked.

"Sure, the money is great. But, I'd just like to know what, and who I'm involved with is all."

Larry methodically swooshed the last piece of crepe, along with the remaining delicious syrupy concoction, and not until he was convinced there was no way he was going to get any more off the plate did he laboriously slide the overfilled spoon into his gaping mouth.   As he slurped the last mouthful down, he answered Jake's query, "All right. I'll make you a deal. You pick up the tab and I'll let you in on the straight dope."

"You're   on,"   Jake   agreed,   wondering momentarily whether he really wanted to know after all.

Larry stood, wiped his mouth one last time and tossed the crimson linen napkin on the dirty plate. "Don't worry Jake. As I said before you got started in this racket, everything is totally legit! I've got an early morning flight so I'm heading out.   Stop theorizing would be my advice, Jakey. Take a good thing while it lasts."   As Larry waltzed out of the restaurant he shouted, "Oh yeah, thanks for dinner!"

Jake sparked up another smoke and ordered a second expresso. He wondered if it would keep him awake. He looked out the window to see a young lady swimming in the pool below, and wondered why no one had told her that she shouldn't be in the pool while lightning was in the area.   Jake's mind drifted to Evelyn. What would she be doing? He looked at his watch, 11:32 local. 9:32 California Time. She would probably be watching a movie or the news. Whatever it may be he wished he were there with her. He would start a nice blazing fire and reminisce about silly stories they had shared many times before, or possibly just enjoy the closeness and peace, along with the occasional crackle from burning logs.

"Mr. McInnes?" a voice asked, bringing him back to reality.

Jake turned to face one of the phoney-looking American tourists who had arrived shortly after Larry departed. "Yeah," Jake answered and studied the man's face and tried to place it. "Do I know you?"

"No. We haven't met." The man replied.

"Okay, so what's the deal? You know my name. You've been watching me for the past few hours and you waited for Larry to leave before coming over here," Jake stated calmly.

"I'm Agent Killian and this is Agent Sowers," the man said, pointing to his left at the person standing next to him.

"Very well. Nice to meet you Agent Killian. What brings you to the lovely Camino Real, Mazatlán?" Jake said trying to feign aloofness.

"As a matter of fact, you bring us to Mazatlán."

"Oh? And why is that?" Jake questioned.

"Because of the person you work for, General Gasdas." Killian paused momentarily to study Jake's reaction.

It was clear he was being studied and he did his best to keep an unreadable poker face.

"Do you mind if we sit?"

"Not at all. Be my guest."

Killian and Sowers sat down.

"Now that you folks are comfortable, would you like to show me some ID?" Jake requested.

The two agents reached into their coat pockets in one fluid motion, clearly indicating to the observer that they had performed this action a great many times. "DEA," Jake read aloud. "What can I do for the DEA? Is it about the operations your agency has with the General?"

"You see, Mr. McInnes, there lies the problem. Even though the DEA has many agreements with the Mexican government, we have no such agreements involving the General."

"Of course you do!" Jake responded quickly. "I've been working with your operation for the past several months." A sinking feeling was settling on Jake, as all his suspicions changed from possible to probable and quickly on to certain.

"As I said before," Killian continued, " General Gasdas is in fact an Army General, but he has nothing to do with any cooperative agreement with the DEA or any other US agency for that matter. Our agency has been trying to develop a case for years now, but he always seems to stay one step ahead of us every time." Agent Killian took a sip of his water before continuing. He also used this technique to give his audience a little time to digest the startling piece of information he had just placed on the table.

"Mr. McInnes, on behalf of the US Government and specifically the DEA, I am officially requesting your assistance in taking down the General and his organization."

"It sounds like a great way to get killed, if you want my opinion," Jake responded. "What if I decline?"

"If you decline and continue to work for Gasdas you will eventually be indicted along with the rest of his people, when the time comes. We could also press charges for the work you have done so far, even if you quit working for him tomorrow," Agent Killian responded.

"And if I decide to cooperate with the DEA?"

"You're a free man!" The agent said with gusto.

Agent Sowers sat silently, absorbing the exchange-taking place before her.

"As I said before. It seems like a good way to get myself killed," Jake said.

"Yes, I suppose it might at first glance. But we will be there every step of the way to make sure no harm comes to you."

"How many informants or recruits have you lost during your career, Agent Killian?"

Killian didn't have to do much memory. The young man's face was forever etched in his mind. 'Could I have done anything to save that man's life?' Killian thought momentarily, and proceeded to answer the question truthfully, "One," he replied as his focus came back to Jake.

"Would you mind elaborating? Who were you after on that occasion? Or even better, did you get the bad guy in the end?"

Killian looked around the room, and then up at the ceiling for half a second, wondering exactly how he was going to answer the question. "It happened a few years ago. Somebody in the organization figured out what was going on and they killed our informant before we had a chance to react. As far as we know, our man was chased down by a second plane and shot down."

"Now that inspires a lot of confidence!" Jake said sarcastically. Then, with the kinda attention you get when struck by lighting it all came together for him. "You were after General Gasdas, weren't you?"

"Yes. But.."

Jake interrupted him, "And I bet your informant was Enrique Carrillo y Salas wasn't it?"

Killian and Sowers looked at each other mystified. "How did you know?" Killian asked.

Jake thought back on the number of times since meeting Omar that Enrique's story had mysteriously surfaced. 'It seems there is a dead man trying to tell me something,' he thought, 'It has to be more than a coincidence.' With determination he looked squarely at Killian and said, "I'll do anything I can to help you get that sack of shit! When do we get started?"

Killian was a little thrown by the reaction. After the preceding conversation he fully expected Jake to bow out. "To begin with," he began, "this will be our last face-to-face meeting for at least a month. If we happen to stumble upon one another without a previous agreement, it is imperative that there be no recognition whatsoever. Is that completely understood?"

"Understood," Jake answered, and again felt the now familiar chill run the length of his spine up to his neck.

"You should be suspicious of everything. Your hotel room, the phone and a lot of other places are most likely bugged. In fact, I wouldn't be surprised if the closest pay phone to the hotel is bugged as well. Here is my number and below it is Agent Sowers' number. They are untraceable," he handed him a card printed with only two numbers and nothing else to identify them.

"Alright," Was all Jake managed to utter. He was too overwhelmed to think of anything else to say

"Try not to contact us.   We'll contact you."
Agents Killian and Sowers were gone and for a
moment Jake wondered if he'd imagined the whole
thing.

A third expresso arrived at Jake's table just as
the sky lit up with an enormous flash of lightning,
followed very quickly by a crash of thunder. Heavier
sheets of rain pelted the window, but he barely noticed
as he inhaled the thick pungent smoke from his filter-
less cigarette.

His mind sought refuge in more pleasant
memories, and started to drift again with the distant
rumbling of the storm. It took him back to one of his
favorite memories of Evelyn. It was a balmy evening
after a long hike around Big Bear. Sometime during a
summer afternoon enormous cumulonimbus clouds
shot to over fifty thousand feet and had just finished
unleashing the day's accumulation on the small
mountain community.

As usual they had stayed at a friend's cabin.
Quiet and secluded, the living room a jumble of old
books and family mementos, a fire raged in the river
stone fireplace. The happy couple snuggled on the
deep leather couch mesmerized by the dancing
flames. They made slow passionate love, with only
one another's pleasure and happiness in mind.

"¿Otro café señor?"

Jake was startled from the pleasantness of a
daydream he didn't want to leave. "No. Just the
check please." Reality flooded back into his mind,
muddy and polluted. Jake stared at his image
reflected in the window. "What the hell are you
thinking?" he asked himself.

Chapter 6.

In Over His Head.

As Jake muscled open the large hangar door, which had once housed the operations of Aces Aviación, it screeched in rusty protest. Amber squeezed through the opening and rushed to greet Omar who was still at his desk even though it was after nine pm.

"You're here late," Jake stated as he sparked up a smoke. "What the hell are you doing?" He refrained from asking 'What the fuck are you doing?' which came more naturally to him, but knew his partner didn't appreciate his bad language.

"I'm working on another version of the budget. I've tried to make ends meet a hundred different ways and keep coming up with the same negative result." Omar took a sip of his tea and continued. "I think you should probably take the 185 and wind down the company. At this point I just don't see any way things are going to turn around."

"This might make you feel a little better," Jake said smiling as he tossed three short stacks of bills on to Omar's desk.

"What's this?" Omar asked as he picked up the money.

"What's it look like! It's money, cash, mulla, dinero. Comprende?" Jake said sarcastically.

"I know that! But where did you get it?" Omar fingered through the fine cotton based paper that American green backs are manufactured from.

"I've been working in Mazatlán, remember? It hasn't exactly been a vacation you know. That's fifteen thousand in case you're wondering."

"As much as I'd like to say, 'I can't accept it', I won't. Things are just too difficult right now to be overly proud. Let's just say Aces owes you and will eventually pay you back."

"Don't worry about it, Omar. As long as we can eventually get things started again, I'll be happy." Jake paused momentarily as he dreaded the next information he was going to break. "How about we go outside. It's a beautiful night and there is something I need to talk to you about."

"I hope you're not going to get romantic on me!" Omar said with a chuckle as he reached for his jacket, feeling more light-hearted than he had for weeks, thanks to Jake's unexpected contribution.

An infinite number of stars sparkled brightly on the clear, moonless night. A light, cool breeze announced the inevitable arrival of the winter season. The last plane of the evening had come and gone and the surrounding desert was deathly silent.

"So what did you want to tell me?" Omar inquired, curiosity getting the better of him.

Over the next hour Jake explained in detail about his unofficial meeting with Agents Killian and

Sowers, and the fact that his partner's assessment of the situation, months before, had been correct. Jake left out the most important piece of information. He knew it would cause his friend a great deal of pain and didn't look forward to bringing such dark memories to the surface, so he kept it until the end of his tale.

"I left out one piece of information that I must tell you. It's about your brother," Jake said carefully. He slowly and methodically retold the story he had heard from the DEA agents regarding Enrique's death. There was no doubt about the authenticity of the facts. Omar simply nodded from time to time to indicate he was paying attention.

As Jake concluded, he waited for Omar's reaction. There was none, he stared blankly and said, "I've got to go," Omar turned and walked away.

"Are you all right?" Jake called after him.

"Don't worry, I'll talk to you in the morning."

Omar drove his father's car out to the desert and up a barren hill overlooking the airport. Flickering in the distance Durango's city lights could be seen. The wind picked up and chilled him further. He was grateful his father always kept a thick jacket in the trunk of the old Dodge.

As he hiked up the steep incline Omar became increasingly angry, saddened, confused, and out of breath. The revelation Jake had just shared with him created more questions than answers. His mind was a minefield of thoughts blowing up at him with each painful step. He desperately wanted to kill the General. But then, if he were caught who would take care of his family? How could he get away with murder? His rational side told him not to be ridiculous, nothing would bring his brother back and it would expose him to the possibility of some lengthy jail time, never a good prospect and especially in Mexico, not to mention being apart from his family. 'I have to come up with the perfect plan to revenge Enrique's death and ensure freedom for myself.' He thought.

Omar walked a little further, until he came across a struggling little mesquite. Its trunk was a scarce four inches in diameter. 'Where the hell did it come from?' Omar thought as he looked around at the barren, desolate section of earth. 'The resolve shown by this crooked little tree is what I need.' And sat next to it looking up through its thick dark green leaves towards the bright stars way above. Most shone a brilliant white, while others had a slight blue hue, a few faintly yellow. As he reflected on the information Jake had hit him with, he unconsciously slouched lower and lower, and finally lay down, hands clasped behind his weary head protecting it from the harsh ground. Sleep silently crept upon him and coaxed his weary eyes closed.

The cold, near freezing, woke Omar some hours later. His watch read 4:14. Realizing Alejandra had no idea where he was and was probably worried sick, he needed to rush home. With the drive home the same tumult of thoughts again rushed his mind. By killing that piece of shit (the General) he wouldn't get his brother back, and he risked losing everything he held dear, including his freedom. A sensible man would let the DEA do their job and stay out of the picture, but he longed to have a part in bring the General to his end.

Jake also awoke, stiff and cold, as the first jet arrived from Mexico City on its way to Tijuana at 5:45 am. The cot in the office was not so comfortable after sleeping in the big bed at the Gascony Hotel. Amber was ready for a walk and she sat staring at his closed eyes to ensure she would be his first order of business. Transient parking was nasally scoured by her bright wet nose one more time. The few derelict planes deserved special attention just in case there was a rabbit or mouse to chase. A brilliant yellow orange sun commenced its daily warming process and started raising the temperature from chilly to pleasant as they made their slow waltzing retreat to the hangar.

Omar came to a halt in the beat up 1967 Dodge Valiant, a thick cloud of burnt motor oil followed him. Amber's ear perked up in curiosity, and she ran over to greet her friend. Her furry butt wiggled in happiness as she knew he was a great ear scratcher.

"Mornin', Omar. You're up early. You all right?" Jake asked truly concerned for his partner's well being.

"I'm doin' all right considering how and where I slept," Omar replied and changed the subject. "Jake, I appreciate the money but I can't take it. That money comes directly from the man that caused my brother's death."

"It's not," Jake lied. "The money I gave you, I received from the DEA for my work with them."

"Jake, you better not be lying about this!"

"Scout's honor!" Jake said with a smile and a quick salute.

"Who are you kidding? The scouts would never accept the likes of you!" Omar said with the first smile in 24 hours. "If there is anything I can do to help the investigation and, hopefully capture of the General, please let me know."

"You can count on it," Jake said as he gave an overly enthusiastic thumbs up.

As instructed by the DEA Jake flew the Pilatus to a small strip, fifty-eight DME North of Mazatlán called La Cruz, a desolate little dirt field next to the highway (if you could give such a fancy name to such a crappy stretch of asphalt). Just as soon as the propeller stopped turning the team of DEA techs started installing the latest and greatest surveillance and tracking equipment on the bird. This was a strict US only operation. No Mexican agents were present. The DEA knew they couldn't trust anyone on this operation.

The satellite tracking and upload system installed was the size and appearance of a standard Whelan Strobe pack. In fact, they had ingeniously used the housing of the unit to contain and camouflage the high tech contents. Both wing tip strobes where replaced with almost identical units. Almost identical, because the new strobes included a miniscule camera lens the size of a pinhead. Additional lenses were fitted just behind the doors and tail, giving a 360-degree view upon snapping each shot. Photos would be immediately uploaded to any number of covert satellites covering that region of the world at that particular time. The first time anyone would view the photos outside of the DEA or the defendant's attorneys (the low-life was bound to have a pack of them) would most likely be in criminal court.

Agents Killian and Sowers were present to oversee the installation and brief Jake on the expected results and proper usage of the gadgets. "This is the triggering device," Killian said as he held up a key chain. A little red and white 747 model/caricature with a tiny light on the nose and a push button on its back. "All you do is press the button on its back and you'll automatically take six photographs. Just keep it in your pocket and fire away. If you hold the button down it acts as a video camera for fifteen seconds. Any longer and it bogs down the system."

Jake paid as much attention as possible, but continually looked around to see if anybody was in the bushes or surrounding areas watching what was going on.

Killian noticed Jake's concern and promptly reassured him. "Don't worry. There's not a soul in this area."

"Would you mind telling me what makes you so sure?" Jake asked unbelievingly.

"We have a Citation orbiting at 35,000 feet with a slew of remote sensing gadgetry. If a lizard farted twenty miles away these boys could tell us what it had for dinner," Killian said straight-faced. Sowers turned before Jake could see her smile. Killian didn't miss a beat, "All right, here's the drill. All you need to do is keep flying just the way you have been. Don't do anything different. Maybe ask for more flights if they're available. Mostly, to begin with, we want photos of soldiers loading the plane with drugs and cash. Got it?"

"Got it," Jake responded with as much enthusiasm as he could muster.

"What we would like more than anything is a nice photo of the General saying 'cheese' next to a big pile of dope."

"How about the money runs?   What do you want me to do there?" Jake inquired.

"Snap as many shots of people delivering and loading anything you think might help the case. Just snap away freely, since it's all digital with an automatic satellite upload, there is no limit to your picture taking," Sowers offered.

"How do I get in touch with you guys if I need you?"

"Very basically. You don't. We will contact you when we know it's safe," Killian stated shortly.

"That sounds like a crock of shit to me! What if I have an emergency?" Jake protested.

"If you have an emergency dial your mother's phone number. Let it ring once and hang up. Then dial 911, pound. One of us will answer your call immediately," Sowers answered on this occasion. It occurred to Jake that Sowers was the more technologically apt of the two.

"How long do you expect the investigation to continue?"   Jake inquired, and then qualified. "Honestly."

"We really don't know. We would suspect six months or so. It all depends on how long it takes to develop the right amount of evidence," Killian replied.

"Now for the most important question of all. What the hell am I supposed to do with my life when this is all over? I'm probably going to have a bunch of pissed off drug dealers wanting me dead."

"We will offer you the witness protection program and a pay out for lost income," Killian stated as if he was reading from a brochure.

"That's very nice. But do you realize that flying is my life. It's all I have ever wanted to do, and after the shit hits the fan it's not going to be the safest job for me."

"Stop beating around the bush, Mr. McInnes. Why don't you tell us what you want, and we'll see what we can do. Let's just make sure it's fair for all parties," Killian responded with a hint of irritation in his voice.

"I'm thinking a fair price would be a million dollars," Jake said.

One of the techs came by and gave the agents a quick thumbs up.

Ignoring the figure stated by Jake, Killian continued, "You're ready to go. We'll be in touch in the next week or two." Killian paused, "Let me leave you with a thought. The effort and sacrifice you are making will result in many people not falling into drug addiction, and the violence that the drug trade brings to our nation."

'Pompous ass," thought Jake as he bit his tongue in an effort to avoid answering in the manner he would like. Instead he just nodded and said goodbye. He was one of the silent majority who truly believed there was no stopping the drug trade as long as there was a demand for the product. The first fight should be within the confines of the US. Stop the use before it starts and control the borders. Redirect the funds allotted to expenditure in foreign countries and use it instead to tighten up the security on US borders and ports of entry. Jake knew that politics would never permit this to happen. Foreign governments loved the influx of US currency brought in by our drug fighting operations and yet hate us at the same. 'Go figure!' Jake thought. 'We can put a man on the moon. We can build a space station. So many brilliant achievements, and yet we can't stop drugs from polluting United States citizens.'

The Swiss-built Pilatus Porter climbed with the ease that excess horsepower provides. Jake steered towards the deep blue Pacific Ocean in search of tranquilizing his troubled mind. Keeping it low and throttled back, he was in no rush to get back to Mazatlán. Amber was happy enough sleeping in the cavernous passenger/cargo compartment. At 500 feet over the deserted surf below, the PT6 was guzzling an ungodly amount of Jet-A. But then what did he care. He wasn't paying for it so he might as well have some fun.

Beach after deserted beach passed beneath him and he realized that as serene and peaceful as it all looked from the air, it had held its position against the might and persistence of the endless tides since the beginning of time. And it had done so with admirable style and pizzazz. Jake felt at home and comforted by the familiar outline below and felt himself relax as some of the tension drained away. The objective of soothing his mind accomplished, he started looking forward to a nice dinner at his favorite seafood restaurant, Los Chatos.

A few days later, Jake found himself a couple of hundred miles farther south searching for the button on the key chain/camera shutter actuator and finally managed to get a nice shot of the lieutenant's sullen face. The man was busy supervising the loading of Jake's aircraft with 'seized' drugs destined for 'destruction'. Or was it more like 'stolen' and destined for 'consumption', Jake thought.

As the second and third shots were squeezed off, the photographer's apprehensions of capture and death seemed to vanish. Killian had told him to snap away with gusto, and that he did. It was strange to think that a satellite thousands of miles above him was uploading the images and retransmitting them. Somewhere.

Jake wanted to make certain the receiving end would like his photography, so they would be enticed into delivering the best retirement package possible. He allowed himself to wonder, 'If in fact I survive this ordeal, what will I do? What would the future hold? Even more important, just how much would the DEA be willing to give me if I actually provide a photo of the General himself caught in a compromising situation?'

Agent Killian and agent Sowers performed their well-rehearsed, wide-eyed, excessive flinch when they heard Jake's request for a cool million dollars and the witness protection program in compensation for his participation in the big bust. Jake was expecting this and told them they didn't have to decide immediately. In fact he would let them know when he actually needed an answer. He knew it would be necessary to deliver at least one good shot of the General. Jake's mind reeled at the possibilities.

A month had slowly ticked by since Jake had set his objectives on obtaining a nice photo of the General. Unfortunately, the man was being uncooperative towards Jake's photographic endeavors. After all, a man of that importance didn't make a habit of going into the field to get up close and personal with the operation. The General always told his men: "I don't give a fuck what you have to do, just get the job done and show me the money at the end of the day!"

During the previous thirty days Jake had shot around a thousand photos of the operations. He also made a list of the clandestine airfields, even though the DEA already had coordinates based on the tracking systems installed in the plane.

The biggest question remained. How was he going to get a photo of the General with the drugs? A hundred ideas crossed his mind as he flew; each analyzed and then discarded due to some deficiency or another. Finally one idea kept coming back to him. It was dangerous, but it was simple. And, he might just take care of two problems at once. Committed to his idea, Jake made an appointment with General Gasdas.

They met at the airport on a Wednesday before Gasdas set off to his usual meetings in Mexico City, "Mr. McInnes, why did you want to see me?"

"I have some information you will find very interesting. And I thought you should be the only one to know since it's a very sensitive matter," Jake let the words sink in.

"Continue," the General instructed.

"I was picking up a load of drugs when.."

"A load of 'seized narcotics'." Gasdas rephrased.

"Yes, well, once the troops had loaded the 'narcotics' in the plane I noticed another pile of bricks hidden next to some bushes. I asked the Lieutenant if that was all he had, and he said yes. The plane could've hauled twice the amount. But I didn't argue, I just took off," Jake paused for effect. The General's normally brownish skin was tinted crimson with anger. "I didn't fly directly back to Mazatlán," Jake continued, "There was a convenient clearing some ten miles away on the far side of a hill. I took my binoculars to see if another aircraft showed up."

"And!?" The General ordered, his face even redder than before.

"A 172 came by low level and landed at the pick up site an hour or so after I left. It remained for twenty minutes or so. When it departed I couldn't help but notice how labored it's departure was. I really can't confirm what he had on board since I didn't physically watch them load, but I can make a pretty good guess."

"Yes, well so can I," the General said as his eyes narrowed. "Which Lieutenant was it?"

"Perez," Jake responded.

"We'll have to pay that lying piece of shit a visit. Be prepared day after tomorrow, you will be taking me," he turned on his heels to leave.

Jake called after him, "Sir. I think it would be better to go three days from today since that is when he is expecting another pickup."

"Very well, Saturday it is," he answered without turning. A King Air in Army livery awaited, its right engine at idle. The left would be started as soon as the door was latched.

Jake spent most of his days reading, mostly because it offered a temporary escape from all of the questions in his mind. Solitaire, on the other hand, helped him to concentrate. His concentration slowly focused on the realization which became sometime ago, when the nagging suspicion had struck that he probably wasn't involved in a legitimate government sanctioned operation and the ultimate confirmation of his doubts by the DEA. Every time that Jake's mind took him in this direction he felt depressed and disappointed that his initial objective of a clean sound adventure had gone so completely awry. Now that he was working towards a cause he deemed worthy of such an enormous risk, he felt motivated and alive. His adrenaline pumped and just like a junky getting his fix, he relished every terrifying moment.

Gasdas didn't bother complimenting him on the silky smooth landing, but then Jake was aware that the General wasn't one to compliment anybody about anything, ever.

Noticing the General was in the airplane, Lieutenant Perez rushed towards it like a dog to its master arriving home from a long business trip. The man panted, scratched and leapt at the door, and finally opened it before the turbine engine wound down. "General, I didn't realize you would be coming today!" the lieutenant sputtered with obvious anxiety in his voice.

"Yes, well, it's been a long time since I have seen the troops and the operation." Turning his attention to the motley crew before him, he instructed Perez to have the men line up. Jake's hand nervously toyed with the photo trigger in his pocket as he snapped away. These were the photos he had been waiting for and he knew couldn't blow this one time opportunity.

Nine men stood at attention. Dressed right. They were a rag tag bunch. Their clothes torn and dirty, sweat stained from weeks in the blistering heat and no place to get cleaned up. Most of them were short and lean, deep brown skin devoid of facial hair and black eyes told of their almost pure Indian heritage. No doubt they had joined the army simply because they were searching for a better existence than that offered in their humble little home towns way out in the Middle of Nowhere, Mexico. By now, after a few years of service they had probably come to realize that they were not much better off.

"Soldiers!" the General started, "you should know your country appreciates your hard work. Each and every one of you is doing a great service, not only for Mexico but also for the World. Only because of your efforts will we be able to end this terrible scourge. In gratitude I am here to present each of you with a bonus of two hundred US Dollars." Gasdas presented the bills to Perez to be passed around. He in turn gave it to the Sergeant, who walked down the ranks handing two bills with Benjamin Franklin's stoic face looking out at them. "Sergeant, Lieutenant, stand along side your men."

Jake continued snapping photos as the money was passed around from hand to hand. He knew this was great footage.

"Now, I have some bad news," the General paused momentarily. "We have a traitor among us. Who will come forward and tell me who this cowardly bastard is?" They all stood fast, hearts beating as if they had just run a marathon. Each tried to refrain from breathing for fear such action would be misconstrued as a step forward. Gasdas took his 9mm Browning from his side holster, ceremoniously loaded the first bullet into the chamber and walked in front of the line up. He stared menacingly into each pair of terrified eyes. Proceeding to the rear of the line he continued, almost shouting, "We can not tolerate deceit in our ranks! We will not allow one bad element to tarnish army honor!"

Gasdas slowly walked behind Perez and shoved the cold steel barrel of the weapon to the base of his neck and gave him a hard shove. Exaggeratedly Perez fell to the ground in the dramatic manner of an injured soccer player. "Get up! Stand before your men and show them what a spineless piece of shit you are!"

Perez's eyes were wide, his mind reeled, he didn't beg for his life. Not because he thought such action was undignified, he was so stunned he couldn't formulate a single syllable. The nine men before him looked on in absolute silence each one weak in the knees with relief at not being in Perez's shoes.

As Gasdas shouted, "We will not tolerate traitors!" Jake squeezed his triggering device so hard he thought he might have broken it. The General also squeezed. A large high velocity hollow point 9mm hunk of lead blasted through Perez's brain and splattered seven of the ten men standing before him. Not a single one dare wipe the brain tissue from his face. Only one threw up, but then who could blame him, he did have a piece of Perez's brain dripping from his lip.

Lieutenant Perez's body lay in a heap before them. "Let this be a lesson for each and everyone of you," Gasdas pointed his 9mm with its remaining 13 bullets at the ready at each one in the line. "Don't fuck with the army! Yaik. Give me one of your cigarettes."

Jake complied and also gave him a light. The General took a long drag. "Soldiers. You will be taking orders from your Sergeant now. What's your name Sergeant?"

"Gonzalez," he stammered meekly as he wished he were a hundred miles away.

"You will be taking orders from Sergeant Gonzalez! You can take two weeks leave as soon as you finish loading the plane. You know what to do! So get going!"

The ten men took off in a mad dash, including the Sergeant, who usually didn't do any lifting.

"Not you Gonzalez. I want to talk with you."

Gasdas told the Sergeant, in no uncertain terms, that he was holding him and his entire family accountable for the success of the operation. Gonzalez mumbled "Yes, Sir."

"Oh," said Gasdas, "you just made Lieutenant. Go ahead and take the insignia off that piece of shit. He won't be needing them anymore."

Despite Gonzalez's reputation for being a tough, mean son of a bitch, he really didn't want to confront the gruesome task of removing the blood spattered bars from the uniform of his ex-boss. Lieutenant Perez lay face down in the dirt, so he pushed him over with the toe of his boot to get better access. In doing so, half of the dead man's frappéd brain oozed through the huge gaping hole left by the hollow point. Gonzalez had to clench his throat muscles hard so he wouldn't projectile vomit his lunch of rice and beans.

Gasdas stood by himself as he watched them load the airplane with neatly packaged bricks of 99.9% pure Cambodian heroin. He silently thanked his lucky stars that there was always a smuggler to catch and thus be able to fulfill the requirements of his exclusive clientele.

He called one of the young soldiers over and took a brick. Taking a knife to it he made a small incision and tasted a few granules. He held the brick in his hand and made a weighing motion. A crooked malevolent little smile appeared for half a second on his thin lips.

Jake, who was poised and ready at that precise split second snared the perfect image digitally and even managed to include the inert frame of Perez in the background.

The return flight was as quiet and uneventful as the previous one. Jake got the impression that Gasdas didn't like gringos much. As he flew in silence, he wondered if the photos were done uploading and the first shots were appearing like magic on the desk of some bureaucrat/agent at DEA headquarters. By the following day they would be in the hands of Agents Sowers and Killian. What would their reaction be? Maybe, now they would agree he deserved the requested million and he'd be off the hook.

Jake played it cool, waiting a couple of days before he made contact with Killian and Sowers. He went down the costera a ways and dialed his mother's number from a payphone; he let in ring once, dialed 911 and then pound. A ring echoed distantly, then Killian answered with a quick suspicious "Hello."

"I'd like to set up a meeting," Jake said making sure he mentioned no names.

"Very well. In person or on the phone?" Killian responded.

"Did you get my special delivery?" Jake asked, not bothering to answer the agent's question, but simply came straight to the point.

"Yes," Killian responded without elaborating.

"Not bad for an amateur. Wouldn't you agree?" Jake toyed.

"Yeah. Not bad at all," Killian said with a tiny hint of exasperation in his voice.

"Are your friends willing to pay my price?" Jake asked, referring to the million-dollar price tag he had originally established.

"I'll be in touch with you in the next few days with an answer." Killian hung up.

Jake continued down the costera a little ways to one of the small seafood restaurants. He had dinner alone as he watched the wavelets leave salty foam along the beach. He hadn't made any friends during his stay in Mazatlán because he wanted to remain detached, anonymous. It felt like the right thing to do. There was no need to leave any kind of emotional trace once the shit hit the fan. His only company, as always, was Amber and she lay contentedly by his feet under the table as he ate his meal. This establishment was the only one that would allow a dog on the patio section and because of this fact alone the proprietor had found a very steady customer in Jake McInnes.

As always, the meal was very good. The seafood and veggies were always fresh, and never overcooked. Unfortunately, his mind refused to focus on the mission of filling his hungry stomach and concentrated on re-running the events of the last few days. He continually saw Lieutenant Perez's brains atomized before his very eyes, and saw his limp body slump to a heap in the dirt. It was the most revolting thing he had ever seen in his life and the fact that he was the direct cause of the man's death now weighed heavily on his conscience, even though he had been one of the most unpleasant people Jake had ever met.

Jake knew full well he hadn't seen a Cessna 172 come in after he had departed. He knew full well Perez had not stolen any of the General's smack. He knew the events would haunt him for years to come. Did the Lieutenant have kids? A wife? What would his mother say to the news? 'We regret to inform you that your son was killed during a military exercise. He served his country....blah, blah, blah....' Jake could vividly see the tears rolling down the old wrinkled cheeks.

Seeking consolation, he knew for a fact that Perez was a mean sack of shit who would find any excuse to beat on his men, and was a worthless human being. Every time he had seen him he had been flogging one soldier or another. Jake continued his mental justification, Lieutenant Perez knew full well the extent of damage the heroin trade caused on the streets of Somewhere, USA. In summation, Perez was just another piece of shit that didn't deserve to be breathing the same air as decent folk.

DEA agent Killian tailed Jake from the Gascony Hotel to the Comercial Mexicana supermarket. He had already established that Jake was not being shadowed. Gliding down the smooth polished floor on aisle number 7 – 'Canned goods' his near empty cart almost making contact with the only other American in the store. Killian stopped momentarily next to Jake, "Meet me at the old hacienda outside of town. Now point towards the back of the store and nod affirmatively." Jake did as he was told.

Killian said 'thanks' a little too loudly and made for the check out with his sodas. A fifth of Cuervos crappy tequila was already pilfered and nicely stashed in his jacket pocket. He'd always had quick hands and had never been caught. Not even when he was a youngster stealing booze for his alcoholic father.

The 'old hacienda outside of town' was an abandoned coconut farm 20 miles north on Highway 15 towards Los Mochis, and a mile or so towards the beach. It was a good location with two possible exits. Also, it was possible to see cars coming all the way from the highway, allowing enough time to mobilize if necessary.

Killian knew what Jake wanted to talk about so he didn't bother with the idle chitchat. "The Agency is willing to pay you five hundred thousand dollars. We are all expecting you to do the right thing."

Jake had fully expected this response and was ready with an answer, "I'm very willing to do the right thing. But do you honestly believe my career as a pilot is only worth that amount? Do you know how much work and sacrifice it has been to become a pilot? You are aware that I will never be able to fly professionally once this goes down? It's very easy to locate a pilot. What do you care how much I'm paid? It's not your money. It's the taxpayer's money! The way our wonderful government squanders it, who gives a damn about sending a paltry million in my direction!"

Killian stood silently for a few seconds, staring thoughtfully at Jake. Studying him. "You know in a way you are absolutely right."

Sowers, who had also been studying Jake, turned to Killian in surprise.

"Your arguments are certainly valid. However, I have only been authorized half a million," he lied, "so I guess it's a take it or leave it type situation."

"Maybe I'll just leave it. And maybe I'll just leave Mazatlán so you pigs can wallow in your own filth together!" Jake was now thoroughly pissed.

"That's your choice Jake. But remember, once we get an operative to cooperate and the house of cards comes tumbling down, you're going to come down with it," Killian said with a small smirk.

Sowers looked startled, her eyes darted back and forth between the two men.

"You can't be serious Killian. I'm risking my life because of you. I could be killed because of you!"

"All right McInnes, take it easy. Let me see what I can do. I might get the higher-ups to go for an extra two hundred thousand or so."

Jake knew they had him between a rock and a hard place. "If you can get me seven hundred fifty thousand you've got a deal," he said even though he was in no position to bargain. But it was worth a try.

Jake and Amber stayed a while longer on the solitary stretch of beach. She slept peacefully by his side as he stroked her fur and felt envious of her serenity. As the day grew old Jake felt lonelier than ever before. He had made a point of not making friends since he viewed his stay as temporary, but now the isolation was getting to him. Idle chitchat with an unknown at some bar was just not going to cut it. A phone call to a friend in the US was out of the question, since his phone was certainly tapped. Not that he would talk about the activities he was involved with anyway. He just didn't want to give the General or his cronies any information about his family or friends.

He missed the blunting effects of a nice cold beer. But then, that wasn't an option. Last time he took that route he woke up two states away in a jail cell in some Podunk town in the middle of nowhere.

Mazatlán's lights burned brightly to the south. Even though he was getting hungry and thirsty he wasn't ready to leave. There was a feeling of safety in the secluded spot. As the waves lapped across the sand he stared blankly and wondered what each of the important people in his life might be doing at that particular moment. He slowly went down his mental list, imagining each one in vivid detail.

Once he finished this lengthy process of conjecture the original troubles again tumbled freely through his mind. He felt a tremendous urge to simply pack up that same night and disappear. After all, other people had done just that with every success and he examined the idea seriously. The problem, he finally realized was, disappear where? The money he had saved would only take him so far. 'No,' he determined. This was the adventure he had been searching for and it was an experience he needed to see through. Coming to a definite conclusion somehow eased his mind and he drifted off. He slept for what seemed like only a few moments and awoke hours later to a bright moon well past half of its nightly journey. His watch confirmed what the heavenly bodies had already told him.

A humid tropical breeze did little to cool his hot damp skin. Every window in the hotel room was open, since the AC hadn't been working for the past week. A persistent ring reverberated around the stark room until the pillow, which covered his head no longer managed to fulfill its vital mission of putting the world off just a little bit longer.

"Yeah," Jake answered with a groggy voice.

"General Gasdas wishes to speak with you." A soldier informed him curtly.

"Okay. When?" Jake managed to reply.

"Now. There is a car waiting downstairs."

"Give me ten minutes. I need to take a shower."

As he left the hotel he quickly put on his shades. The day's sun was too bright, and too hot for 10am. Combine this with a serious caffeine deficiency and Jake's irritability factor was high. "It's Sunday. What does the General want on a Sunday?" he asked the driver/soldier whose only answer was to shrug his shoulders.

Dressed in what appeared to be a silk paisley robe Gasdas was eating his breakfast alone by the pool as Jake walked up. His mouth bulging with food, he pointed with his chorizo-laden fork indicating that Jake should sit down.   Jake filled the fine porcelain cup in front of him with coffee from a plastic restaurant-style thermos and waited for the General.

An instant before he shoved the large piece of chorizo into his mouth the man managed to briefly utter some words, "Who was the man you were talking to last night in the Comercial Mexicana?"

Searching for the right answer Jake said, "Last night at the supermarket?"   And put on his most puzzled face.

His mouth still contained a large portion of the Spanish chorizo, which had been confiscated in Mexico City two days earlier from a man who had been visiting his ancestor's village in the old country. "Yes, last night. One of my men happened to be there and saw you talking to a known DEA agent. Now answer my question! Why were you talking to him?"

Jake responded quickly since it was obvious by the bulging veins in the General's temples that he was getting very agitated. "The guy simply asked me if the fruit was safe to eat. That's all." Jake remembered clearly that Killian had been very brief.

"That man is a DEA agent and I think you know exactly what I'm talking about!" Gasdas said, particles of food coming out of his mouth. Gasdas stared at Jake searching for the slightest indication of acknowledgement. He unholstered his service 9mm and pointed it at the pilot, "You don't want to mess with me, Mr. Yaik. I'll blow your brains all over the floor, just like Perez. Do you think I care?" His evil beady eyes scoured him.

"I don't understand General. I thought we were working with the DEA?"

"Don't play stupid with me McInnes. You know very well that this operation isn't sanctioned by the DEA or any other agency, and you are just another money grubbing sack-a-shit just like everybody else!" Gasdas took a long breath. "Now tell me. What did he really say to you?"

"I'm telling you the truth. I've never seen the man before in my life," Jake said a conviction worthy of an academy award.

"I'm not sure I believe you. If my people see you talking to anybody, gringo or otherwise, that looks even the slightest bit suspicious, you are a dead man. ¿Me entiendes?" the General asked.

"Yes, Sir, I understand perfectly," Jake said respectfully.

"You can leave now." The General waved his gun in the general direction of the door.

Jake caught a cab, and thought long and hard whether there had ever been a time when he had come so close to joining the ranks of the deceased. Reality set in and he noticed that his shirt was drenched with sweat, his hair pasted to his scalp.

"Are you all right Señor?" the cabby asked as he watched his passenger in the rear view mirror, "If you are going to throw up, please let me know so I can pull over." The driver obviously had too much experience with young gringos 'borrachos'.

"I'm fine," Jake replied. "I just have a bit of a cold," he lied.

"Are those your friends behind us?"

Jake slowly and as casually as possible turned to look out the rear window.

A Volkswagen Jetta with two of the General's goons followed a few car lengths behind making little effort to remain undetected.

"No. Not friends of mine," Jake said still looking at the pursuing vehicle.

"Well Jake, they've been following since you left the General's house," the cabby said in perfect English.

Jake turned around quickly, and tried to get a better view of the driver, "Do I know you?"

"It must be the beard," the man declared. "I caught you off guard the first time we met and on that occasion at least you had Amber looking out for you. Where is she anyway?"

Jake pieced the provided clues together. "You're the Costa Rica guy! The one I met in the Sierra after I made my emergency landing!"

"Bingo."

"What are you doing in Mazatlán?" Jake inquired as he looked back at the Jetta one more time.

"I can't live on rattlesnakes all the time you know. I needed to make a little money so I came into town. A little female companionship may also have been a factor," he said as he noticed Jake staring out the rear window. "Would you like me to lose them?"

"No!" Jake said quickly. "I'm in enough trouble as is."

"How about we go somewhere and catch up on the last year's events then?"

"I'd like that but I don't want to get you involved," Jake explained.

"Don't worry about me. But I'll tell you what. I'll drop you off at your hotel and I'll come back tonight to pick you up once the goons back there are nice and tired of sitting around. There is an underground parking lot in the apartment building next door to your hotel. Since both buildings are the same height, just go from one roof access to the next and make your way down to the garage. I'll meet you there at 9:30."

The Nissan Sentra taxi with tinted windows pulled up to the Gascony Hotel. "How much do I owe you?" asked Jake.

"Don't worry about it, we'll get even eventually."

"This is the second time you've been in the right spot at the right time to help me out. It's kind of uncanny, but man, I really appreciate it!" Jake gave him a pat on the shoulder and got out of the car, quickly climbing the steps to the lobby without looking back.

Amber was very happy to see him and anxious to go on a potty run. Jake went out to the balcony to check on the Jetta. It wasn't parked outside, but that didn't mean much. The gringo pilot and his dog first went to the roof access to make sure it was open and then walked down the emergency staircase to the lobby. There he found one of Gasdas' men reading the newspaper as he sat in one of the sofas. He saw Jake and 'casually' followed him as he peered just above the paper. Jake decided it looked like a scene in a poorly acted B rated film.

Jake walked over to the man. "I'm going down to the beach to walk my dog. Are you coming?"

The goon stared momentarily at Jake, a bit flustered that he had been noticed and a little surprised at the gringo's blunt approach, "I don't know what you are talking about, Señor." the man replied.

"Sure you do. And it's all right. I understand the General's apprehension. Tell ya what. If it makes you feel any better, I won't approach you again. All right?"

"I think that would be best," the man said quietly.

Jake and Amber continued their walk through the old quarter and down to the beach. Amber played fetch with her favorite ball and took a swim in the warm Pacific Ocean. After a while Jake sat by a palapa and read while Amber dozed and her fur dried. For the first time in what seemed to be a long time, and despite his current predicament, he felt a little more at ease. Most likely a reflection of meeting up with his old friend. Loneliness in combination with a challenging situation can be very stressful, he decided.

Looking around to see if the goon was still watching, Jake located him a few seconds later slumped on a bench with his head cocked off to one side in what appeared to be a very uncomfortable position. As Jake approached he could hear the man snoring. His mouth hung slightly open and a little drool oozed out of the lower corner of his mouth. Jake thought, for a guy that looks pretty fierce when he's awake he sure doesn't look very impressive now. He gave him a little tap on the shoulder, which made the man jump out of his skin. "What, what?" the goon asked startled.

"It's time to go," Jake said as he continued to walk down the street.

The man finally realized where he was and what was happening. He quickly looked around to make sure he hadn't been caught napping and rapidly followed in Jake's footsteps.

As the time approached for Jake's scheduled visit with his friend, he noticed how slowly time seemed to pass. At nine fifteen he gave Amber a quick pet and a scratch before he opened the door of his room and peeked outside. He wore a dark blue shirt and the newest darkest jeans, he didn't want to be too obvious about it but he did want to blend in with the night. The emergency staircase was right next to the elevator; as he reached for the doorknob a bell signaled the elevator's arrival at the seventh floor. Jake's heart skipped a beat and he quickly turned around as if he had been waiting for the lift to arrive. A young couple smiled at him as they walked by.

The escape route worked fine, and the Nissan cab was waiting for him even though he arrived seven minutes early. Jake opened the front door to get in. "You should probably travel in the back." the voice inside said.

They made their way out of town, doubling back several times and made some quick turns through parking lots to make certain no one was following them. Thirty miles to the south of town, fifteen past the airport, was a little fishing village called Calderas. Very few people knew of the tiny family restaurant just off Avenida Constituyentes. It was a nice quiet place for a homemade meal. The friends chatted chatted casually for a while and then Jake explained in gory detail all the events since their last encounter deep in the forests of the Sierra Madre Oriental.

"I can imagine just how much you would like to run for the hills, Jake. But by helping put this scumbag away you will be doing a great service to society."

"Don't you think it's a waste of time? After all, this bad guy will just be replaced by another bad guy, and on, and on. The only thing accomplished is the great possibility of getting myself killed, and at the very least the certainty of not being able to work as a pilot again. Unless of course I move to Africa or BFE."

"Well, you're not going to die, and about the piloting thing, you'll just have to find a better place to do it."

"You seem very sure of that statement," Jake said.

"I've got contacts."

"Yeah. I'm sure you do," Jake said incredulously.

"The biggest problem with the drug trade is the undeniable fact that there is an enormous demand for the product. And while the demand exists there will always be someone willing to supply it. That's capitalism. It's also human nature."

Jake thought about the words his friend had just spoken. "I agree. And that's the reason why I think I'm wasting my time."

"Unfortunately, at this juncture the DEA also has you on accessory. So, unless you are willing to risk your freedom, you are more or less committed to the program."

"True enough," Jake agreed with a tired ring of resignation in his voice.

"On one of my many hikes through the Sierra, I came across a poppy field in a very remote area. The five acres were deep in a valley, but still on a very steep slope. Even an inexperienced person in these matters, such as myself, would believe such a location to be ideal for this kind of activity. Anyway, an old man, maybe seventy-five or so was tending the fields. You would think he would be angry and hostile to an intruder, but he wasn't. In fact he was very welcoming. This really surprised me, and I wound up staying for a few days. It was very interesting to hear his side of the story.

"His leathery face was evidence enough of a hard life working in the fields. It wasn't a sad face, and it certainly wasn't a happy one either. I would best describe it as a resolute face. It told the onlooker, 'this is what I have been dealt and this is how I'm making the best of it.'"

Jake sipped a cup of instant decaf with a little too much sugar.

"Believe it or not but the guy's name was Juan Valdez!"

"See, now I think you are bullshitting me!" Jake said as he tore off the filter and sparked up his cigarette.

"Juan told me that of the 25 children God had given him only 14 remained. Most of them died as infants, or toddlers. Doctors were hard to come by, and furthermore, way beyond their budget. By the time he was 54 years old his direct descendants numbered almost a hundred. He noticed that each new generation was no better than the one before. Each one continued to hand plow the fields with the help of a single burro, and nothing more. He knew that if he ever had the opportunity to do something to get a boost out of this cycle of poverty, he would grab it with both hands in order to change their inevitable future.

"A middleman happened to come to the area and told him about the wonders of the poppy. Old Juan of course knew it was a drug. From our conversations, he had no idea just how powerful a drug it is. But he did know that it didn't do anybody any good," he took a sip of his lemonade, and continued, "He was told by the middleman that he knew some people in 'El Norte' who wanted this product, and if they couldn't find it here they would find it some place else. And that someone else would benefit in a big way."

"Old Juan thought about this long and hard, and finally decided he would grow one small crop. Just enough to buy a used tractor and some seed for the next season. He searched, and found a little piece of land in the middle of nowhere. In fact it was the plot where I found him. He planted half of the five acres he had commandeered, and within a matter of months he was ready to deliver. From making three or four thousand for the whole year, he netted forty thousand for that one small crop. The following year he tended to his fields the way he would for a regular crop and produced almost three rotations, and expanded to the full five acres. The $150,000 dollars he made was split between his children and grandchildren. And in search of cleansing his soul, he gave $20,000 to the church."

"I can completely understand why a poor farmer, who doesn't have two dimes to rub together and no hope for the future, would get involved. But I can't understand how the guy at the other end of the distribution chain can stick this shit in one of his veins," Jake commented.

"Mexico only produces around nine thousand pounds of heroin a year, but is the port of entry for a great deal more. The real scary thing is that Mexico's four and a half tons per year equates to only two percent of the worlds production."

"How the hell do you know so much about the heroin trade?" Jake inquired.

"I was curious after I met Juan, and researched it on the Internet."

"With staggering numbers like that there will always be people willing to grow and sell the product," Jake added.

"And transport it. Just one kilo of pure heroin, say in Durango, which happens to be the heroin capital of Mexico, sells for ten to thirteen thousand dollars. By the time that same kilo of smack arrives in San Antonio, Texas it sells for around sixty thousand! Let me tell you, a great many people are willing to do that and a lot more for fifty grand."

Jake added, "By the sound of it, the only way to control the drug trade is by getting rid of the demand."

"Easier said than done."

"So here I am putting my life on the line to shut down a supply chain that will pop up somewhere else, with someone else in command as soon as this one's out of the way. Why the hell am I doing this? I'm wasting my time, I'm throwing away my career, and I could lose my life!"

"I wouldn't say that Jake. At the moment it's all you can do. You are doing an admirable thing. Don't be disillusioned with it all, if nothing else, you are doing your part."

"I'm glad we met up, it's great being able to talk things over with a friend. It makes me feel like I'm not really going insane after all." Jake raised his cup of coffee to his lips, a thick column of smoke burst from his nostrils. "Would you mind calling my DEA contact and setting up a meeting for tomorrow night? It's just hard for me to do anything while being watched so closely."

"Sure, Jake and I'll pick you up at the same time tomorrow. Deal?"

"Deal."

Chapter 7.
No Turning Back.

The Nissan Sentra with polarized windows and dressed up in taxi garb was parked in the exact same spot as the night before. Jake frantically ripped open the door and jumped in and laid flat on the back seat. He quickly locked the doors.

"You seem a little out of breath there Jake. Are you being followed?" He asked calmly.

"No, I don't think so," Jake said as he peered just above the seat level. "Did you see someone?"

"No, but you're in such a state I thought it would be best to ask."

"I'm a nervous wreck is all. This shit is really starting to get to me." Jake fumbled with his cigarettes, and dropped one on the floor. He found it a second later and lit it without thinking about the kinds of germs it may have picked up from the taxi's well-trodden floor.

"I'm sorry, Sir, but there is no smoking in the taxi."

"What!? Are you kidding!" Jake said as he removed the nicotine stick from his face.

"Yes, in fact I am. I figure at least one of us needs to have some fun," he said as he shifted gears, and released the clutch just enough to see Jake's head jolt back.

"Did you call my contact?" Jake inquired as he scoured the cars from behind his Ray Bans.

"Yes I did. But I'll tell you, this Killian character was a little pissed that I was making the call."

"Oh, well. Fuck him if he can't take a joke."

The two cohorts in the Sentra taxi drove around town, made a few U turns, and some unnecessary jaunts through some parking structures with two exits. Once they were certain no tails were on them, they proceeded towards the rendezvous point. On the way a gorgeous young lady waved for him to stop.

"Jake!" he said with urgency, "Look at her. She just motioned me to stop. Maybe you should take another cab the rest of the way."

"She's young enough to be your daughter, you pig. Now drive," Jake admonished but couldn't help staring.

"You're no fun, McInnes."

After a forty-five minute drive east, north east, an old dilapidated hacienda came into sight, it was overgrown by large tropical hardwoods and thick vines. Heavy, humid air scented and alive with the nutrients provided by decaying leaves and other organic material filled the visitors' senses.

Jake got out of the car by himself and walked in front of the car's headlamps. A flashlight a hundred yards or so away flashed at him. He started to walk. He was as nervous as he was during his first solo. His mind raced at warp speed. It played nasty little games with him. What if it was an ambush? What would happen if it were the General behind the flashlight? How quickly would they kill him?

"Señor Yaik." A voice came from his left. Jake almost jumped out of his skin. The voice didn't sound like Killian or Sowers. The flashlight shined in his eyes again. "Is that you Killian?"

"Yeah it's me. Where you expecting anyone else?" He didn't wait for an answer. "Come over this way."

Jake identified the voice this time and calmed down somewhat. "What's up with the mystery location, Killian?"

"Hell if I know. Your buddy chose it, and we spent the afternoon checking it out. And by the way, that was a very dumb move, bringing someone in without consulting us," Killian said, his voice telling of the annoyance he was feeling.

"I didn't have a choice. My room and my phone are tapped, I've got a tail on my ass 24/7. Did you have a better plan?" Jake complained.

"I suppose you did the best you could under the circumstances," Killian acknowledged begrudgingly. "Anyway, you called the meeting. Whaz up?" Killian said.

Jake thought about Killian's demeanor, and his voice. He could almost swear he could smell some booze over the chewing gum. "What's up? What the hell is that supposed to mean? I just told you. I'm being followed and my room is bugged because they think I just might be a snitch. That's whaz up!" Jake snapped in frustration and then continued. "So what's happening with my money?"

"The Agency is willing to give you seven hundred thousand, but," he let the 'but' sink in, "Only if you can get the General to the US."

"You know, you guys are so full of shit. How the fuck do you suppose I'm going to accomplish that?"

"We haven't come up with a plan just yet. But our experts are presently working on it. They'll come up with something in the next few days. So don't worry. Just keep working as usual, and we'll be in touch."

"No. The General has you marked as a DEA agent and someone saw us together in the supermarket. I'll be in touch. Do not contact me! And if you do, all bets are off!" Jake walked away briskly. He got into the cab, its engine had been running and the air conditioning blasting. He welcomed the cool interior.

"So. How'd it go?"

"This one'll blow you away," Jake said and proceeded to narrate the conversation which had just taken place.

"I think that's do-able," said his friend as soon as the last word had been launched from Jake's mouth.

"You must be crazier than the DEA!" Jake responded and continued, "How do you suppose it might work?"

As the two friends drove back to Mazatlán and the underground parking next to Jake's hotel, they drafted the plan in thick brush strokes. Soon they would fill in the finer details.

Jake quietly worked the following months keeping a very low profile and contacting no one, until he was pretty sure the heat was off him. During that time he refined his plan and took more photos of the operation. Contact with Killian and Sowers was nonexistent. He couldn't help but enjoy the flights, regardless of whether they were drug runs or money runs. Either way he no longer felt the anxiety of the initial days, and felt confident no crazed bandits would attempt storming such a heavily armed group of soldiers.

On a few occasions, as Jake flew around the country, he pretended to be an aerial tour guide, paid to take customers sightseeing. He imagined the commentary he might provide his passengers regarding the landmarks they were passing. 'On the right you have the Balsas River. It's not Mexico's longest, but it is world famous for its annual jet boat race. Hosted for 31 years straight it's had celebrity racers such as Paul Newman participating on several occasions.' 'Whatever keeps me sane is all that matters. Soon it'll all be over.' Jake thought.

It was time. Jake had kept his nose clean, and regained whatever confidence may have been lost. He requested a meeting with General Gasdas. It was set for Thursday. Dinner. If it didn't work, he had no idea where he would go from there. All he could do was sell it the best he knew how.

The black suburban picked him up at the hotel. Jake wore his nicest pair of khakis with a golf shirt, accompanied by a pair of penny loafers he had bought for the occasion and would probably never wear again.

He felt completely out of place and self conscious without his jeans and tennis shoes.

General Ignacio Gasdas Sanchez sat regally on the plush chaise longue on his patio. He was looking at the city lights below while listening to the waves. "Mister Yaik. You requested a meeting. What do you want?"

Jake was expecting at least a couple of minutes of small talk, maybe even dinner before delving into the touchy subject he wanted to talk about. He had hoped for a little more time to read the General's mood. His prepared speech was flowery and reverent, copying the style he had heard Omar use when talking to people who felt they were superior to everyone else. On one hand it appeared to boost and massage their oversized egos, and on the other he noticed it appeared to get Omar what he wanted.

"As you know General, I have been working with the operation for a year or so now…"

"And you think you are entitled to a raise?" Gasdas interrupted.

"No, no. I'm not looking for a raise," Jake continued with his rehearsed speech. "With the utmost respect you deserve and forgive me beforehand if I am out of line, but it is hard not to notice certain events over the months."

"Cut to the chase, Yaik. You are not Mexican, so stop trying to sound like one. What's on your mind?"

"There's this gentleman I know in LA. He's a bit of an accountant."

"Why do you think I need an accountant?" Gasdas interrupted again.

"Well, he is an accountant, but he doesn't work as one. We just refer to him as such because he makes money appear and disappear without a trace. And it seems he also has very reasonable rates." Jake stopped to let his words take effect.

Gasdas studied Jake; his eyes darting back and forth as if searching for something, "And why do you think that would be of interest to me?"

"I thought you might be interested in comparing prices with whoever you are dealing with now," Jake stated matter-of-fact.

Gasdas turned quickly and called one of his goons, "Did you check this man for wires?"

The bulky man hesitated for a couple of seconds and looked from side to side like a child caught with his hand in the cookie jar, "Um, no. General, I thought..."

"That's the problem. Don't think. Just do as you are instructed. Now check him!" Gasdas rasped, the irritation clear in his voice.

The big goon grabbed Jake forcefully by the arm, "Against the wall," he barked.

"After that display of idiocy it really doesn't work very well to be threatening. Just pat him down," Gasdas admonished.

When the guard finished he declared him to be clean. General Gasdas waved him off and continued as though nothing had happened, "Now, Yaik. This friend of yours, 'the accountant', how much does he charge?"

"Ten percent," Jake said smoothly, watching disbelief and greed chase across Gasdas' face.

"I don't believe it! The man I deal with now charges almost twenty for the amounts I send. Your friend is either a phony, or the best. Where does he take delivery?"

"In Laredo if you like, or LA. And if you want to find out if he's a fake or the best, you can decide for yourself. He would be willing to come visit and talk face to face," Jake said.

"And what's in it for you, Yaik?"

"I want one percent of the cleaned portion."

"That's almost two hundred seventy thousand a month!"

"Yes, but I'm saving you a bunch more than that," Jake came back quickly.

"I'll give you fifty thousand a month and that's it!" The General offered.

"Deal," Jake offered his hand to seal the agreement.

Gasdas reluctantly shook it and thought, 'Stupid gringo. I would have given him the full two hundred seventy thousand if he had pushed a little.'

Shimmying and shaking, the rickety old VW Beetle taxi made the short trip over the cobblestones from the General's villa to the Gascony Hotel, and yet the distraction didn't prevent Jake from going over and over the events that had just transpired. He couldn't believe the man had taken the bait so easily. Either Gasdas was setting him up, or his greed was insatiable. In any case, there was no turning back now. The wheels were now in unstoppable motion and not only was he gambling with his life, he was gambling with just about every dime he had to his name.

Now that he was living the life of the truly adventurous he wasn't so sure that it was all it was cracked up to be, but Jake recognized that it was a little too late to change his mind. This basic realization hit him as he dealt the thirty-first game of solitaire of the evening. Unaware of the wonderful warm night as he sat on the balcony, he made mental notes of each step of the plan. Going over each facet and committing it to memory, he hashed out each uncertain element until the plan was as complete and perfect as he could possibly make it.

Friday. It used to be Jake's favorite day. After all, you had the whole weekend to look forward to. The possibilities were endless. Or at least when you were young it seemed that way. Jake had a money run and the flying, if nothing else, was great. Even though the usual two thugs with their loaded AK47's were in the back. At least it was a smooth ride, and they wouldn't be barfing their brains out. With the Pilatus' low wing loading the lightest turbulence made the most seasoned pilot wish he was on the ground. Jake had exactly the opposite of Larry's fuck' em all attitude, always provided the guards with O_2 for the higher cruising altitudes. He felt bad for the poor bastards. He could just imagine the raging headaches they must have by the end of a long work day with Larry.

As usual, today's route took them to ten different airports, and finally back to Mazatlán by 23:40. A very long day of flying, but he preferred that over a day of wondering what to do with himself. When he flew, problems seemed to distance themselves in proportion to the altitude gained.

Looking down from his perch the world appeared friendlier, simpler. The hustle and bustle of the towns and cities passing under wing were invisible from his perspective.   No horns were being blasted a millisecond after the light had changed. There was no shouting. There was nothing. And nothing can be a good thing.

Unfortunately you can't remain in the skies forever. Eventually you'll run out of gas and your feet will inevitably touch the ground. Hopefully when they do you are sufficiently recharged to face the realities of everyday life once again. At least for the length of time between flights.

Jake awoke late Saturday morning, drained by the previous day's trip. Regardless of his precarious situation, the fresh sunrise brought him a sense of great possibility. He had a deep feeling that things would work out after all. The home stretch was near and imminent.

With intense purpose and bounce in his step Jake walked the short distance to the old market square. It was alive with activity. Each tiny outlet, measuring around fifteen by fifteen feet, was crammed with items for sale. Some had fruit, others vegetables. Being a port city there were many seafood shops. Clothing, some plain, others fancy. Hardware. It was all available in this one stop shop and bargaining was expected. Jake's eyes absorbed true commerce. One of the things he enjoyed about Mexico was the fact that no one got a free ride. You work. Your family takes care of you if you can't. Or you die. Darwinism in its purest form.

Jake purchased a plastic cup brimming with fresh fruit, but passed on the fiercely hot chile powder they usually doused it with. As he walked along taking in the sounds and distinctive smells, Amber at his side, he savored the fresh mango slices and sweet pineapple followed by the lush papaya, as always a hint of lime juice added the necessary tang.

So far, he had refrained from smoking, but now the urge was hitting him hard. He silently cursed himself for being weak. How was it possible that he could beat an addiction like booze, and be completely unable to contend against these little cancer sticks? He stuffed one in his face, still pissed, and lit the little fucker; he sucked on it hard as if he was trying to kill it with one drag. It was time to find some thick strong coffee. He knew just the place. Now if he could just find a copy of the LA Times.

As he walked out of the usual, and only good, coffee shop, he noticed the now well-known Sentra Cab with dark windows parked on the other side of the street. He was right on time. He was still wearing the silly Panama Jack hat. Jake watched as he tipped the brim of the hat, the prearranged signal meaning "all's clear". Even so, Jake took a quick look round to see if anything was out of the ordinary. Amber leapt into the vehicle first.

"Beautiful morning for a walk!"

"Is everything in place?" Jake inquired.

"You make it sound a lot more complicated than it is. All we're doing is making phone calls from my place. And I've done that many times before!" He said with a mocking smile.

"I guess I am getting carried away."

About in time for a late lunch the elements required to complete the first phase of the ruse were in place. Along with them came a large void in Jake's savings account and he knew the expenses would continue. "Are you ready to head out to Tijuana tonight?" Jake asked.

"Reservations are made and paid. Now all I need is some cash for expenses while I'm there, the Armani suits and of course the other items we already talked about."

"Armani? Who said anything about Armani?" Jake asked knowing full well how much a couple of suits from this expensive designer would cost, "Couldn't you pick something up at the Men's Warehouse?"

"Jakey, if you want to look the part it's got to be authentic."

"All right, all right," Jake said as he mentally calculated and unconsciously shook his head. He retrieved a thick wad of cash from the knapsack he was carrying and counted off $26,000. "I know this is more than enough, but you should probably buy some fancy-ass shoes, a couple of rings and a gold Rolex watch. Make sure the watch is real, for some reason watches are very important to Mexican men and they know what they are looking at. The stones in the rings can be fake, good fakes."

As night fell Jake left his hotel and walked along the costera. He wanted to use the time to go over the plan one more time. His watch, a cheap Casio with a built in calculator, showed 19:35. He looked skyward as he heard a jet overhead. Most likely his friend was on board. He hailed a 'pulmonia' cab and made his way to the General's place.

Once the soldiers had established his identity, and jotted down his arrival in their log he was waved in. As was customary, Jake waited for forty minutes before Gasdas would see him. His private office, which overlooked the veranda and the ocean, was grander and more tasteful than its owner could ever be. "Mr. Yaik, you wanted to see me?"

"Yes General. The man I was telling you about, the accountant, he can visit you next Wednesday."

"Wednesdays are not good for me. I have meetings in Mexico City. Tell him I can see him on Thursday morning. I'll be back by then."

Jake knew all about General Gasdas' weekly meeting. But wanted to create some organized conflict, "I'll see what I can do. But let's plan on that."

Mexicana's Flight 525 departed Mazatlán's International airport a few minutes late. The rickety old 727-200 with too many hours on it to be worth the risk for a US carrier, shimmied and shook as it slowly gained altitude through the pockets of hot air left by the blazing day. Each passenger contained within the long aerial sausage was extremely quiet. Some focused on the harsh thumps provided by the unstable air, others sought forgiveness from a higher being in case of an extreme eventuality. With a particularly bad bump a woman towards the rear of the aircraft let out an unconscious yet extremely loud yelp as her seatbelt dug into her chubby legs. The man in seat 25B wished he had taken a potty break before boarding. Suddenly things smoothed out and people nervously looked around with awkward little smiles and wiped their sweaty hands on their pants, or the nearest available absorbent surface.

He was also apprehensive. Not about the flight, there was nothing he could do about that. He was nervous about returning to the States after so many years. When he was growing up with Myles and Lynette Burrard in Santa Barbara he had loved his adoptive country. But after the way American bureaucracy had treated him upon his adoptive parents death, he could only categorize his feelings as hate. But now, with the passage of time, which truly cures all, he felt somewhat indifferent and slightly curious.

Tijuana, he decided after a few hours, was in fact the asshole of the world. Or, at least it was in his book, until something worse took its place. An old Caprice Classic station wagon, its bright crushed velvet interior pockmarked with cigarette burns, burned more oil than gasoline but managed to make its way to a hotel. "I need to get across to 'El Norte'," he said to the cab driver, when he felt the moment was right.

"You want me to take you to 'La Linea' (The Line)?" The cabby asked a little confused.

"What I need is a coyote. I don't have any papers."

The cabby was surprised that a nicely dressed man would have such a problem. He studied him via the rear view mirror. Hesitant that it may be some kind of a set up, maybe a cop looking to shake him down for the fares he had earned that day.

"No, Señor, I'm sorry, but I can't help you."

A twenty-dollar bill appeared in front of the cabby's face. "Do you think Mr. Jackson could refresh your memory?" he asked as he wondered how the hell he managed to remember who was on the front of a twenty.

This middle-aged driver, like most of those who shared his profession in TJ, had his share of run-ins with the local Judicial Police, and was still skeptical about the authenticity of the man in the back seat, regardless of the convincing argument provided by the venerable Mr. Jackson. "I honestly don't know of anyone, but I can take you to a bar downtown where I have heard you can hire a coyote." The man quickly snatched the twenty for the information provided, "Do you want me to take you there?"

"Sure."

The bar, 'Los Huleros', which had nothing to do with rubber, was perfectly camouflaged in its run down squalid surroundings. A drunk sat on the curb trying to stabilize his spinning head with his hands. A large pool of barf between his feet represented the last four days of wages earned at a sweatshop on the south side of town.

As he was about to enter the establishment he read a sign painted directly on the stucco by the entry which warned: No children, no women, no people in uniform. And someone had added with a felt tipped pen '¡No Culeros!' (No Assholes!). Now he wished he had dressed down for the occasion. His clean jeans, nice fresh Nike's along with a stylish golf shirt made him look out of place and caused three quarters of the patrons to turn and stare at his arrival.

The bartender, he noticed as he walked up to the bar, was obscenely obese and before he could utter word one the man confronted him with a thick raspy voice, "What the fuck do you want?" For some strange reason placing emphasis on 'you'.

He wasn't entirely sure if he was asking him what he wanted to drink, but answered anyway. "Gimme a fuckin beer, and chase it with a fuckin tequila." And quickly added for good measure, "You fat fuck!"

Some of the patrons at the bar turned to look at the stranger in disbelief.

"Ho-ly fuck! If I didn't know any better I would say you are from Alvarado, Veracruz," the bartender said with an almost imperceptible smile.

"As a matter I am, you nasty fuck!" He lied and continued, "I left when I was a teenager. Now I suppose you are going to tell me that you and your whoring sisters are also from the old town?"

"By the sounds of it, you know my family!" the bartender said, now with a big grin, and flicked his cigarette butt across the room, hitting some drunk who was way beyond feeling anything.

"I need to get across to 'El Norte'. Which of these assholes can help me?"

"Talk to that dumb looking 'hijo de la chingada' over there."

"The guy with the bug eyes?"

"Yeah, the one that looks like he's got a broom stick stuck up his ass! Tell him you're from the old town."

The man with the permanent surprised look on his face also had a speech impediment, which made it sound like he was talking through his nose. He refrained from engaging in much of the conversation for fear of ridicule, but enough was said for the man to agree to get him across the border (special home boy pricing) for $400, plus an extra $300 to get him past the secondary checkpoint, dropping him off somewhere in Santa Ana. It was agreed that they would meet the following night, 8pm sharp (if such an exact time ever existed in Mexico) at Los Huleros.

As he left the dirty, dilapidated establishment an overwhelming need for a shower hit him. He found himself a room with a bath in a nice yet affordable hotel just off Avenida de las Americas. It was a well-known fact that TJ could be a dangerous place, so for dinner he kept to the touristy places where he would most likely be safe.

Half an hour earlier than the agreed time he was waiting at Los Huleros. He nodded at the fat man behind the bar as he sat down at the 'surprised man's table. "How many people are you taking across tonight?"

"Just seven," Surprised said as he took a long chug of beer.

At a quarter to nine Surprised stood up, got the seven's attention by making a circular motion above his head and headed for the door. A rickety old Econoline Van, which was parked just down the street, would be the evening's ride. After what seemed to be a long ride, although his watch told him otherwise, they arrived at the proposed crossing point east of town in the mountains, which separate the desert from the coastal area. Seven men, no women, each of them looking for work and the money this work would bring, so they could send it back to their families in Mexico and maybe provide them with a slightly better life. Working for peanuts a day, well over six million illegal immigrants would send around ten billion US dollars a year to their families. In fact, this is one of Mexico's biggest sources of income second only to the income from oil exports.

It was a fair exchange. After all, the illegal Mexicans performed most of the tasks the Americans wouldn't dream of doing and without the brazeros backbreaking labor California wouldn't be the agricultural powerhouse it has become.

Once the van dropped the group off near the border they made their way on foot and in absolute silence and darkness. The small group of nervous men hiked for five hours; a sliver of a moon was the only source of light. They came across a small dirt road just as they had been instructed and a mile later the same Ford Econoline awaited. They piled in gratefully and tried to rest as the van made a slow arduous progress along the back roads of the Cleveland National Forest. The driver refrained from using his headlights and as daylight started to encroach on the night's domain, lights were no longer necessary and he was able to increase his speed. Much to the chagrin of his passengers who were violently tossed around the empty interior.

By noon the seven bruised and exhausted illegals were safely in Santa Ana, California. To the untrained eye, you would have sworn you were still in Mexico. All the store signs were in Spanish and walking down the street all you could hear was Spanish. In fact the only real clue to the fact that you were not in Mexico was that the streets were wider, slightly cleaner and all traffic signs were in English.

Three days slipped by as he searched for the appropriate props that would substantiate the visuals of the ruse. The two Armani suits were purchased directly from the store bearing that name on Rodeo Drive, along with shirts, ties and shoes. Both suits needed some minor alterations to obtain the perfect fit, so he had to return the following day. The jewelry, on the other hand was acquired at an upscale pawnshop near Century City. Each piece qualified as not too gaudy, yet not too classy. It could best be described as "pimp light".

Memories of his youthful days in Sta. Barbara were ever present during his short stay, and finally he caved in to the desire to revisit his past. After a short train ride up the coast, and then a cab ride, which cost about the same, he was walking along the happy streets of his childhood. Things hadn't changed much. The trees were bigger, the cars were newer and fancier than he remembered.

He had purposely asked the driver to let him off a few blocks shy of the old Burrard house. For some strange reason it seemed more appropriate to approach slowly on foot rather than suddenly get out of a cab right in front of it. As he approached the corner of Florencia Drive and pushed back the hibiscus, which invaded the sidewalk, his old home came into view. For a millisecond he felt like a child again coming home from school. What had Mom made for supper? And then the thought vanished. He stared, his expression frozen, eyes glazed. Happy memories flooded his mind, the bad ones long cast away as useless material and he smiled a genuine unconscious smile.

"Are you looking for someone young man?" an elderly woman inquired.

'Young man', he thought, and smiled again. "No. I used to live here," he said pointing at the house.

"Humm." The lady muttered as she thought. "You wouldn't be the boy that lived with the Burrards would you?"

He was shocked. That was eons ago. How could she possibly remember?

"Terrible tragedy. Lovely people," she said as if the events had taken place the week before. With the assistance of a cane the little old lady hobbled away without another word, in a bit of a daze, one knee high rolled down around her ankle. He raised his hand as if he wanted to stop her but she was well on her way. It was too late, and it was time to head to Van Nuys Airport to catch his flight back to Mazatlán.

All 34,000 pounds of sleek Citation X exuded speed, class and the wicked aura of tons of cash. His mesmerized mind was drawn back to reality by the soft purr of the flight attendant. A delightful slender creature who could very well have graced the pages of the Victoria's Secret catalogue. This thought sent his imagination into overdrive, as he clearly envisioned her in a naughty lacy undergarment with the inevitable garter belt. Suddenly his collar felt too tight, and a bead of sweat popped to the surface.

"Sir. Are you ready for departure?" The sultry yet sweet voice enquired for the second time.

He looked into her oversized aqua blue eyes and simply nodded. He decided he wouldn't be able to trust himself to speak.

The interior of the twenty million dollar jet still had a wonderful new leather smell to it. The rest of the aircraft was the most sumptuous and elegant thing he had ever seen. "Please have a seat at your convenience. As soon as you are comfortable we will depart. Would you like a drink, Sir?"

"Maybe a Jack and Coke." There! He said something. Something with no sexual connotation whatsoever. As he continued to look around only one thing came to mind, well two. 'How did Jake manage to pull this one off? This must be costing an absolute fortune,' he thought as he removed his new Armani jacket.

"Here, let me help you with that," she gently took the beautifully cut jacket and hung it in the fore cabinet, which, as the rest of the interior, was made of elm burl with brushed platinum trim. She handed him his beverage in a nice crystal glass, Baccarat of course, "Would you like a pair of moccasins so you'll be more comfortable?"

He was both surprised and mystified by the question. It took him several seconds to realize what she was saying and then formulate an answer. "Ahh, yes. Thanks." Was all that stumbled out? 'Get a handle on the situation! You look like a bumbling fool!' He reprimanded himself.

She handed him a new pair of butter soft leather and sheepskin moccasins. And then proceeded to go over the safety features of the plane. He couldn't concentrate on a word she was saying; all he saw were the lovely motions of her full pouty lips. He felt like a sex maniac.

A fifty or so year old gentleman came out of the cockpit and walked purposefully to the VIP. "Hi. I'm Captain Taylor," they shook hands. "If you are ready for departure I'll get things going. Oh, and you still want to go to Mazatlán, correct?"

"Yes, that's right," he responded somewhat puzzled.

The pilot noticed the look and clarified. "I've got in the habit of double checking because some of our clientele tend to change their minds even while we are enroute," he waited for a moment to see if this would be the case and upon determining it wasn't he continued, "If there is anything we can do for you please do not hesitate to let us know." The captain smiled at his passenger, and made his way back to the state of the art cockpit.

Excess thrust continued to push the biz jet through 37,000 feet on its way to 43. 'How does a person, or a company justify this level of extreme opulence?' he asked himself, as he got comfortable as single passenger of the multimillion-dollar craft. He was determined to enjoy every minute of this once-in-a-lifetime journey. Upon reaching cruising altitude Kristy inquired about his comfort and what he might like for dinner. Would it be salmon medallions in a light dill sauce or maybe a chicken breast with seasoned greens in a white wine sauce?

"Which would you choose?" he asked.

She thought for a few seconds, believing he was interested in her personal opinion, finally responding, "I'm partial to the salmon myself."

"All right, I'll have the chicken."

Somewhat confused by this exchange, it suddenly dawned on her, "Oh, I'm not allowed to have lunch with the customers," she said with a smile.

"Didn't you ask me earlier if there was anything you could do? 'Just ask', you said. Well I don't like eating alone and I'm asking if you would mind having lunch with me." The second Jack Daniels and Coke were smoothing the edges and trimming him out.

"No customer has ever asked me to have lunch with them. Would you mind if I consult with the Captain?" She didn't wait for an answer, and none was provided.

By the bounce in her step and the smile on her face it was obvious that the Captain okayed the lunch. She joined the handsome middle-aged man and allowed herself to dream for a while what it would be like to be whisked away as a passenger on a private jet. The miles smoothly and effortlessly ripping by beneath their feet, "So what does it feel like to be a big cheese?" She smiled a girlish, naughty grin and savored the meal.

He studied her youthful expression and beautiful figure, and felt mildly perverted for the thoughts that were going through in his mind. He would've loved to seduce her but first off he was working, and secondly he was almost old enough to be her father.

The flight to Mazatlán was the shortest two hours of his life. As he committed the plush interior to memory he wished the flight would never end. It had been a unique experience, which he was quite certain, would not repeat itself during this lifetime. As the aircraft came to a halt, General Gasdas, accompanied by Jake pulled up to greet the 'Accountant'.

In his mind, he had rehearsed his departure from the plane in detail. Completely casual, slightly aloof maybe, possibly a hint of pedantry. After all the Citation X was supposed to be his, and this was just one more monotonous flight. Strolling down the steps he made a light wave to the crew and said: "See ya in a bit," Just a little louder than would be considered normal.

Jake approached and shook his hand, "I'm so glad you could make it, Mr. Andropolous. I'd like you to meet General Ignacio Gasdas." The two powerful men shook hands and studied one another's' eyes. Both tried to decipher the secrets that must lie within.

"Beautiful aircraft, Mr. Andropolous," the General offered as idle chitchat.

"Yes, it is," he said somewhat cavalierly. "Will we have our meeting here or in Mazatlán, or is there some place you would prefer to go in my jet?"

Jake's guts cramped as he waited for the reply. He really didn't want to pay another $14,500 just to toddle around the countryside in a grand gesture.

"No, we shall talk at my villa." Gasdas emphasized the word 'villa'.

Jake wondered if he had externalized his huge sigh of relief.

"I won't be needing you for the moment. I'll be in touch when I'm ready to depart," Andropolous spoke a little louder than usual to the confused pilot. 'What the hell is he talking about?' he wondered, but nodded politely as he turned away.

Andropolous strolled through the General's villa and complimented him on his exquisite taste. Surrounded by enormous bouquets of tropical flowers the three men sat in the ornate living room. The seven mahogany French doors were wide open allowing the Pacific breeze to cool them and play with the light sheer curtains. A uniformed maid had placed a pitcher of fresh orange/lemon juice and a silver carafe of coffee on the low table before them.

"General, I brought you a little something." Andropolous picked up his alligator skin brief case and gave the General a small intricately detailed rosewood humidor containing twenty reserve Cohiba cigars, "You do enjoy a nice cigar I hope? You strike me as a man who has a cigar from time to time."

He had not smoked a cigar in years. "Absolutely!" Gasdas lied. "Yaik, you should leave us now," the General said condescendingly.

"General Gasdas, if you wouldn't mind." Said Andropolous leaning forward slightly, "had it not been for Mr. McInnes here we would never have made contact. I would appreciate it if he stayed."

"Very well," Gasdas agreed reluctantly.

"It's my understanding that you have somewhat large amounts of cash available to you on a regular basis from a discreet origin, and you might be looking for some assistance in reestablishing its background."

Gasdas understood about half of the words spoken but pieced the rest together. "Yes, that's correct, I need some cash laundered," he stated bluntly, putting it in a depured version of Mr. Andropolous' expression. "Jake told me you charge eight percent."

Andropolous studied the General, "The correct amount is ten percent.   And that's final.   I do understand, however, that this may not work for you," he reached for his briefcase as he rose to his feet. "I can still stop my plane for the return flight. My crew was going to pick up my partner, but they should still be there," he flipped open his cell phone and quickly punched in a couple of random numbers.

"Very well, ten percent it is," Gasdas mumbled. "Tell me, Mr. Andropolous, what guarantees do I have that you are legit?"

"I'm sure you have your sources. If they have any inside knowledge they will have heard of me."

"That's the problem, no one has," the General said not really knowing one way or the other.

Without skipping a beat, he answered, "Then I'm sorry to tell you General that you do not have good sources."

After a brief visual stand off Andropolous continued. "Here's a thought if it would make you feel more at ease why don't you personally accompany the first load of cash and do an on-the-spot verification that your money has been transferred to your offshore bank account and everything is in order."

"I don't like going to the US," was his instinctive reply.   "Let me think about it, I'll let you know tomorrow."

Jake   and   Andropolous   stood   to   leave. Andropolous shook hands with Gasdas. The General didn't bother to shake hands with Jake. He was, after all only an employee. "The lieutenant here will see you out," he announced and immediately headed towards his office. The soldier suddenly appeared from nowhere and ushered them to the door.

The same soldier that had driven them from the airport to the Villa explained that he had orders to take Andropolous wherever he wished to go, he would take care of everything, and that only the best would do for the distinguished guest. Furthermore, a hotel reservation had already been made and paid for in advance in the typical way Gasdas 'paid' for most things around town, with a shake of his holstered 9mm and an evil eye. Needless to say most people didn't insist on seeing real money. The presidential suite was a luxury he was not used to. Only his alter ego, Andropolous was accustomed to such a lavish existence.

Jake and his accomplice had previously decided that any conversation would most likely be recorded, and given today's technology, very possibly videotaped as well. In a very professional and business like manner they shook hands and bade each other a restful night.

Andropolous made a number of pre-arranged phone calls to his 'office', which subsequently 'patched' him through to several of his high rolling customers and many banking institutions located primarily in the few remaining tax havens around the globe. Each call had been carefully written, choreographed, and finely performed. Any eavesdropper would have the impression that millions of dollars were being shifted around with the expertise of a very skilled practitioner in the art of moving money.

As he made his calls, Andropolous wondered how many businessmen realized just how easy it was to tap a phone line in a hotel, intercept a fax or an email for that matter. Intercepting conversations and data are more common practices than many business people care to acknowledge. Needless to say, the perpetrators are even less anxious to let on their dirty little secrets.

Money launderer extraordinaire, Andropolous ordered an exquisite meal, along with the finest wines available to the hotel restaurant. He sat on the large veranda of his suite and savored each morsel and sip as if it were his last. With a nice buzz from the overpriced wine he ordered a few DVD's and watched movies before turning in for the night. The partners in the ruse had agreed that this would be the safest course of action. Especially since it would be a little more than awkward if someone recognized Andropolous' past as a cab driver.

The telephone's pleasant digital sounding ring eased him from his sleep. Still half asleep a soothing female voice informed him that some gentlemen were downstairs to escort him to his meeting. Jake was standing in front of the clearly homosexual clerk as he relayed this information to the guest up stairs and he had to smile as the young man said the word 'gentlemen' and watched as his mouth and nose crinkled slightly with distaste, unconsciously revealing his feelings towards the goons standing by the front desk.

Andropolous decided to wear the deep olive green double-breasted suit with a tan shirt and fancy paisley tie. The rich brown Italian leather shoes tied in with the accent colors from the silk tie. He put on the two gold rings and one platinum ring, each flashing an assortment of well-placed cubic zircons. The gaudy gold Presidential Rolex with the diamond bezel was very reminiscent of what a wealthy pimp might view as 'classy'.   Andropolous put on a very convincing swagger as he passed through the nicely decorated lobby and entryway. Gasdas, who stood surrounded by his men and a few acquaintances, was indeed convinced that he was dealing with a man of the world. Everything about him spelled 'money'.

"Buenos dias Señor Andropolous. I hope you had a restful night," Gasdas said with the first smile Jake had ever seen cross his lips.

Jake was sitting across the hallway, not wanting to be near Gasdas or his cohorts, and thought it was all very amusing. He had never seen the General be nice to anyone. It was very obvious that he wanted something from Andropolous and found himself in the unusual position of having to be civil for once.

"Yes, thank you for asking. Mazatlán is a lovely town," Andropolous answered.

Not being used to exchanging pleasantries Gasdas was a loss for words, "Yes, yes," was all he could manage and then continued on a different subject. He dismissed the people around him and proceeded, "I have decided that we should start doing business. As you suggested, I will come to Laredo next week with the first load of cash. You will be able to make the transfer directly to my account. Is this not correct?"

Not wanting to be overly anxious Andropolous informed the General, "I'm very sorry but I have meetings in Zurich next week.   How about the following week? Would that work for you?"

Gasdas, not used to being second fiddle, but still too interested in getting a better deal for his money acceded, "Very well. The week after next. But instead of eighteen to twenty million it will be all most double. Will that be a problem?"

"No, not a problem." Andropolous said very casually looking in another direction. "Where are we having breakfast?" he asked nonchalantly.

Breakfast was a quiet affair. Neither man wanted to reveal too much or elaborate on his own affairs, so they talked a little about weather. It was a simple and safe subject in which anyone can safely participate.   Unfortunately the conversation stifles quickly when all you have to talk about is Mazatlán's almost unchanging climate and soon the topic was redirected to military history, a subject which Andropolous figured the General would be comfortable with and in which he would not have to participate very much.

His assumption was correct. Not only was the General very content to talk about the exploits of famous Mexican generals, but also he liked hassling Jake. Gasdas especially liked to talk about Pancho Villa, "The only man ever to attack an American city and not be caught for doing so!" he loved to say, laughing loudly afterwards. The other 'Caudillo' he idolized was Emiliano Zapata, "Even though he was just an Indian," Gasdas would say and subsequently launch into his rehearsed speech that although Zapata was a man born into extreme poverty, he was able to see the terrible injustice of a few vast landowners oppression of the poor and how he dedicated his life to the redistribution of that land. His war cry: "The land belongs to those who work it!" With his life's objective accomplished with the success of the Mexican Revolution of 1910, he was murdered in cold blood in April 1919 in an ambush arranged by his own government at the Hacienda Chinameca. Gasdas never tired of telling this piece of Mexican history and his bodyguards who had heard it countless times, knew it word for word.

Jake thought his friend's selected topic was perfect. It gave them a chance to relax, albeit briefly, from being in a state of permanent defense. The schemers knew the General would check on the 'Accountant's' destination and casually mentioned the fact that Andropolous' partner was using the Citation and he had elected to return on a commercial flight to Tijuana to meet with some bankers and businessmen.

With little fanfare the parties cordially parted company, and one of the fleet of black Suburbans was provided for Andropolous to take him to the airport to catch his flight. Everything was set for the next phase.

Upon his arrival in TJ he made certain that he wasn't being followed. He changed into his 'Indian costume' and made his way to the bus station. The bus to Hermosillo was slow, hot and smelly. He looked forward to the airplane ride back to Maz. in the morning. He couldn't help comparing this portion of the journey with the luxury of his trip in the Citation, it was certainly an enormous difference.

Omar had no idea why Jake had asked him to meet with him at La Cruz, North of Mazatlán, instead of Mazatlán International. But then that is what friends do for friends, no questions asked.

Jake stood leaning against the car smoking his third cigarette. The day was blisteringly hot and the sky was filled with smoke from the surrounding sugar cane fields being burned before harvest and the noxious, sweet smoke brought visibility down to a mile or maybe less in a few areas. As he leaned against the Sentra he heard the drone of the 185's engine. He had been around airplanes for such a long time that he could recognize the sound of an individual aircraft, and the engine he heard was definitely the 185 he had 'borrowed' from the Nevada desert almost two years ago. 'Two years' Jake thought. It had gone by so quickly and yet in some ways it seems to have passed painfully slowly.

Omar approached the deserted strip from the upwind side. 'Strange', Jake thought. There was the lightest of breezes but the smoke could certainly tell him which way he should land. Omar was carrying excess speed and this told Jake that his friend was just having some fun. The wheel landing was perfect. Then he made the plane do two identical hops followed by touching down only the port tire for fifteen yards and then the starboard for exactly the same distance. The engine gunned, and Omar had a hard time keeping her on the dirt. By the end of the runway he let her gain enough altitude to throw in two notches of flaps and haul back on the yoke, and most importantly not hit the rudder during the hard rotation. The pristine 185 shot into the skies like a raped ape. As he approached five hundred feet agl and the airspeed was lowering, he kicked full right rudder and pulled the throttle to idle. A little slip to increase his rate of descent and a perfect three point landing two yards from the end of the runway.

Omar taxied up to the car and pulled the mixture. He jumped out. "How'd ya like that?" He said with a big smile on his face. Enthusiastically wiggling her tailless furry butt Amber raced over to greet him.

"Like what?" Jake asked, pretending he hadn't noticed a thing. "Oh, do you mean your awful landing? Well at least you got it right after the go-around!" Jake said with a smile, and shook his friends hand.

"You're so full of shit!" Omar announced like it was a big revelation. "Alejandra sent you some cookies," he reached into the plane and handed him a nice size bag.

"After that landing they are probably crumbs by now!"

The partners chatted about the latest events and had some coffee from Jake's thermos. They also ate half the chocolate chip cookies Alejandra had baked. "I asked you to fly over to tell you what's going on and to see if you could take care of Amber for a few weeks, maybe months."

"Don't worry we would love to have her. You know how much Cynthia loves her!" Omar said referring to his daughter.

Jake gave Amber a long pat, scratch and shake, followed by a hug. He wasn't entirely sure if he would see her again. She happily got into Omar's plane but quickly became disillusioned when she realized that Jake wasn't coming.

Now that Amber was in a safe place Jake felt more at ease. However, as the big day grew near his anxiety level skyrocketed to new heights. He was increasingly grateful to the person who invented the sleeping pill, because without help he wouldn't have caught a half wink of sleep for the past five nights.

Three thirty AM. The sun not up and the port city still very much asleep. Jake, regardless of the assistance of his medication is wide-awake. This time he is extremely grateful for whoever came up with the bizarre idea of patiently picking these funny little red berries, drying them, toasting them, crushing them and finally extracting their flavor by pouring boiling water over them. 'What a strange person he must have been. But just the same, thanks,' Jake thought in a momentary reprieve from his constant mental iterations regarding the day ahead.

At 5am, as Jake maneuvered the now very familiar Pilatus Porter onto active runway 26 the airport was completely silent. The two goons he had seen on many of his previous trips were seated on the bench at the back of the cabin looking forward. Their flack jackets, helmets, 9mm Browning side arms along with their AK47's were ready for use at a moment's notice. Gasdas decided the previous night not to join them on the first few pickups. It had been agreed that they would hit the first six airports and then head back to Mazatlán to pick up the General. Then two more pickups before heading on to Laredo, Texas for the big drop off.

The routine by now was just like clockwork and each pickup was uncomplicated and carried out with the professionalism and attention to detail one would expect only from the fighting elite from industrialized nations. Only one of the delivering units was a couple of minutes behind schedule, but time was made up on the ground and in the air. The Colonel in charge asked, almost begged, that Jake not mention the delay to Gasdas. 'El Piloto Contento' (The happy pilot), as he was known among the deliverers, in thought more than in speech, readily agreed.

Only one instrument approach was required for the morning's milk run. And as Murphy, the bastard, would have it, it happened at the most difficult airport. Uruapan, Michoacán. Surrounded on three sides by mountains, the approach to runway 02 offers the lowest terrain, but unfortunately it's also predominantly upwind. The missed approach is also pretty hair-raising but then Jake didn't have to perform it.

Upon their arrival back at Mazatlán International at 14:05, the Porter was loaded down with duffle bags containing cash to the tune of twenty five million US dollars. Stuffed in the cargo hold, along with and overlooking the cash sat the two expressionless goons. Coincidentally, and unbeknownst to them, they both had 4 daughters and 3 sons apiece, and both knew the mountain of money before them was untouchable. Amazingly the thought of stealing it for themselves never once crossed their minds.

Gasdas marched towards the Porter as Jake jumped down from the cockpit. He noticed the General's funny gait, a little more than chubby; he really couldn't keep his arms straight down by his sides. Jake wanted to chuckle but bit his cheek instead.

"Yaik, we are taking the King Air. I don't want to fly in that thing!" he announced referring to the Pilatus Porter. Gasdas knew that if there were any problems in the US, he could say he was on official business since the King Air bore the colors of the Mexican Army.

"But I don't have a twin rating," Jake lied.

"So what? Nothing is going to happen. If you can fly the Pilatus into the bush and land safely on the tiny strips, as I have seen, you can certainly fly a King Air into big airports without a problem. Now tell the soldiers to transload the cash!" The two soldiers who had guarded the cash all morning overheard the General's instructions and didn't bother waiting for Jake to redirect the orders before they got to work.

Jake knew the Pilatus was rigged for the mission, and furthermore, didn't want to lose the tracking devices or the camera equipment. "General, the other problem is…" Jake didn't have a chance to finish the sentence.

"Look, Yaik. I didn't ask for your opinion in the matter. We are taking the King Air and that is final. However, if you don't think you are capable of flying the airplane by yourself I can get Larry to co-pilot for you," Gasdas offered.

Jake was certain that Larry's presence would cause tremendous complications and he quickly informed Gasdas that he could handle it. Despite Jake's lack of experience flying King Air's, its benevolent flight characteristics made flying it a non-issue. As Jake flew, or more appropriately supervised the autopilot, he studied the POH for the more important points. Gasdas and the two goons remained in the back along with the mountain of cash. Having stopped in Durango and Torreon the hold now contained around twenty nine million dollars. 27,000 feet and smooth as silk. Laredo was an hour away as Jake looked around and then gave a quick twist to the cabin altitude controller, moving it up to 15,000 feet.

"Why are you wearing your oxygen mask?" Gasdas inquired with a bit of a smile. Indicating to Jake the first signs of hypoxia.

Jake removed it to answer the question. "I've got a bit of a headache and the pure O_2 helps it," he put the mask back on and again increased the cabin altitude by five hundred feet. Gasdas, feeling dizzy and happy nodded at the pilot. Jake continued to raise the cabin altitude by five hundred feet every minute, so they wouldn't notice their ears popping.

Slowly. Another twenty minutes crept by and the cabin altitude was now even with the outside, 27,000 feet. Jake again turned to check on his passengers. They were all out cold. There was no turning back now. He undid his safety harness and reached into to his flight bag. The eighteen by six inch diameter canister contained nitrous oxide and the three face masks. It was enough to knock out three grown men for a few hours.

The handheld GPS, which was velcroed to the yoke, still showed a direct line to Laredo. His nimble fingers changed the direction to the coordinates on the matchbox in his pocket. 257° degrees. He set the heading bug in that direction and preselected a descent of 2,000 feet a minute once he received clearance for Saltillo approach. As he crawled from the tight cockpit he accidentally bumped against the yoke and the plane lurched upwards violently for half an instant.

Very gently he placed the masks on the men and turned on the valve. The tiny indicator showed the correct flow of nitrous, just as the dentist had indicated. Hopefully they would receive an equal amount through the homemade distributor Jake had manufactured from a Tupperware container, glue and used aluminum – 4 hydraulic line. He took the AK 47's and the 9mm side arms from the three men, and after removing the magazines he hid them in his flight bag. Jake then cautiously made his way to the rear of the plane where the big black canvas duffle bags awaited. The autopilot retrimmed itself with the change in weight in the cabin. He tossed half the bags into the head, and the other half were pushed as close as possible to the door so he could get it out as quickly as possible. The fewer minutes he spent on the ground the better. As he returned to the cockpit he saw the altimeter going through 15,000 feet, he retarded the throttles since he was well into the yellow arc and closing in on Vne. He thought about increasing the rate of descent but decided there was enough time. The GPS confirmed his mental calculation, ten minutes to the rendezvous point. An enormous dry lakebed extending almost two hundred square miles among a sea of cactus was not a difficult landmark to find.

As the twin turbine aircraft descended through 10,000 feet the turbulence from a hot day bounced them around. Jake looked back to see if his passengers were stirring. Not even a twitch. If he didn't know any better he would swear they were dead. 'It wouldn't be a great loss to humanity that's for sure,' Jake thought as he turned back to concentrate on the flying.

Just after the turbulence associated with lower altitude thermal activity started he disengaged the autopilot and set up for the approach. Jake gingerly touched down and placed the props to a flat pitch, and let the plane slow to a halt.

He left the engines and the air conditioning running. Searching out the windows, there was no one to be seen. He shut down the engines and proceeded to open the door/jet way. A blast of desert heat from the furnace outside hit him and instantly replaced the comfortable air-conditioned interior.

Before he even started to toss the duffle bags out he was sweating profusely and he was well drenched by the time the familiar sound of the 185 came into earshot. Before long Omar was parked next to him.

"While I was flying in this direction I was monitoring this area's frequency and I thought I recognized your voice. But when you announced as a King Air I was completely confused. What happened to the Pilatus?" Omar inquired.

"Oh nothing. The prima donna General doesn't like the Porter and insisted we take the King Air."

Omar saw the great heap of duffle bags and asked with astonishment. "All those bags are filled with cash?"

"Believe it or not," Jake said, "And that is only half!"

"Is it all in five dollar bills? Or what!?" Omar asked thinking that was the only way there could possibly be that many bags.

"No. It's mostly hundred's, fifty's and just a few 20's. The total pickup today was around twenty nine million dollars. I think we should take sixteen mill to split between the three of us!" Jake said enthusiastically.

"I still don't like it Jake. The origin of that money is dirty."

"Hey, thieving from a thief is not a crime. After all, if we give it to the DEA they'll just squander it!" Jake rationalized.

"Now, when you get to Laredo and they bust the General and his bodyguards, don't you think he's going to say something about only half the money being present?" Omar inquired.

"First, the DEA is going to confiscate any and all money present. Secondly, why would they believe what he has to say anyway? And if that isn't enough to convince them I have this forged pick up log saying we only picked up thirteen million! Ha!" Jake said with great pleasure.

In hindsight Jake wasn't sure whether he heard the gunshot first or felt it rip through his leg. He knew he had been hit, not so much because it hurt, but because he was on the ground and when he touched his leg there was blood. It startled him. 'Wait a minute,' Jake thought, 'where did he get the gun and why is he awake. If he's awake the soldiers will quickly follow.'

The partners stared at the groggy General as he held the snub nose 38 in his hand.

When Jake had placed the masks, which were hooked to the nitrous oxide, he hadn't noticed the slight kink in the tube going to Gasdas, or that the General was receiving only about a tenth of the dosage required to keep him under. Once the aircraft had landed the oxygen rich environment became available, it was only a matter of time before he regained consciousness.

Jake had stuffed one of the 9mm Browning's in the back of his belt. He felt the large heavy frame pressing into his spine. Only problem was, by the time he reached back, retrieved it, slid a cartridge into the chamber, aimed and fired, Gasdas would have ample time to pump the last five bullets into him from his 38.

Gasdas looked very unsteady and sat down on the stairs. His words slurred as he ordered. "Get your hands up."

Jake's leg was now really starting to hurt, especially since he had struggled to his feet and put some weight on it. The two men slowly complied. "I can explain this," Jake said placing himself deliberately between Gasdas and Omar, "We had engine trouble and…"

This time he heard the loud bang first. Luckily it whizzed past him, possibly missing by an inch or so. "There's nothing to talk about you piece of shit!" Gasdas slurred as he started to take aim again.

With lightning speed Omar tore the gun from Jake's belt, and in one fluid motion, loaded, cocked, pushed Jake out of the way and blasted away as he raced forward. All thirteen remaining bullets were rapidly expelled from the firearm as quickly as Omar could yank back on the trigger. Six pieces of lead found their mark in the General's body, another five riddled the King Air fuselage and another two would be forever lost somewhere in a dry lake bed in northern Mexico.

Gasdas also managed to squeeze off another few rounds, but none reached a target of any consequence.   The snub nose 38 tumbled to the desert floor, while its owner remained sprawled on the Jetway.   His breathing was labored, blood gurgled loudly and flowed profusely from two of the three holes, which had punctured his left lung.

Jake walked up and looked at the holes. First he stuck his finger into one and then another, "Nice shooting ace! You know she won't pressurize now. I hope you didn't hit any hydraulic lines, or any other important shit for that matter."

As funny as Omar thought it was a few months down the road, at that particular moment he wasn't able to laugh. He walked over to the dying man and looked into his fast dimming eyes. He wanted to ask him if he cared at all about the heartache, pain and suffering he had caused his own family and the countless other families affected by the shit he'd helped export.

There would never be a direct answer since at that precise moment General Ignacio Gasdas Sanchez joined the ranks of the dead. And in any case Omar knew the answer.

"So I guess that makes us even," Omar mumbled to the corpse of his brother's murderer.

Chapter 8.

Even.

As the tiny wavelets provided by the transparent Caribbean Sea lapped the side of the shiny new aluminum pontoons, it created a sound mildly reminiscent of a calypso steel drum. Only monotonous. But as you added the soft rustling of the palms and the occasional squeals of an operatic monkey, it became a soul-soothing symphony. Jake was parked, semi-dressed and semi-permanently on a particular stretch of sandy white beach, a mere forty feet from the dock that lead to his beautiful practically new 2001 Cessna Caravan. With a mere 310 hours on the Hobbs she was new to the world.

After three months of ownership he was still amazed that she actually belonged to him. And best of all, free and clear. Even though business was by no means brisk he really didn't care. Amber seemed to not care much either, but then she usually didn't get torn up much about anything. She lay close and napped.

Costa Rica seemed to suit them fine, the people were friendly, the weather was great, and the cigarettes were cheap. Now he wondered if his friend would ever suddenly stroll down the beach, right out of the blue, as he tended to do from time to time. He looked up and down the beach just in case.

She handed him a chilled coconut with a slice of pineapple and a little pink umbrella. A bottle of ice-cold water was poured into Amber's dish. As she sat down in the comfortable chair next to Jake she urged him on, "So keep going, you left off when you were landing in Laredo."

As Jake came to a nice easy halt in front of the customs building the big King Air was surrounded by every known law enforcement agency he could think of. Customs was present because it was their building, DEA was there because it was their operation, the local police was there because someone had blabbed and they didn't have anything better to do, the Marshals were there because American currency was being brought in and it could be counterfeit, you know.

He had already radioed ahead and informed Killian that there had been some trouble, he hadn't elaborated since he wanted to get the hell out of Mexico before he did. As Jake opened the hatch Killian was intently inspecting the bullet holes in the fuselage. "What the hell happened?" Killian shouted as he climbed the jet way and pushed Jake back. Before he took another step he saw the General's cooling corpse sprawled in the center aisle, "What the hell happened?" he asked again.

"During the flight the General started getting agitated and told me to land. Once we were on the ground he accused me of setting him up. I have no idea why this fact suddenly occurred to him. But then he pulled a gun and shot me," Jake said calmly. "So I..."

"Where?" Killian asked looking for traces and quickly noticed the large bloodstain on his jeans.

As Jake was pointing at the stain, he continued. "So I shot back. And, well, here he is."

Flustered and angry Killian tried to calm himself, "We'll talk about this later. First we need to get you to a hospital."

"St. Andrews hospital discharged me the following day and Killian was there to pick me up and continue the grilling. Let me tell ya, he was pissed! He had wanted to debrief the general and tear down his whole chain of distribution. Needless to say Gasdas wasn't going to be doing any talkin'.'"

Killian debriefed the pilot for several days. Jake presented the coordinates for all the pickup zones and gave the names of as many men as he could possibly remember. They wanted the name of every person that appeared in the thousands of photos uploaded. "It was ridiculous! And the whole time I was treated like a common criminal."

"Don't get upset. You're here on a beautiful beach now with no worries," she said soothing him.

"One thing that really pisses me off is the fact that they refused to pay me the seven hundred thousand. Killian said I didn't fulfill my end of the deal. Which was to deliver the General to them in the US. As I see it, I did. Dead, but I delivered him!"

Jake took a moment to calm down and spark up another coffin nail, "I didn't want to fight it. After all those months of stress all I wanted to do was take it easy. Anyway, all I got in return for my efforts was a document from the federal government absolving me from any complicity in the in the entire operation, or anything related to the case."

Once the DEA had finished with Jake, and he was free to go, he needed to get back to Durango to meet up with Omar, and then on to Mazatlán to meet up with his friend. The biggest problem was how to do this without having the Mexican authorities pass this information on to the people who were surely after him. The liaison officer for the Judicial Police, representing the powers-that-be had informed Jake in no uncertain terms that they were very happy to be rid of a low life like Gasdas and he would be a welcome visitor to Mexico whenever and wherever he pleased. But Jake knew better. There were more than a few powerful individuals who would be very interested in seeing him wrapped in chains and at the bottom of Lake Chapala.

So far there was no reason to believe that anyone was on to Omar, after all Jake's name had never figured in the incorporation papers, the Cessna 185 or anything else for that matter.

Sporting a fresh paint job, Omar flew the 185 with the original N-numbers proudly displayed on its side, N54NE, to a deserted strip in the desert just outside Nuevo Laredo. Amber had insisted on accompanying him, or so he said. She jumped at Jake ecstatically happy to see him and then barked at him in disapproval of his absence.

Omar had the controls on the flight back, and as always never engaged the autopilot (even if there was one). If there were ever any words he would never forget from his friend, they would be those uttered in complete happiness after Jake offered to fly when he got tired. The twenty thousand hour bush pilot had remarked, "That is exactly what I want the day before I die. I want to be able to say, 'I am tired of flying!'"

Upon their arrival at a secluded dirt strip just outside Durango, they immediately went to Omar's house where Alejandra had a warm meal waiting for them. The overfilled duffle bags were neatly pilled in the guest room where Jake had spent several nights when he had first arrived in Durango. After dinner they divided the take into three equal portions. Each of the partners in the operation received a touch over five million.

Jake stayed the night. Most of it was spent chatting about the failed partnership and the great adventures they had shared. Before Jake left the following morning the two friends agreed to stay in touch and visit one another from time to time. When was the only question.

Having split up the cash three ways and before leaving, Jake visited several banks and rented safety deposit boxes. He left most of his own cash and took his friend's cash to Mazatlán with him. The short hop to Maz. was an enjoyable one, he hadn't had the controls of an airplane for several weeks and it felt good. He landed on the old dirt road that lead to an abandoned sugar cane plantation. It was the place where his last meeting with Killian and Sowers had taken place.

He stashed the 185 in the old shell of the hacienda and hid the cash in a hole he dug and covered it under a pile of rocks in the corner of what had once been a magnificent ballroom in the early 1940's. Having completed the arduous task to his satisfaction, he was drenched in sweat and not really excited about the long hike down to the highway to either hitchhike or find a cab into town.

After two weeks of looking over his shoulder, and staying in the crappiest hotels Mazatlán had to offer he gave up on his search. He wasn't particularly worried about his friend because not only did the landlady say he had simply packed up his few belongings one day and checked out, Jake had this overwhelming certainty that he was all right. He had no idea why he should feel so sure but at some profound level he was certain of the fact. It was time to move on, and Jake was getting worried that someone might identify him if he stayed any longer.

After an uneventful flight, Jake was back in California having spent over two years trying to get himself into trouble. Customs in Calexico was a non-issue. The agents, as always, were friendly and no one questioned a thing.

A scarce hour and a half flight time before he pulled the throttle back to idle. The 185's engine purred on the long descent from 10,500 feet, and Jake's last touch down in the plane he had come to love was a greaser. He felt a sickening pit in his stomach at the prospect of leaving her in the same place he had found her. She deserved a better, more loving home.

As the little bell above the door rang, Jake remembered that it was there the first time he walked into the establishment. The young man behind the desk had his back to him, feet on a bookcase, and didn't acknowledge his presence. He was too busy playing with his portable computer game and listening to some crap he referred to as music. Jake heaved a crumpled piece of paper at him to get his attention. "Where's Hamish?"

"Hamish? Who's Hamish?" The young man asked with a 'why-are-you-bothering-me' attitude.

"He owns the place," Jake said with irritation in his voice.

"Oh, that guy!" he said as he pointed to the photograph of a dashing young man in a crisp RAF uniform, "He died a couple of months ago," the kid said carelessly.

The flippant way he said 'Oh, that guy,' made Jake want to jump over the counter and slap him silly. But what was the point? 'I suppose I was an insolent little shit just like him at one time', he thought as he harnessed and eventually subdued his anger.

He paid for two years of hangar fees. Jake just couldn't face the prospect of his beautiful 185 sitting outside. For the last time he pulled the canopy cover he had purchased for the plane and gave the side of the cowl a pat and said a sad goodbye to his friend.

Waking late the following morning, after the bus ride from Overton to Las Vegas, he consulted the Yellow Pages and later made his way to the attorney's office. The polished brass lettering on the side of the building confirmed he was in the right place. LB Curtis and Associates.

For an hour Jake thumbed through a number of Newsweeks and Times before he was allowed to see Mr. Curtis, even though he had promised Peggy, his receptionist that his business would only take fifteen minutes.

The office was plush and decorated with impeccable taste. "Mr. McInnes. What can I do for you?"

"It's about your plane. The 185 at Overton Airport."

"Oh. Yeah, that was my Dad's plane. I just can't bring myself to sell it. Bunches of people have asked me but I've always said no. Actually you are the first person asking about it for quite some time," Curtis said as he tried to think exactly how long it had been. "It was always a dream of mine to learn to fly, but now I just don't have the time and she's probably in such an awful state I wouldn't have the time to fix her either."

"Well, Mr. Curtis. Maybe now is the time. She's in perfect flying condition. She has a nice strong engine, new interior, new paint job. You have nothing to do to her but fly!"

The man looked completely baffled. So Jake explained, not in complete detail but enough of what he had done, and finally offered to pay for the hours he had used the plane.

"You know, Mr. McInnes. Do you mind if I just call you Jake?" He didn't wait for an answer either way, "Jake, that's the ballziest and most amazing story I've ever heard. I just wish my old man was here to share it." Curtis thought for a moment. "And you know, just maybe he was. No, I couldn't possibly take your money."

The two men shook hands. Before departing Jake said, "Now that you have worked so hard to be successful, you should really take the time to pursue your dreams. After all, you only live once!"

LB Curtis' thoughts wandered and he nodded as he thought about Jake's advice. Jake made a silent exit before the man came back to reality.

Jake McInnes sat looking out the window of the Greyhound bus as the stark, yet beautiful desert whizzed by. He certainly could afford the flight to John Wayne Airport in Orange County, but he wanted the extra time the bus trip would give him to gather his thoughts, and determine exactly what he was going to say. It wasn't that he hadn't had enough time, it had more to do with the fact that the time was nearing when he would finally see her again.

Thank **you** for taking the time to read these words.
I hope you enjoyed reading them as much as I
enjoyed writing them!

This book is the first to my name.
If you enjoyed this story please
recommend it to a friend.
I would be very grateful if you did!

Following are the first few pages of my latest book.

GONE!

I hope you enjoy it.

Bad Decisions

When Red noticed that the prop stopped turning, he knew the engine wouldn't be starting anytime soon, especially after the loud wham the rod made as it departed the side of the cowl. He moved his right hand away from the panel to flip off the alternator, and in the same manner as when he had departed the little airport on the outskirts of Phoenix, it almost fell in his lap again. "Okay, last time I'll try that then," he mumbled to himself as he established what he guessed might be best glide. But then he had never flown a Luscombe 8A before, so what did he know.

Looking out into the pitch black darkness of the desert below he noticed just a few lights in the distance dotting the ground. 'Why the hell am I flying this piece of shit in the middle of the night anyway?' Red wondered as the utter silence which surrounded him and was only slightly interrupted by the wind rushing past the descending aircraft. 'And for that matter why do I get myself entwined in mindless conversations with sauce monster lounge lizards like Lilly? Or was it Debbie? Maybe it was the fact that she was rubbing her oversized breasts on me when she asked for my opinion about the latest episode of Survivor. Like I even give a shit.'

Randy 'Red' Pratt checked his altimeter. Five thousand feet. He nagged at himself with the old adage: There's nothing more useless than the runway behind you and the altitude above you. He realized that he should've been flying at ten thousand. But he wasn't, so there wasn't much point in bitching at himself about it now. He continued shining the red beam emanating from the tiny flashlight a buddy had given him for Christmas around the panel and found the VSI more or less where it should be. He and the repossessed hunk-a-junk he was flying, or more appropriately gliding, were descending at 650 feet a minute. Red and the Luscombe would be on the ground in eight, no seven minutes.

He tried to take comfort in the fact that the desert down below was relatively flat, although it was dotted with its share of hard rocks and prickly cactus. Let's just call it an interesting lottery. Nothing, rock or cactus and he couldn't consider any of them a big win.

Red was cramped in the tight confines of the small airplane, not surprising at six foot three and two hundred and twenty, all right, thirty pounds. He knew he should lose some weight, stop drinking and stop smoking. 'Well, I might be doin' all three momentarily,' he thought as his rapid and inevitable descent continued. 'Why didn't I follow a little closer to I-10? At this point it would've made life a lot easier.' But he hadn't, so there wasn't much point in bitchin' about that either. Suddenly, at what his brain calculated to be a glide-able distance he could swear he saw the headlights of a car. If he could just manage to squeeze a little more distance outta this hunk, not only would he possibly make it, he probably wouldn't even have a long, hot walk through the desert tomorrow morning.

ᙏᙅᘒ ᙏᙅᘒ ᙏᙅᘒ ᙏᙅᘒ ᙏᙅᘒ ᙏᙅᘒ ᙏᙅᘒ ᙏᙅᘒ

Larry, aka 'The Lushman' Anderson was hunched deep in the crushed velour seat of his 1973 Cadillac Sedan de Ville. The cruise control was set for forty, from experience he knew he could survive a crash at forty. His cigarette was two thirds gone and irritating his eyes. Also irritating his eyes were the two roads before him. Which also, from experience, he knew deep down were really one and hopefully deserted as usual at 2am. During the previous two years, in other words since he had moved out to the middle of nowhere, or BFE as he liked to refer to it, he had never once seen a highway patrol in the area. But then, there was always a first time for everything. He hoped it wouldn't be tonight. He was tired, but he was feeling pretty darn happy. After all, it had been a pretty long time since he last won at Thursday night poker, and let me tell ya, a buck-twenty four on the positive side is still considered winning!

It wasn't until Red had skimmed, or more appropriately, momentarily landed on the aircraft carrier/Cadillac roof and touched down in front of him that Larry's alcohol impaired gray matter computed the fact that what was in front of him was an airplane and not a UFO.

Despite the fact that Red braked nice and easy it was still too fast for 'The Lushmans' self-medicated reactions and he plowed into the Luscombe, snapping Red's head back. The empennage of the Luscombe was flattened in the process. Both vehicles came to a stop after the impact without further damage. Larry stepped out of the car before putting the big caddy into park, and continued to push the little wounded Luscombe a few feet. He recognized his mistake faster than his previous one (but then he was going considerably slower) and took care of business by diving into the car and slapping it into park, which completely sapped his very last reserves.

Red came around to the driver's side where Larry had given up and remained almost comatose in the vehicle.

"Hi! How ya doin' this fine evenin'?" Red inquired in a friendly manner. 'After all I just landed on this guy's car', he thought.

"Gu, good officer. Wha, what can I do ya for. Do for ya?" Larry slurred unaware of his speech impediment. "W, was I spu, speeding?"

Red couldn't help but laugh, "No pal, not at all. Would you mind giving me a ride?"

"No!" He said a little too loud, "not at all. Jump in!" Larry said enthusiastically.

"How about I drive?" Red asked fearing for his life. He had just cheated death once that night, and he wasn't about to tempt the grim reaper more than once per twenty-four hour period.

When the caddy impacted the Luscombe the empennage folded under itself at a 90-degree angle. Red decided this would be perfect for trailering and upon popping the cavernous trunk he plopped the deformed tail into it and tied it down as best he could with a set of jumper cables he had found jumbled into a corner.

Larry surrendered his driving privileges in exchange for a bit of shuteye on the vast back seat of the Caddy where he promptly feel asleep. Red started driving, the Luscombe following backwards in tow. He constantly looked back to make sure the cargo was still in place. Red searched for a good place to leave the crippled plane, but couldn't find something that met his mental picture of 'a good place'. Maybe a tiny airfield would miraculously appear, possibly a sign on the side of the road would announce one of the dozens of abandoned world war two training airports scattered around this desert. Miles and miles of straight deserted roads stretched before him with not a soul in sight. He smiled at his lucky stars as he sparked up a smoke. He was glad to be alive and unscathed.

In the very same surprising, rapid, and some what rude manner in which Red had descended upon the poor and unsuspecting Larry, the illegally over wide and overloaded Peterbilt with a Caterpillar D15 on its back raced down the back road hoping to avoid detection of the highway patrol or the weigh stations. He appeared just as the road crested from a little gully and just like a chainsaw would cut a beer can in half, the big semi-trailer ripped the right wing off the little Luscombe and sent it into the ditch after a couple of nicely performed somersaults. It landed on its back in a cloud of dust.

The semi driven by Bob 'Boom-Boom' Taylor slammed on the brakes and quickly became enveloped in a cloud of acrid smoke.

Red, still inside the big four door Cadillac, having almost come to a stop before the impact, sat for a couple of seconds reflecting on his own idiocy, and rubbed his face with both hands and exclaimed at the top of his lungs: "FUUUCK!"

Larry, who had been sleeping the whole time in the back seat, awoke seconds after the impact. "W-where are we?"

If you would like to be first in line to purchase S. Featherstone's latest novel

GONE!

Please send the following information:

Name, address, city, state or province, country & email.

And send it to: info@delascenizas.com